Your Witch Is My Command

WISHING FOR A MAGICAL MIDLIFE
BOOK TWO

TEE HARLOWE

M&F BOOKS

Copyright © 2023 by Tee Harlowe

All rights reserved.

No part of this book may be reproduced in any form or by any electronic or mechanical means, including information storage and retrieval systems, without written permission from the author, except for the use of brief quotations in a book review.

Cover design by Karen Dimmick/ArcaneCovers.com

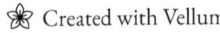 Created with Vellum

Introduction

Hi, and thanks so much for your interest in *Your Witch Is My Command*! If you want to get all the latest updates, fun bonus chapters, scenes, art, and more, then join Tee Time, my biweekly newsletter, at www.teeharlowe.com!

Happy reading,
Tee

Chapter One

Students rushed onto the grassy lawns in front of their school, happily chattering and hugging like it had been an entire year since they'd seen each other rather than just a couple months.

I sat in the car next to Remy as we watched students gather together, phones out for selfies, some sitting and scrolling through their Instagram or TikTok feeds, others looking at their schedules, checking to make sure they had all the supplies and books needed for the start of another year.

I pushed my emergency blinker button and parked the car in the round circle driveway that sat in front of the school. The ancient brick buildings rose up, three in all, tall and looming with pointed peaks and stone gargoyles lurking on ledges, overlooking the grounds. I'd attended this very school, and being back here brought up so many memories, both good and bad. Mainly good.

"You ready for this?" I asked Remy as she looked at her new school: Whispering Willows Magical Academy—the best this town had to offer.

Remy's brown curls grazed her shoulder, and she turned to me. "This really isn't a big deal, Mom. I know half these kids already from hanging out with them over the summer. Everything is gonna go great." She reached over and patted my hand. "It's okay to be nervous, but I'll be alright, promise."

Yes, admittedly, I was nervous about Remy starting a new school her senior year. She'd so easily left behind our life in Portland and accepted this new life in Whispering Willows, and I think I was still waiting for the hammer to drop. But ever since Remy found out we were witches, that Whispering Willows was home to a supernatural community full of fairies, vampires, werewolves, and so much more, she'd been, well . . . fine. Too fine. It was making me *not* fine.

"It's just another day." Remy grabbed the door handle. "Let's not make a big deal about it." She hopped out of the car, door still open. "You don't see anyone else's parents here fawning over their kids, do you?" She blew me a kiss and adjusted her purple backpack. "See you after school at the shop?"

I nodded and smiled. "Yeah, hon. Of course."

A gaggle of loud voices drowned out the chatter of students.

"Bones, you idiot!"

"You're the one who insisted we all ride together," another voice said, this one a thick Irish accent.

"Because I'm environmentally conscious. Carpooling is the responsible thing to do."

Oh. Oh no. Remy had the same look of horror on her face that I felt in that moment. I turned in my seat and my fears were confirmed: Martin, Bones, Myrtle, Helen, and Gene all marched toward us, Gene looking surlier than usual, which was saying a lot, given that the vampire's entire M.O. was prickly with a side of grumpy. Helen kissed him on the cheek, and he flashed a ghost of a smile. Except when it came to his wife, the only person on the planet who could bring out the sunshine in him.

"What are they doing here?" Remy hissed at me, darting glances back at the group, students beginning to take notice. "I thought we told them absolutely no stepping foot on school grounds?"

I shrugged helplessly as they strode with purpose toward us. Martin had a phone in his hand, and—I squinted—did Bones have a video camera? Oh lord. This would not go well for Remy, who desperately wanted to blend in today more than any other day.

"Remy!" Martin called, his green skin flushed with excitement as he practically vibrated. "Remy! We're here for your first day of school!"

Remy winced, students now blatantly staring, their gazes bouncing between Remy and the ragtag group currently fiddling with the video camera Bones held.

The half-giant towered over them, and Martin, half his height, jumped and swiped at the camera. "Give me that!"

Bones only held it higher, which made Martin angrier, of course.

"Will you two pull yourselves together?" Myrtle asked in that unmistakable Irish accent. "You're embarrassing Remy." Her golden tracksuit glittered bright in the sun, matching her rectangle glasses and poofy yellow hair. Wrinkles upon wrinkles lined her ancient face as she frowned. "Now how do I work the camera on this phone?" Myrtle banged the phone with her hand, muttering at it.

Remy groaned and smashed her face against the car. "Kill me now," she mumbled.

Okay, time to do some damage control. I got out of the car and met the group on the sidewalk. "Hi everyone, um, I thought we agreed we weren't doing this?" I tried to keep my voice light and cheery while also conveying a "this is really not the time" tone, which would hopefully hint that they needed to turn around and go home.

It did not.

Helen smiled, her blue eyes dancing with amusement. "I told them. I told them this was a bad idea."

Martin waved off her words. "Oh pish posh. We weren't going to miss Remy's first day of her senior year of high school." The imp sniffled, tears in his eyes. "They just grow up so fast."

He buried his face into Bones's arm, wailing loudly, while Bones patted him, using his other massive hand to stick the camera in Remy's face.

I rolled my eyes. "Martin, you've known Remy for three months."

The imp was mischievous and also incredibly dramatic. If he didn't own a successful B&B, I'd say he could make a good living as an actor.

Martin straightened at that, wiping the tears from his face. "And she's grown so much in those three months."

Three months. I couldn't believe we'd left Portland just three months ago. It was supposed to be a short trip to sell my mother's shop of wishes and use the money to start over. Instead, Whispering Willows had reeled us in like fish. Now here we were, making this place our home, these people our family, building a whole life here.

"I still don't know what *I'm* doing here," Gene said. "I'm supposed to be sleeping, in my cushy, dark, wonderful coffin."

Helen shot her vampire husband *a look*. "We're here to support Remy, dear."

Gene ran a hand over his bleach-blond hair and tugged at his leather jacket. "I can support Remy while I'm sleeping."

"I'd be okay with that," Remy chimed in. "There's Megan. Thank god. I have to go, everyone!"

With that, she darted off toward her friend.

"But we didn't get the pictures!" Martin said, pink flushing his green cheeks. "I made a sign and everything." He held up one of those hokey first-day-of-school signs, an idea he no doubt got from Pinterest.

I sighed heavily and tapped my foot against the pavement.

"It was too much, wasn't it?" Martin asked, the sign hanging limp at his side. He turned and flicked Bones. "I told you the sign was too much, but you were all silent and staring."

That generally was what Bones did. The half-giant wasn't much of a talker.

Bones just grunted in response, flipping the lens on the camera closed with his big meaty hands that could easily crush my windpipe with one squeeze. Luckily Bones was a gentle giant. The strong-but-silent type.

I flung out my arms. "All of this was too much. You guys weren't supposed to show up on Remy's first day of school. Do you know anything about teenagers?"

They all looked at each other for a moment, mumbling variations of "no."

"Sorry, Clara. I guess Remy is the first teen any of us have spent a lot of time with," Helen said. "I mean, I'm busy demon slaying, and this guy"—she jabbed a thumb at her husband—"is like four centuries old and spends most of his time with other vampires."

I rubbed my temples.

Martin crossed his skinny arms over his chest. "Are you implying that Remy is embarrassed by us?"

"Yes, one hundred percent," I said. "And I'm not implying. I know it. You guys were supposed to meet at the shop after school today, where we were going to privately celebrate Remy's first day of school. Instead, you humiliated her."

"No we did not!" Martin held a hand to this chest.

Helen's phone dinged. "Oh, look, Martin, you're a meme." She pointed her phone at the group, and we all gathered around.

"What the feck is a meme?" Myrtle asked, scratching her head with her long, manicured nails. "I'm getting hungry. Ready to bugger off and go hunt." The werewolf could go from nice to raging in a moment's notice when she got hungry.

I turned my attention back to the phone Helen was holding. Martin had, indeed, been made into a meme. A student had snapped a picture of him and Bones fighting over the camera and posted it on social media. It was already trending. I looked at the photo and caption. The green imp was mid-air, swiping at Bones and trying to reach the camera. The caption read "when you're small but got that big D energy."

"What is big D?" Myrtle asked, her head cocked.

Gene smirked, and Helen guffawed. I groaned. This was a nightmare.

Martin sniffed and ran a hand through his thick salt n pepper hair. "Does this make me internet famous?"

I rolled my eyes. "Okay. Enough. All of you. Go home. We will see you later, though I don't know if Remy is going to feel like celebrating after you all intruded on what was supposed to be a quiet, easy morning."

Everyone grudgingly dispersed, except Helen, who walked with me toward my car. Her spiky blonde hair gleamed in the emerging sun, and like her husband, she wore all black. "Mind if I catch a ride?" she asked.

I motioned for her to get in.

"I can't believe you went along with that charade," I said once we'd gotten in the car.

She splayed out her hands. "Well, Martin was getting us all amped up about it. Said it would be a huge surprise, that Remy would love it. You know how convincing that imp is."

"He's also an idiot."

An idiot who loved my daughter like she was his own, which I appreciated, of course, but sometimes he took things too far. I put the car in drive, and we wheeled out of the circle driveway and away from the school. I watched it grow smaller and smaller in my rearview mirror. The aroma of coffee beckoned me. I grabbed my cup, now cold, and took a sip.

"Well, he got us all hyped up, and we thought Remy would love the surprise, but clearly just because we all love and adore your daughter does not mean we know how to raise her."

I patted Helen's arm. "You had good intentions. It just wasn't the best timing."

She smiled apologetically.

So much for our perfect fresh start. Hopefully the rest of the day went better than the morning had.

Chapter Two

The bell to The Wish List jingled as Helen and I stepped inside, my breath catching in my throat. It never got old, knowing that this place was mine, that I got to live out my dreams granting wishes and helping people in need.

A mop swished its way across the wooden floors, polishing up the last section near the door before spinning back into the closet. A cast iron cauldron sat in the corner, my favorite relaxing spell rising from it and misting the air. Shelves lined the walls with little crystal balls waiting to be enacted with wishes.

I walked to the long marble counter near the back wall and grabbed a rag to polish the surface. It was hard to believe just three months ago, I'd dragged Remy back here with the intent of selling this shop and running from this place as fast as my legs could carry me. Instead, here I was: living out my family's legacy and granting wishes, just like I was meant to do.

"So do you want to talk about it . . . or . . . ?"

Helen's voice yanked me from my thoughts. "Talk about what?"

Helen raised an eyebrow. "Whatever is bothering you."

I scoffed. "Nothing is bothering me! Life is perfect, Helen. Better than perfect." I gestured to the shop around me. "I couldn't have dreamed up this life if I tried. I'm back in Whispering Willows, own The

Wish List, get to grant wishes. Remy loves it here, wants to embrace her heritage, become a Witch Granter like me." I shook my head. "I don't know what you're getting at, but I'm starting to think you like drama as much as Martin does."

That imp loved to gossip.

Helen studied me for a long minute. "I guess it feels like you're trying hard to convince yourself of something. I just don't know what... or why."

"I'm just happy with the way things are. I don't want to . . ." I scrunched my nose, thinking about the words I was looking for. "Rock the boat."

"Rock the boat?" Helen repeated.

"Yes! I want things to be easy, uncomplicated, drama free. Is that too much to ask?" I walked around the counter and leaned down, my elbows pressing into the cool stone. "And I while I'm busy *not* rocking the boat, you need to focus on what you do best: killing demons. Leave the thinking to me."

"Ha ha ha." Helen picked at the edges of her black shirt. "I don't even know if I'm the best one for that job anymore. You think I'm too old to be the Demon Slayer? I've been doing this for twenty years now. I'm sixty-five. My husband is four hundred years old. Maybe I should retire, find something more relaxing to do."

I tried to picture Gene and Helen laying on a beach somewhere and snorted. "You could never do relaxing. Gene would pick a fight with a fish just to have something to do."

Helen laughed. "Now I would pay to see that."

"Me too," I echoed.

Helen sank onto the purple couch that sat in the middle of the room, along with two purple chairs and an antique coffee table. "I don't know. Maybe someone younger needs to come into town and take up the mantle, become the new Demon Slayer."

I shook my head, firm. "You're the best person for the job because you love Whispering Willows and will protect this town at any cost."

Helen gave a little shrug. "Maybe you're right. I do love my job. Nothing's as satisfying as driving a sword straight through a demon's head."

"You're also perfect for the job because you're slightly psychotic," I said, which made Helen laugh, her eyes crinkling around the corners.

"So you're sure nothing is bothering you?" Helen asked, turning around from where she sat to look at me.

"No, everything is perfect."

I set down the rag, turning and straightening the crystal balls sitting on the shelf behind me. That was exactly the problem. I had everything I could want, so what if I went and ruined it all? Not just for me, but for Remy too. She was finally happy, had found a place where she fit in, found her calling as a witch. One misstep and this new, wonderful life could come tumbling down. I had to watch every step, every move, I made. It was a lot of pressure.

I didn't want to sound ungrateful, though, and it sounded like Helen was dealing with her own issues, so I kept the thoughts to myself and did what I do best: changed the subject so I didn't have to mull over it.

"I think I want to clear out the basement and renovate it so that Remy has a dedicated place to practice her magic. Her own little witch cave. I want to surprise her with it for her birthday."

Still about a month away, but it was her eighteenth birthday. I needed to do something big, something to make up for her last two birthdays being complete crap.

Helen dropped her arm away from her face. "You didn't tell me that."

"Well, the residents of Whispering Willows aren't exactly known for their secret-keeping skills. I tell you. You tell Gene. He tells all the vampires. It somehow gets back to Martin. And then, boom! The whole town knows and my surprise is spoiled."

Helen's mouth dropped open, her icy blue eyes boring into me. "I can keep secrets from Gene!"

Green mist from the cauldron floated past my face and dissipated in the air, momentarily relaxing me.

"Uh-huh. You couldn't even keep Gene's own surprise birthday party a secret from him."

"He hates surprises!" Helen said. "I was being considerate by telling him."

I pointed a finger at her. "Do not tell anyone about this. Including your gossip-loving vampire husband."

Helen zipped her lips and flicked her hand like she was throwing away the key. "Just don't overdo it, Clara. You spent the last year working yourself to the bone trying to provide for Remy. You finally have a job you love, a life you love, a support system. Don't repeat your past mistakes."

I wasn't. I wouldn't. Yes, I had to work three jobs after my husband died to support me and Remy—and to pay off Greg's secret gambling debt. But this was different. I wasn't fighting to survive anymore, I was fighting to live. I was working hard to keep a life that made both me and Remy happy. There was nothing wrong with that.

I tapped my fingers against the gritty edge of the cauldron. "So if you don't want me working too hard, does that mean you're going to help me clean out the basement?"

Helen's face fell. "Yeah, I walked right into that one, didn't I?"

I gave her a sweet smile, and she just rolled her eyes and sat up. "A few boxes, and then I'm leaving. I am not going to get sucked into spending my whole day helping you clean down there."

I walked to the basement door, an extra bounce in my step as I opened it and descended the creaky stairs.

Creak. Creak. Creak.

My feet hit the hard cement floor, and my hand fumbled for the light switch in the dark, finally finding it and flicking on the dim light. Helen's feet padded against the stairs until she came to a stand next to me.

"Wow, this is going to need a ton of work. How are you going to renovate this place in just one month?"

Well, I hadn't figured that out yet, but I would. As soon as I got all this junk cleared out. Decades of random artifacts and trinkets collected by various ancestors lay in neatly packed boxes that filled the room.

I ignored Helen's pessimism and looked at the stacks of boxes. "Okay, so I'm thinking three piles: junk, things Remy might want to keep, things I want to keep."

Helen surveyed the space, wrinkling her nose. "I'm already regretting this."

I took a few steps into the room, my eyes adjusting to the dark.

"Let's start over here." I pointed to the left of us. "And then work our way around."

Helen marched over and opened a box. "Well, well, well, this might be interesting after all."

She picked up a matchbook and then a candlestick. I turned to focus on another box when I heard the sizzle of a match being lit and whipped around just in time to see Helen lighting the candle.

"Helen, no!"

The flame lit, and suddenly a tornado appeared in the middle of the room, swirling bigger, bigger, bigger, catching boxes and throwing them against the wall. Objects fell from the boxes, clunking on the floor, a knife flew past my head, and I ducked right before it could plant itself in my skull.

Helen grabbed me and we huddled in a corner as vases, plates, paintings, lamps flew around the room in a frenzy.

"The candle!" I yelled.

"What?" Helen yelled back, the whirring of the windstorm drowning out our words.

"Blow out the candle!"

Helen looked at the candle in her hand and let loose a huge breath, dousing the flickering flame. All at once the tornado vanished, and the boxes and objects dropped to the ground.

I surveyed the damage: boxes had been smashed, ripped open, artifacts littering every inch of the floor.

I glared at Helen, and she looked from the candle to me, then the candle again.

"How was I supposed to know lighting a candle would conjure . . . that?" She waved her hand at the mess in front of us.

I snatched the candle from her. "Helen, this is a basement full of relics from ancient, powerful witches. Half these objects are likely spelled."

"Well, you should've warned me. My specialty is slaying demons, not cleaning out witch's basements."

"I'm using you for your muscles."

She sniffed, slightly mollified. "I am pretty strong."

I patted her arm, then let out a big sigh. "Now what? Look at this mess. It's going to take me even longer to clean it all up."

Helen cocked her head, her gaze catching on something. "What's that?" She pointed to the back of the room.

Something gold glinted from the back wall, in between bricks that had moments ago been covered by the stacked boxes. A little wink of light flashed in and out.

I squinted, something niggling in my memory. "Wait a minute."

I picked my way over all the clutter and debris until I stood in front of the back wall. The little shimmer of gold blinked in and out. I dug my fingers between the brick and pulled, handing it to Helen as I stared at the object sitting in front of me.

"What is that?" Helen's asked in awe.

"It's a lamp. A golden lamp," I said, shaking my head. "Remy and I found it weeks ago, when we were down here cleaning."

"So why is it back here, in this wall?"

"I don't know." I shook my head, my memory over the whole thing foggy. "I think I put it back here? I can't remember." I turned to Helen. "Why can't I remember? That's weird, right?"

She nodded. "Definitely weird. Especially if you're telling me it just happened a few weeks ago and you literally just . . . don't remember?"

Gold twinkled under layers of rust and grime. Dents peppered the lamp's long spout, now bent, and rust covered the handle.

I tried to remember that night Remy and I had stumbled upon it. "I think . . . I think I told Remy it was just a piece of junk," I said. And then I'd just put it back in the wall, like it was no big deal that I'd found a freaking golden lamp in my basement.

"This is powerful Witch Granter magic." I tapped my chin. "Well, golden lamps are more common in the Middle East. Long ago, before there was a Council or any kind of law regarding magic, people would try to capture Witch Granters. In the Middle East, they used golden lamps, spelled with dark magic to trap Witch Granters, who they called jinn. They'd release the jinn when they wanted a wish." I shuddered. "It was evil. Obviously it's banned today, illegal to do this sort of thing." The lamp felt cold in my hands. "But why would a golden lamp be here in my basement?" And why had I completely forgotten about the fact that Remy and I had discovered it just weeks earlier?

Helen reached out to touch it, and I grabbed her arm. "Wait!"

She froze, looking at me.

"Don't touch it. Maybe there's a spell or something on it, a forgetful spell. As soon as one of us touches it, we'll forget about it and put it back here, where it'll continue to stay hidden." I turned to Helen, eyes wide. "That must be why I didn't remember it."

Except now that I knew of the spell, it wouldn't have the same power over me. I should be able to safely touch it without forgetting it again.

Helen frowned, retreating her stretched-out arm. "This sounds like powerful, dark magic, Clara. We have to figure out what it's doing in your basement."

I groaned. "Why do I have a feeling this has to do with my mother? Everything lately seems to be connected to her." After discovering my mother had been abusing her power as a Witch Granter when I was just nineteen years old, nothing surprised me anymore. She'd died five years ago, but she still managed to cause so much trouble in my life. I'd loved my mother so much, still did, but I couldn't forgive her for all the awful things she'd done, all in the name of power.

Helen planted her hands on her hips. "You know, your mom is not the only one surrounded by drama, Clara. You're like a magnet for it."

Well, I couldn't deny that. The last three months since we'd arrived in Whispering Willows had been eventful, to say the least. I'd come to The Wish List after being gone for twenty years, ready to sell it, take the money, and use it for me and Remy to start over. Instead, I found out due to an ancient family spell I was bound to the shop and couldn't sell it until I figured out how to undo the spell, which led me on a wild goose chase all over Whispering Willows as I tried to figure out how to do exactly that. Of course, while trying to undo the binding spell, I somehow fell back in love with Whispering Willows—and so did my daughter. I finally did figure out how to undo that binding spell, but it was too late. I wanted to stay, to make this place my home.

My perfect life.

I eyed the lamp, wishing that forgetful spell might still have a power over me. No such luck. The magic wouldn't work on me now. "Maybe we should just put this back." I lifted the lamp toward the wall. "Just because the forgetful spell won't work on me anymore doesn't mean I can't still just ignore it."

Helen grabbed my arm, stopping me from returning the lamp.

"Clara! This is dark magic hidden here in your basement. You can't just ignore it!"

"Why?" I whined.

Doing something about it might mean ruining the perfectly good life we had.

Helen just looked at me. "Because you can't just have dark magic like this hanging around in your shop."

I rolled my eyes.

Helen stared at the lamp, then nodded decisively. "We're going to visit my husband. If anyone would know about dark magic like this, it would be him."

I sighed, shoulders slumping as Helen dragged me out of the basement, away from what was supposed to be an easy, drama-free morning.

Chapter Three

I trailed Helen as we marched down Main Street, filled with little shops, palm trees lining the sidewalk, the salty ocean air tickling our nostrils. Once upon a time Whispering Willows had been the joke of the supernatural community, still was to an extent. Our town had been run over by demons, was known to be dangerous, home to a thriving black market where dark magic and dark dealings were traded frequently.

But the new mayor had turned this place around, invested in the people and our strengths. Now we had a downtown filled with every little shop you could imagine: jewelry, ice cream, potions, clothes, and so much more. I'd always loved Whispering Willows because it was my home, but now it was a place I could be proud of.

Helen took a sharp turn off Main Street, veering into an alleyway, away from the ocean and deeper into the heart of Whispering Willows.

"Listen," I said, lamp dangling in my hand, "I love seeing your husband more than anyone, but I don't think this is something we should explore. Let's forget about the lamp. Throw it back in the basement. Better yet, let's throw it in the ocean. Let it sink to the bottom and be done with it. If I'm right and that thing put a forgetful spell on me and Remy when we touched it, that's bad news, Helen. Real, real bad. Someone went to extraordinary lengths to make sure this thing was never found. There's probably a good reason for that."

Helen ignored me as we passed a dumpster full of animals digging through the trash.

A raccoon stopped its rummaging and stared right back at me. "What are you looking at, lady? Do I come to your home and stare at you while you eat?"

I ducked my head. This town was definitely full of some characters.

"Hello?" I asked Helen. "Am I speaking to a brick wall, here?"

"Clara." Helen continued to drag me with her ironclad grip. "You quite possibly have dark magic just hanging out in your basement. That's not okay."

We stopped in the middle of the alleyway, arriving at a black door with a half-giant standing outside, long shaggy black hair hanging to his shoulders, bulging muscles peeking out from his tight black T-shirt.

He took one look at Helen and opened the door, not even asking for a password, which was usually required to enter The Black Hat. Smoke immediately punched the air, pungent and thick as Helen and I waded our way through it, pulsing music vibrating the walls and floors around us. We walked through a long hallway with black walls, a black floor, a black ceiling—well, there was a reason the nightclub was called The Black Hat.

The hallway opened to a large space, with cozy U-shaped booths lining the walls. Splatters of water hit my face, and I looked over to the pool where sirens and tritons lounged, their tails splashing about. Cages hung over the dance floor, fairies dancing inside, each flap of their wings shaking dust over us that gave patrons a little zest, a high of sorts that would fill a missing need in their life. It would have no effect on me since nothing was missing from my life. I had everything I needed—what I didn't need was this stupid lamp and the mystery that came along with it.

It'd been a long, long time since I'd stepped foot in this place. Actually, the last time I'd been here was with Helen, twenty years ago. She arrived in Whispering Willows as a tourist on vacation, dealing with the fallout of her marriage ending. And that's when she'd found out she was a Demon Slayer. She didn't accept it at first, claimed she was only here for the weekend, but had eventually realized this was what she was meant to do.

"You look like you're lost in the past," Helen said.

I swallowed and stepped forward, gaze scanning the room. It was empty for the most part, being ten o' clock in the morning and all. A few regulars sat in shadowed corners, the dance floor completely empty save for two very drunk girls, strutting and stumbling like they were still partying from the night before.

"Just a lot of memories from here."

She grabbed my arm and pulled me from the dance floor and toward the stairs that led up to a second floor overlooking the first. From there we walked into a back hallway and finally came to red velvet curtain, two goblins guarding it, smoke curling out from underneath. Like the bouncer, they saw Helen and automatically parted the curtain. You got a five-star experience at The Black Hat when you were married to its owner.

Red and black velvet couches lined the walls where fairies, werewolves, vampires, leprechauns, every kind of supernatural in existence, lounged, many of them smoking pipes and puffing out the smoke in big rings. All employed by the Serpent.

In the center sat a throne, where a very grumpy-looking Gene resided. We'd officially entered the Serpent's lair. A leather jacket hugged his shoulders, and he wore tight leather pants. His gelled blonde hair glinted in the light, his jaw strong and sharp, a frown turning down the corners of his lips.

I jabbed my thumb at Helen. "Blame your wife. I told her we should leave it alone, but she was all *no, we need to go visit Gene right away—*"

He held up his hand. "Ah-ba-ba-ba-ba." He leaned closer as we approached. "Are you insane?" he whispered. "Coming into my business and using my given name *that nobody knows?*"

I bit my lip. Right. The only three people who knew his name were Helen, me, and Remy, and after being gone from Whispering Willows for twenty years, I had a hard time remembering that everyone else referred to the vampire as the Serpent.

"Serpent." I laughed uncomfortably. "I'm sorry your wife insisted on waking you up. Especially after you were already up bright and early this morning for Remy's school visit. All you need to do is tell her to leave this alone, and we'll be on our way."

Gene's dark eyes narrowed. "Leave what alone, exactly?"

Helen nodded at me, and I brought the lamp out from behind my back.

He stared at it, no expression on his face. "Why is *that* here?"

If anyone could smell dark magic, it would be the Serpent. He used to deal it exclusively on the black market, a middle man who bought dark magic from witches and then sold it to other supernaturals. Once he met Helen, he cleaned up his life, bought The Black Hat, and turned it into a profitable business. But even if he no longer walked on the dark side, the Serpent had a certain reputation he liked to maintain.

"You can feel it, right?" Helen asked, voice far too excited. "The dark magic?"

He nodded. "Fucking hell. Why do you have that thing?"

"We found it in the basement of The Wish List," I said. "But the good news is we can just put it back. Forget we ever found it. Wash our hands of it."

He rubbed a hand over his face. "Oh god. You're a magnet for trouble, you know that? A golden fucking lamp. In your basement. Oh, this is bad."

"I told you he'd be grumpy if we woke him up for this," I said to Helen out of the side of my mouth.

Gene really took not-a-morning-person to a new level.

"Just tell Clara what she should do," Helen said, then started pacing. "I mean, why would someone cast a forgetful spell on this thing? Why would they hide it in The Wish List? What were they afraid of?"

Gene sighed, his shoulders slumping. "It's too early in the morning for this. I just wanted to sleep in my coffin. But does anyone care about what I want? No."

Helen raised an eyebrow at him.

Gene held up his hands. "Okay, okay. You need to see the mermaids. They might know how this lamp ended up here, or at least can tell you what to do with it."

"Mermaids?" I asked. The mermaids weren't who came to mind when I thought of someone who might know about a golden lamp.

"Yes. The mermaids," Gene gritted out. "They're the most well-traveled of the supernaturals, have regular dealings in the Dead Sea, where the magical lamps originated. These things are rare, Clara. Very rare. You need to figure out why you have one in your possession."

"Are you sure we shouldn't just forget about this?" I asked. "Come on, guys. Do you really want to invite more trouble to Whispering Willows?"

"It's already been invited." Gene gestured to the golden object. "What are you so afraid of, exactly?"

I rolled my eyes. "Oh, I don't know. That I'm going to get wrapped up in yet another dangerous adventure that will put everyone I love at risk. Life is good right now. Why do we need to go and mess it up?"

"Great." Gene stood and clapped his hands. A leprechaun jumped at the noise. "So glad you woke me to ask my advice and then blatantly ignore it. Now, I'm going back to my coffin." He approached us and swatted Helen's butt. "And if you're going to wake me up again, love, you better be naked next time you do it."

Well, there was a visual. Helen might not have been my biological mother, but she was like a surrogate mother to me, and therefore, I didn't want to be privy to her sex life with Gene—didn't want it on my radar at all.

Helen shot him a coy smile, and he kissed her on the cheek and walked out the curtains with a swagger to his step.

I stared at the lamp cradled in my hands. How could such an old and tarnished piece of metal cause so much trouble? I didn't want to go see the mermaids about this. I didn't want to deal with it at all. Maybe I still wouldn't have to.

Chapter Four

The bell to The Wish List jingled, and I wrenched my gaze away from the golden lamp sitting on the counter and looked up to see a familiar witch standing in the doorway. She was older, skin pale, big gold hoops dangling from her ears, long gray hair hanging down past her shoulders.

"Dara," I said, surprised. "Welcome to The Wish List. What—what are you doing here?"

It was so odd being back in Whispering Willows and constantly running into people from my past, especially ones I never expected to see.

Dara folded her hands together in front of her, fidgeting from foot to foot.

"I'd like to buy a wish," she said in a small voice, and I gestured to the purple couch that sat in the middle of the shop, already feeling uneasy. I hadn't seen Dara in years, hadn't even thought about her. The last time I had seen her, she'd been getting high off dark fairy dust, stumbling and laughing, ignoring my pleas for her to clean up and get her life together. That had been over twenty years ago. She didn't look high now, didn't look like an addict. Still, my hackles raised at seeing her here, in my shop.

"Why don't you take a seat?" I asked.

She shuffled over, and I joined her with a clipboard and some forms.

"Dara, are you... aware of the cost that comes with a wish?"

Wishes weren't cheap, not in terms of money—or in terms of your soul. Wishes were the most powerful form of magic, and, well, magic always came with a price. In this case, the price was a piece of the soul.

She gave a firm nod. "Yes."

I wondered where she'd gotten the money to pay for something like this. Dara had blown most of her savings on drugs after her husband had died, spiraled down a dark path. But I had been gone for twenty years, and I knew better than anyone, people could change. I had to give Dara a fair chance, let her answer my questions, and I would evaluate if she was a good candidate to receive a wish, just like I did with everyone. She deserved that much, at least. Besides, this would be a good distraction from that damn lamp, its presence heavy and looming.

I'd spent the last hour staring at it, wondering what I should do about it. Yes, Gene and Helen had advised me to investigate, figure out where the lamp had come from and why it ended up at The Wish List. But just because that's what they advised didn't mean that's what I had to do.

I took a deep breath and set the clipboard and a spelled quill down on the coffee table in front of us. The quill righted itself, poised to take notes as I went through each question with the witch. I started with the basics: name, address, type of supernatural, any medical history I needed to be aware of, a quick prick of blood, and then we were ready for the most important question:

"What do you want to wish for?" I asked, because I had to, but also because I was curious.

She tapped her foot, hands clenched in front of her, knuckles white. "Clara, Emerson is coming back."

My breath caught in my throat at hearing the name. A name I hadn't heard in a long, long time. My high school best friend, well, ex best friend, was coming back to Whispering Willows?

I swallowed a few times. "So what are you wishing for, exactly?"

"I want to wish that my daughter will find happiness. I think—" Dara looked down at her hands in her lap. "Well, I think she's been lost for far too long. And she's traveling here for her aunt's funeral—"

"Aunt Kathy?" I gasped. Aunt Kathy was Emerson's idol, or at least she had been when Emerson and I were still on speaking terms. I shook my head. "Sorry. I didn't mean to interrupt."

Dara's eyes welled with tears. "Yes, my sister died. Some boating accident off the Amalfi Coast. It's going to be hard for Emerson. The funeral. And coming home. I know she's going to be so angry. Any time I've tried to reach out she's been so full of hate, and I'm afraid it's going to ruin her. I want to wish for her happiness. And maybe, well, maybe if she's happy we could have a better relationship. Or a relationship at all, really."

The quill scratched furiously, recording her answers to my questions.

I stayed silent, letting everything Dara said sink in. Emerson was coming back. Her aunt had died. She was angry. That part didn't surprise me. Emerson had been angry right up until the day she'd disappeared. No phone call, no text. Nothing. There one day, gone the next. That had effectively ended our friendship.

It was selfish of me, but I didn't want to deal with this. It sounded like Emerson had a lot going on, and I didn't need to get in the middle. Not now, not when Remy and I were just getting settled into our lives, and especially not after finding that lamp. I already had enough on my plate as it was.

"Dara." I leaned forward. "The thing is, you were an addict, and wishes are addictive. Exactly like drugs."

Witch Granters knew the dangers of wishes, but many supernaturals didn't, and for the most part, it wasn't something I told clients, not if I didn't think they were at risk of becoming addicted. But Dara, well, she was a big risk.

Dara's eyes widened. "I didn't know."

I nodded. "You get a high from wishes, and if you're someone prone to highs like that, you could want more, become desperate. Make wish after wish, give away piece after piece of your soul until there's nothing left. Until you become a Hatter."

Her eyes were as big as plates now. "A H-hatter?"

"Someone who's become addicted to wishes to the point that they lose themselves and go mad."

"Like the Mad Hatter."

"Yes, that's where the term originated."

Dara chewed on a fingernail. "What happens if I give up too much of my soul?"

I bit my cheek. "You turn into a demon and then the Demon Slayer will most likely have to kill you."

Scratch that. Helen would definitely kill her.

Dara's hand lifted to her mouth as she processed the information, but after a few seconds, a look of determination settled across her features. "That won't happen to me. I'm clean now. I've been clean for years. I've gotten my life together, and the only piece missing is my daughter. It's my fault she's so angry, so jaded."

I believed it. Emerson and her mom had a complicated relationship, and I always knew not to ask questions. It was a touchy subject for Emerson.

"Please, Clara." Dara pressed her hands together. "I won't even be able get another wish. You won't let me become addicted."

Oh, sweet naive Dara. Unfortunately, there were Witch Granters out there who doled out wishes as they pleased, not caring whom their actions affected, only wanting the money and power that came from granting wishes. My own mother had been one of those Witch Granters, preying on innocent people, taking pieces of their soul and using it for dark magic.

"I don't know," I said. This seemed like a bad idea. Something in my gut told me to say no. "Maybe Emerson needs to make this journey herself. If she's so angry, so full of hate, then it sounds like you two have a lot to unpack. You can't expect a wish to just do that for you."

Dara shook her head. "No. I don't have that kind of time. Emerson will only be here for the funeral, then she'll leave Whispering Willows, and I'll never see her again. She won't even give me her phone number, let alone her address. I had to ask one of Kathy's friends to tell Emerson about her aunt's death, about the funeral. If Emerson ever meant anything to you, you'll do this. Wouldn't it be amazing to have your best friend back?"

In theory, yes. But in reality? Hell no. Emerson coming back meant drama. I was officially living the drama-free life. Why did no one seem to get that memo? Besides, we hadn't spoken in over twenty years. We were probably completely different people at this point.

I gave a tentative nod, not wanting to hurt Dara's feelings.

"So you'll grant me the wish, then?" Dara asked, and I looked from my clipboard to her.

I had to be impartial as a Witch Granter. Dara was clean, she said it herself. And if this were any other person whom I didn't know, I'd grant the wish. I couldn't treat Dara differently just because we had a past. "Yes." I swallowed. "You'll get your wish."

Relief flooded her eyes, which made me happy. I hoped this would do what Dara wanted and change Emerson's life for the better, strengthen their relationship. But other than granting this wish, I wanted to stay out of it.

I bustled behind the counter and grabbed a delicate crystal ball from the shelf, holding it out in my palm. Dara's eyes grew wide upon seeing the little crystal with lines of color zipping through it.

"All I have to do now is enact the crystal with your wish," I said to her. "Just focus on what you want, and I'll do the rest."

I picked up my black obsidian wand and tapped it to the crystal ball. Sparks of green and blue color shot through the crystal, more frantic now, bouncing off the glass, the color glowing brighter and brighter until it filled the entire shop. Suddenly, the blue light receded, zapping back into the little crystal ball, reflecting in the witch's wide eyes.

"The crystal is now enacted with your wish," I said gently and handed her the ball. "Bring the crystal to your mouth and whisper your wish."

She stared at the little crystal, unsure. "It's that simple?"

I nodded. "It's that simple."

Well, not really. It was simple to an outsider, but it was actually incredibly powerful and rare magic that very few witches possessed.

I stretched my hand out further, and she reached for the crystal, but before she could grab it, a puff of black smoke filled the air. The crystal fell from my hand and, in what felt like slow motion, dropped straight to the ground. I yelled and reached for it, but it was too late. The wish smashed to the floor.

"No!" I cried as the glass shattered into a million little pieces, the wish inside leaking out all over the wooden floorboards, bubbling, and then slowly dissipating.

I stared in shock at the carnage, then looked around for the source of the black smoke, which was now receding . . . straight back into the golden lamp.

"What just happened?" Dara asked, eyes wild. "Do you have to make another wish?"

Tears welled in my eyes. I couldn't believe it. This had never happened. It simply *didn't* happen. Witch Granters didn't drop wishes. Once a wish was enacted, it wanted to be granted, to find its source. Accidents like this weren't possible. I sent a sideways glance over to the lamp . . . Unless some other kind of magic, a mischievous kind, was at play.

"I . . ." My throat felt dry and scratchy. "I'm so sorry, but a wish cannot be enacted more than once."

It was the law of Witch Granters, in our code book.

Dara's mouth turned down into a frown. "But what does that mean? I can't ever get my wish, then? Can't help my daughter find happiness?"

My heart hammered in my chest. "I am so, so sorry," I said again, not knowing what else to say. "Please, come back. Tomorrow, maybe. We'll figure this out. I promise."

But she was already backing away, anger reddening her cheeks. "I came to you, came to The Wish List, because I was told you were the best. But this . . . this is . . ."

It was inexcusable.

I reached for her. "Please let me find a solution. I will figure this out, I promise. I won't stop until we find a way to make this wish come true, to help Emerson."

Dara just shook her head in disgust. "I should've known it was too good to be true. No, I'm done with wishes, done with having any kind of hope for a good, happy future. This is my lot in life, and I just need to accept it."

No, no, I couldn't let her believe that was true.

But before I could speak, she turned and fled the shop, while I stared after her in horror. Dara's dreams, her hopes, were just crushed, and it was all my fault.

Chapter Five

The door to the shop jingled, but I made no attempt to move from my position on the couch, where I lay with an arm draped over my eyes.

"We're closed," I croaked, voice hoarse after crying for an hour, brainstorming every solution I could think of to help Dara, only to come up with absolutely nothing.

"Mom?" Remy's voice floated through the air, and I heard her shoes squeaking across the floor and then the rustling of her sitting down on the purple chair next to the couch.

I let my arm fall from my eyes and looked at Remy, who straightened like she'd just been shocked by an electric zap.

"Why are your eyes so red and puffy—have you been crying?" She tutted at me. "Did you watch one of those sappy romance movies again? I told you not to watch those anymore because all they do is make you cry. I mean, come on Mom, you know they have to break up before they can get together for good. That's how they work."

I slowly pushed myself to a seated position and waved away her words. "No, no, it's nothing like that." I sent a glare at the golden lamp sitting on the coffee table, looking so innocent. I should've just gotten rid of it like my instincts told me to. But I'd been stupid and listened to Helen and Gene, actually contemplating trying to solve the mystery of this thing. It had been idiotic, and I'd ruined Dara's wish because of it, possibly ruined her only chance at reconciliation with her daughter.

Remy glanced at the lamp, then back at me. "You better start from the beginning."

So I did. Remy listened, no judgement passing across her face.

Now she leaned forward, squinting at the lamp. "Wait a minute. That's so weird. I do kind of remember finding this lamp a few weeks ago. How did I completely forget about it?"

"Because it's spelled," I said. "Why, I don't know." I shook my head. "But we have to get rid of this thing now before it causes any more trouble—" I paused when a spurt of black smoke shot from the lamp. Remy and I both ducked, and I squeezed my eyes shut, mind whirling with possibilities of what the lamp could possibly be doing now.

I heard a soft trickle at first and slowly sat up to see rain pouring down in the corner of my shop, a dark cloud overhead. The lamp created a rain shower in my store. Seriously?

"Wow," Remy said. "That thing is trouble."

"We're getting rid of it. Right away. I don't care what anyone else thinks. This lamp has got to go."

Remy's eyes darted from me to the lamp. "Are you sure, though? I mean, Aunt Helen and Uncle Gene are right. That's clearly dark magic, and shouldn't we be trying to fix it rather than just ignore it?"

"Not you too," I said. "Remy, it's not our job to fix this."

She bit her lip, not looking sure, and then my gaze caught on her purple backpack seated at her feet.

"Oh my god! Your first day of school!" I dragged a hand over my face. "How was it? Did you make new friends? Did you like your teachers? Did you meet any boys? I'm so sorry I forgot to ask. I was so wrapped up with all of this"—I waved my hand to the lamp—"that I didn't even think of it."

Definitely not winning any Mother of the Year awards over here.

Remy laughed. "It was a pretty typical first day." She tilted her head, brown curls brushing her shoulder. "Well, except for the part where I learned about magic and the history of Whispering Willows. In Portland I learned about World War II; here I'm learning about demon and vampire wars." She paused. "Yes, I liked all my teachers, except for my math teacher, who assigned us homework on the first day. Who does that? No, I didn't make any new friends, but I did learn I have three classes with Megan, which was awesome. No, I didn't meet any new boys." Pink tinged her cheeks at that last remark.

I leaned forward. "Liar."

She looked away, her curls covering her face, so much like my own with those freckles dotting her nose and wide green eyes. She could be my twin, except for my stick-straight, and graying, brown hair, so opposite of her beautiful curls.

"Oh my gosh," I said. "You are definitely lying. Who's the boy?"

She looked back at me, a rueful smile on her face. "Okay fine, there's this vampire . . ."

I groaned. "Not a vampire!"

She pointed at me. "Uncle Gene is a vampire."

"Exactly!"

Gene was arrogant, grumpy, stubborn, and generally hated everyone and everything with the exception of Helen and Remy. He tolerated me.

Remy swooned in her seat. She actually swooned with her hands pressed together and her eyes all dreamy. "He's tall and handsome and smart. He answered every question correctly in our science class."

Oh, she had it bad, and I wasn't sure how I felt about that. I remembered having an all-consuming crush in high school on one particular boy, and while it worked out well for me when we finally got together, it had been torture crushing on someone who didn't notice me for the longest time. And it distracted me from my schoolwork. I still remember getting grounded when my grades had started dropping.

"So did you talk to him?" I pressed.

She crossed her arms. "No, not yet. I'm biding my time. I'm not just going to go talk to him the first day of school."

" . . . Why not? Isn't that what you're supposed to do?"

Remy just rolled her eyes. "You really don't know anything, Mom."

Well, that was true when it came to teenagers and trying to decode their weird dating habits and relationship rituals.

I drummed my fingers against my thigh. "Okay, so, what's the verdict? How did Whispering Willows Magical Academy do?"

Remy tapped her chin. "Like on a scale of one to ten?"

"Sure."

"Let's go with a solid eight."

I raised my eyebrows. "That's promising!"

Remy smiled. "Yeah, I think it is. And that's with the little setback this morning. Martin is a meme at our school now, and I'm afraid he's going to find out, let it go to his head, and try for even more ridiculous stunts to get more memes made about him."

I didn't tell her that ship had already sailed, and the imp definitely knew he was a meme and was definitely pleased.

I held up a hand. "I had a stern talk with everyone about that. They will not be making any more surprise visits at school."

"Did Bones actually have a video camera?"

"He did."

"And did Martin seriously bring one of those cheesy first-day-of-school signs?"

"He did."

"And did Uncle Gene actually get out of his coffin for that visit?"

"He did." Though that was mostly because Helen, who was freakishly strong, dragged him out and made him come.

Remy's gaze landed on the lamp. "Well, that sums up my day. Now, what are we supposed to do about *that*?"

I thought about my meeting with Gene earlier in the day. The warning he gave. The one I wasn't going to heed.

"I think we need to borrow Martin's boat," I said.

Remy wrinkled her nose. "Martin's boat?"

I nodded. "We're taking a little trip out to sea."

Chapter Six

Martin pushed the oars through the choppy waters of the Pacific Ocean, cool mist spraying our skin and the occasional splash of water landing inside the rickety old rowboat where we sat. Martin had insisted on rowing us out to sea himself, claiming that he was the only one who could steer his boat.

Thankfully, I convinced Remy to stay behind at The Wish List and watch over the shop while I was gone. I didn't want her anywhere near this sad excuse for a boat that could capsize at any moment. I'd tried to sneak away by myself, but Helen showed up at the shop and insisted on coming. Like I needed a babysitter or something to go on this mission.

A mission I wasn't telling Helen the truth about because I knew she wouldn't approve of what I intended to do, but semantics. Gene and Helen wanted me to talk to the mermaids, to find out information about this lamp, but after what it did to Dara's wish, I couldn't risk keeping the thing around.

"I can't believe I'm rowing you out to sea *again*," Martin said, referring to just a few months ago, when he'd rowed me and Helen to the middle of the ocean for a very different mystery I'd been determined to solve. "If Karissa sees me out here, she's going to kill me."

I rolled my eyes. "Did you ghost her again?" Last time we were here, Martin had showered the siren with kisses and promises, empty promises, apparently. I didn't get it. She was beautiful, way out of Martin's league, and for some reason, completely obsessed with the imp. So naturally, he wanted nothing to do with her.

"You know, you're very nosy," Martin said. "My love life is none of your business. Besides, Remy said it sounded like me and Karissa weren't compatible. You know your daughter is very wise. She's helping me work through quite a lot of things. Did you know that because my own mother abandoned me and sold me to the Devil that I now seek relationships where I can leave before I'm left?" He continued rowing. "I can't believe that took two centuries to unpack."

"So you can't discuss your relationships with me, but you have no problem talking about them with my daughter?"

Helen's head hung over the boat as she vomited, the sound providing background noise to our conversation.

"You know, I know a leprechaun who knows a faerie who knows a seer who could open a portal and dump that thing in hell." Martin nodded toward the golden lamp that lay in the bottom of the boat, on top of a towel. Although I was immune to the forgetful spell, I was wary of touching something that emanated dark magic, so I'd used the towel to transport it.

"I'm not opening the portal to hell, Martin." Someone already made that mistake a hundred years ago, and it turned Whispering Willows into a demon hub for almost a century, until Helen finally arrived to claim her position as Demon Slayer and keep the demons in check. "I have other plans."

Martin mumbled something under his breath while Helen heaved again, then sat up, her skin pale and a sheen of sweat across her face. "You're going to take Gene's advice and ask the mermaids?"

I fiddled with my hands, pressing my lips together.

Helen narrowed her gaze at me. "What do you have planned, Clara?"

I was saved from answering by her face turning almost as green as Martin's as she leaned over the boat and vomited again.

Martin scoffed. "Why did you come out here if you know you get seasick? You're getting bile on the side of my boat that I just polished."

Nothing could polish this old thing, but Martin was very protective of his rowboat.

Helen wiped her mouth as Martin slowed his rowing. "I'm here to support Clara," she said. Liar. She was here to watch me and make sure I didn't do anything impulsive, which was exactly what I planned to do.

"Support her from land, send her a nice text, wave her off. This level of support isn't necessary." Martin stopped the boat.

Helen's fist curled, and I was afraid she might punch the imp, which I would actually love to see, but not on this boat. A fight might very well sink this thing.

"Okay, okay." I held out my hands between them. "Let's just stick to the task at hand."

A task I technically still hadn't told them about . . .

A seagull landed next to us, snapping up a fish that jumped out of the water with its big orange beak.

"Oh, look at that," Martin said, smiling and cooing at the bird.

Out of nowhere, dark smoke swirled from the lamp's spout, rising into the air, captivating all of us as we watched its slow-moving path—straight toward the seagull.

"Shoo," I yelled, making a frantic motion with my hands at the bird as I watched the smoke float toward it. "Go, fly away."

The seagull paid me no mind, munching on its lunch, the fishtail twitching in its mouth.

The dark smoke circled around the seagull, encasing it fully until we could no longer see the bird. Martin's eyes were wide, and I attempted to reach out, push the bird from the dark cloud, but Helen grabbed my arm and pulled me back.

"You are not getting sucked into that weird smoke cloud."

The black fog hovered there, no sound coming from the bird, before it finally receded, flying straight back into the lamp. We all turned our attention to the seagull, and I feared for the worst, but there it sat, crunching on the fish like nothing had happened

The seagull looked at us. "La la la," it screeched.

Then we screeched.

Then it screeched back at us.

"La la la la laaaaaaa," it said over and over.

"The seagull can sing," I said, horrified.

"It can sing out of tune." Helen covered her ears. "Make it stop."

"Fi fa fo. La di daaaaaa," the bird sang, the sound somewhere between a garbage disposal and nails against a chalkboard.

"Oh this is weird, even for Whispering Willows," Martin grumbled.

I glanced back at the lamp. "Do you think . . . did the lamp do that?"

The seagull's singing got louder.

"Well, last time I checked, seagulls don't belt out tunes, so yes, I'd say the lamp definitely did that," Martin yelled.

The seagull cocked its head, then opened its large beak and started singing a godawful showtune.

Martin covered his ears. "Make it stop, make it stop, please. I'll do anything."

Helen reached out and poked the seagull with an oar, which only made it sing louder.

"Row!" Helen yelled over the awful noise. "Go, go, go."

Martin grabbed the oars, and rowed through the choppy waters until the singing stopped piercing my brain, a distant wail now.

Martin pointed at the lamp. "That thing needs to go."

I could not agree more.

Water bubbled around us, foaming and frothy until I saw the shimmers of a tail flipping in the water.

Martin groaned. "Great. Karissa found out I'm here. Are you happy? You're about to witness a very awkward exchange, and it's all your fault."

I put a hand to my chest. "It's my fault you ghosted the mermaid?"

But the head that popped out of the water wasn't Martin's ex. Helen's face went even whiter, if that was possible. It was hers.

Green and blue scales covered muscular arms and a rock-hard chest, leading up to a strong jaw, piercing eyes, and wavy brown hair. It had been twenty years since I'd seen Aiden, but the triton had aged well.

"Helen," Aiden said, his voice polite, restrained.

Helen flashed him a strained smile. She'd been the one to break his heart after falling for the Serpent, a move that no one, including myself, saw coming. In fact, after Helen had told me she and the Serpent, aka Gene, were getting married, I'd tried to talk her out of it, sure she was making a mistake, reeled in by the whole bad-boy vibe Gene had going on. But here we were, almost twenty years after the Demon Slayer and

Whispering Willow's most notorious vampire fell for each other, and they were clearly the perfect match.

Helen patted her short blond hair, gelled into spikes today that made her look every bit the fierce Demon Slayer she was.

"Awkward," Martin said out in a high-pitched voice, and I elbowed him.

Aiden turned his stormy gaze onto Martin. "At least she had the decency to break it off with me face-to-face."

My mouth dropped open, and so did Helen's. Martin and Aiden? Seriously? "Have you slept with *everyone* in Whispering Willows?" I asked the imp.

Martin sniffed. "I don't see gender, just the person on the inside."

"You mean how hot someone is," I corrected.

Martin frowned. "That's what I just said."

I rolled my eyes.

Aiden tore his gaze from the imp and cleared his throat. "What brings you all out here, exactly?"

I picked up the white towel, which cradled the lamp, trying to hide it away. "Nothing for you to worry about. Just taking a nice trip out to sea."

Helen glared at me. "What are you doing?" she asked.

"Nothing," I said out the side of my mouth. "Mind your own business."

Helen reached for the towel, and I held onto it tighter. She tugged, harder than necessary, and I went flying forward, the lamp rising up into the air and plunking back down in the boat.

Aiden frowned at the golden object, his eyes wide. "Why do you have a magic lamp in your possession?"

I threw the towel over my shoulder. "It's a long story, but I'm handling it."

"No you're not," Helen said, then looked at Aiden. "We thought you might have some information about lamps like this one?"

Aiden pushed a hand through his thick dark hair. "I do. My clan is very familiar with these abominations."

"You know what?" I said, grabbing the towel and scooping up the lamp. "I'm good. I don't need to know. Knowledge is dangerous."

Martin scratched his head. "I think the saying is knowledge is power."

"Will you shut up?" I hissed.

Aiden just crossed his arms. "Do you want my help or not?"

"No," I said at the same time as Helen said, "Yes."

"Oh, for god sakes," Martin mumbled.

Helen cut a glare in my direction. "We'd appreciate anything you could tell us," she said to Aiden.

The triton stared at the lamp cradled in my lap. "I sense dark magic, something twisted inside that lamp."

In? I gulped. I hadn't thought about the fact that something could be inside of it, and that little tidbit sent chills skittering up my arms.

"These golden lamps originated in the Middle East," Aiden said.

That much I'd already known.

"Supernaturals would spell the lamps to trap a Witch Granter, and once they were trapped in the lamp, they became a jinn, no longer a Witch Granter."

Or a genie, the more well-known term here in the United States.

"A mermaid once traveled here from the Dead Sea," Aiden continued. "She told us a tale of a golden lamp her clan had found in a shipwreck. They summoned the jinn trapped inside the lamp, hoping to try and help the jinn, but it was too late."

My stomach dropped.

"What do you mean too late?" Helen asked.

"The jinn had been trapped for almost a thousand years and had gone completely mad. They had no choice but to leave it there in the lamp. They buried it, hoping no one would ever find the object and abuse its power."

"That's awful," I whispered.

Helen and I looked at each other. I'd filled her in on what happened at The Wish List earlier today, how the lamp made me destroy a wish. Did that mean there was an actual jinn trapped in this lamp, a former Witch Granter? There had to be something else going on here, though. Someone hid that lamp in the basement, put a forgetful spell on it for a reason. It might not have anything inside of it, other than dark magic.

"Have you ever heard of lamps misfiring?" I asked, unable to help myself.

Aiden frowned. "What do you mean?"

"A lamp that fires out spells that destroy things, causes mischief?"

Aiden shook his head. "I haven't heard of anything like that. But like I said, I sensed dark magic when I first saw that lamp."

Guilt niggled at me, but I didn't even know why. This lamp was nothing but trouble. I didn't owe it, or whatever may lurk inside, anything. Yet I still felt a responsibility to it.

Then I thought about how the lamp had ruined Dara's wish, the anguish on her face at knowing she lost an opportunity to reconcile with her daughter. This lamp could destroy my entire business, destroy every wish that I tried to grant. I couldn't let that happen.

Mind made up, I lifted the lamp as Helen reached for me and yelled no, and I dropped it into the ocean, watching as it sank further and further away, no longer my problem to deal with.

Chapter Seven

I paced back and forth outside The Wish List, darting furtive glances inside, too afraid to go into my own shop.

"What the feck are you doing out here?" Myrtle approached, today her tracksuit bubblegum pink, her rectangle glasses equally glittery and pink. "Aren't you supposed to be granting wishes and living out your dream and all that jazz?" She nodded toward the sign, which was flipped to Closed.

Yes, yes I was supposed to be granting wishes. Except for the very unfortunate fact that I'd arrived that morning to see the golden lamp sitting there on the counter, taunting me. The same golden lamp I'd just chucked into the ocean yesterday.

Myrtle pressed her face up against the glass window, looking inside. "Now wait a minute. I thought you texted that you'd thrown the lamp to the bottom of the ocean. Good riddance to that thing. Gives me the heebie jeebies." She shuddered.

I gulped. I had. I'd even told Remy we would go out for pizza to celebrate being rid of the menace. Imagine my surprise when I arrived at The Wish List this morning to see the lamp, covered in seaweed and sand, sitting on the counter like it had never left. I told Myrtle as much and she scratched her head.

"Bad omen, that is. You need to get rid of it."

I threw my arms in the air. "What do you think I've been trying to do?"

"Hey, why aren't you granting wishes?" Helen said as she approached, coffee in hand. Behind her, palm trees lined the sidewalk, swaying in the gentle breeze, the beautiful sun shining down. It was another nice day in Whispering Willows. If only I could actually enjoy it.

Myrtle pointed at Helen's leather jacket, which had something on it that looked a lot like pink, slimy entrails. "You got a little something, dear."

Helen looked down and flicked it off. "Whoops, nothing like some demon intestine to start your day."

Myrtle wrinkled her nose. "Another demon, eh? They've been popping up a lot lately."

Helen waved her hand. "Demons come in waves. Sure, there are a few more than usual lurking in Whispering Willows lately, but I've got it handled." The bags under her eyes told a different story. She took a long sip of her coffee. "Back to you. Why is The Wish List closed?"

I gestured toward the lamp, and much like Myrtle had, Helen pressed her face against the glass. I was going to need to invest in some glass cleaner.

Helen turned back around. "But you threw the lamp into the ocean yesterday. I saw you do it, even though I told you not to."

"She did," Myrtle said.

"So, then why is the lamp . . .?"

"We don't know!" Myrtle blurted out. "Got another mystery on our hands."

Helen groaned. "Don't say that word. Please. The M word needs to be banned in this town." She gave me a pointed look. "I won't say I told you so, but . . ."

"It won't go away," I said. "No matter what I do, that lamp is determined to keep causing trouble."

"What kind of trouble?" Myrtle asked just as a spurt of black smoke shot from the lamp and flew toward the window with surprising speed.

"Duck!" I yelled, and we all crouched down, except for Myrtle, slower than the rest of us in her old age.

The black smoke floated right through the window and hit her head, and I yelped, dashing toward her as the smoke swirled around her hair. When it dissipated, I gasped in horror.

"What?" Myrtle patted her head. "What's wrong?"

Helen stood slowly, staring. "Oh my."

"Um." I pointed at her hair. "The lamp might've turned your hair green."

"Green?" Myrtle asked, frowning. "What kind of green?"

"It looks like vomit," Helen said, taking a sip of her coffee.

"Great," Myrtle said. "Now I'm going to have to change my tracksuit to match. I don't have any puke-green tracksuits."

"I'm so sorry." I shot a glare at Helen. "This is exactly why I want this thing gone."

Helen took a deep breath. "You clearly can't ignore this, Clara."

"I'm with Clara." Myrtle still patted her hair self-consciously. "No investigating anything."

Helen sighed into her cup. "She needs to figure out what it's doing in her shop and who put it there. Then maybe it will stop being such a menace."

The lamp's presence made me uneasy, just lurking there, the stench of dark magic wafting from it, tainting my shop.

"I don't want to learn about it. I have to get rid of that thing ASAP."

Then life could go back to normal. No. Rocking. The. Boat.

Helen pointed a finger toward the tall library in the distance. "You need to do some research."

I groaned. Not the library. The one with the ancient librarian who hated me. I just got back into her good graces by returning a page that had been torn from one of her precious books, and it felt too soon to face her again.

Helen continued, "If there's anywhere you're going to learn about a golden lamp and how to destroy it, it'll be the library."

I held up a finger. "Or I can go visit the mermaids because they seem to know quite a lot about these lamps. They can tell me what to do with it. Aiden was really helpful."

Helen choked on her coffee, and I rolled my eyes while Myrtle thumped her back. "Oh for god sakes, Helen. It's been twenty years since you two had a fling. You're very happy with Gene, and I'm sure

Aiden has moved on." I shook my head. "You're acting like some bumbling teenager."

A black car drove by, and I instinctively dove behind a bench, heart pounding. "Is it gone?" I whispered.

"You thought that was the mayor, didn't you?" Helen said, voice accusatory.

"No." Yes. Yes, I did. The mayor . . . who happened to be my ex. Helen shot me a satisfactory smile. "We just broke up like two weeks ago! You and Aiden haven't been a thing for two decades. It's not the same."

"Uh-huh," Helen said, sipping her coffee.

"So what if you broke the triton's heart?" Myrtle asked Helen. "You got the love of your life in the end, so who cares?"

Helen gave a half shrug. "I'm just bad at confrontation is all. I might've waited until Gene and I got together to have the breakup conversation with Aiden. After I sort of just stopped talking to him?" She cringed.

My mouth dropped open. "You're as bad as Martin. You never actually broke up with Aiden?"

"Everything happened so fast! Gene and I were on some mission, trying to save Whispering Willows from the portal to hell opening up, demons overtaking us, and our town being swallowed into the earth, and you know, one thing led to another, and I kind of just never let Aiden know we were over? I mean, I did eventually, but it might've taken me a while. Besides, we weren't officially dating or anything. It had just been flirting up to that point, but he felt like I led him on."

I stared at her for a minute, trying to process everything she'd said. "You'd think the older we got the better we'd be at relationships, but that's not really a thing, is it?"

"That's why I avoid 'em altogether," Myrtle said cheerfully.

"What are you guys doing?"

We all jumped, Remy's voice bringing us back to the present.

"Just chatting," I mumbled, then slung an arm around Remy's shoulder. "How was school today?"

She shrugged. "Same as yesterday." She kissed me on the cheek, then kissed Helen, and then Myrtle. "I promise I'll let you know if anything worthy of gossip happens."

"That's all I ask," I said.

Remy gasped as her gaze landed on the lamp. "What is that doing back here?" She pressed her face against the glass. "I thought it was supposed to be at the bottom of the ocean."

I gestured to all of us. "Join the club, kiddo. We've got another mystery on our hands."

One I had no intention of pursuing. The mermaids could help me dispose of this thing once and for all. I was sure of it.

Remy rubbed her hands together. "Ooh, sounds juicy."

Helen snorted.

"So where do we start?" Remy was already unslinging the backpack from her shoulder, ready for action.

"You're not starting anywhere." I pointed at her. "I know the teachers at the Academy, and that means I know you have homework. Me, however, I'm making another trip out to sea."

"You're going back to the mermaids? Seriously?" Helen asked. "What about the library plan?"

I brushed her off. "I don't want to learn about the lamp. I just want it gone." And to get my life back to being drama free.

Besides, golden lamps were such rare and ancient relics, they weren't well studied in our world. In fact, I bet the library wouldn't even have information on something so old and obsolete.

"Scaredy cat," Myrtle coughed, and I just glared at her.

I looked at Remy. "How about this? You do your homework, and then we can go together? Not in Martin's boat, though. I'm not letting you step foot in that thing, no matter how safe Martin claims it to be."

Remy just rolled her eyes. "Sure, but we already have plans tonight."

I tilted my head. "We do?"

"It's Welcome Back night at school. You know, you get to come and meet my teachers and hear all about what we're going to be learning this year."

Right, where I'd' be running into yet another ex, who just so happened to be my daughter's homeroom teacher. So much for keeping things drama free.

Chapter Eight

I walked into Whispering Willows Magical Academy, bracing myself for whatever emotions might hit. Two decades. It had been over two decades since I'd stepped foot in this place. There'd been a time when I couldn't wait to escape, finish school, take up my mantle as a Witch Granter and follow in my mom's footsteps.

Two sweeping spiral staircases rose up on either side of the enormous entryway, a white- and black-checkered floor beneath my feet, shiny and reflecting the lights of the chandelier hanging above. Pictures of past headmasters and well-known teachers lined the walls. High above, the vaulted ceiling featured a twinkling starry night. Long ago it had been spelled to reflect the weather outside: sunny days, overcast skies, beautiful, starry nights. Parents brushed past me as I stood in the foyer, taking it all in, memories rushing at me so fast I couldn't stop them.

Me walking in here for the first time at fourteen years old, in awe at the grandiosity of it all.

Me sneaking Emerson in here because she wanted to see what the private magical academy was like compared to her public school.

Me walking in here with my mother for parent-teacher conferences.

My high school boyfriend pulling me into a dark corner for a quick kiss.

If only I'd known the ways my life was going to fall apart just a year after graduating. But I couldn't have known. I couldn't have guessed that my mother, the woman I worshipped, who I wanted to be just like, was going to drop a bombshell that would blow my life to pieces.

"Mom?" Remy came to a stand beside me, waving at her new best friend Megan, who walked up the stairs with her parents.

Megan's dark skin glowed under the starry night ceiling, and she shot Remy a bright smile and gave a wave. I waved back. It made me happier than Remy would ever know that she'd already found a friend like Megan. They were attached at the hip ever since they met just a few months ago. "You ready?" Remy asked.

I nodded. "Absolutely." I grabbed her hand and squeezed, and together we walked up the staircase.

Tonight was about Remy. After her dad died over a year and a half ago, I was never able to make it to any conferences, school nights, shows—nothing. I'd missed everything so I could work extra hours and afford the life we'd had before my husband died. Now, I could make up for that. This was Remy's senior year of high school, and I wanted her to know I was going to be by her side every step of the way. No matter that there was a cursed golden lamp sitting in my family's shop. I would not think about that tonight, wouldn't let it ruin this. Tonight was about meeting Remy's teachers, learning about her classes, her senior project, and I was going to be fully present for all of it.

We got to the top of the staircase, my breathing a little more uneven than Remy's, who hadn't even broken a sweat. Okay, a lot more uneven. Fine, I could barely breathe at this point, okay? We should've taken the elevator, but I hadn't even thought about it until we were halfway up the stairs, and my knees were yelling at me to please stop and rest.

"C'mon." Remy pulled me down a hallway lined with maroon runners and filled with glass cases showing off trophies won at various competitions, witch hats from famous witches who had attended the Academy, and what looked like science projects. A mock volcano exploded from behind the glass, smoke pouring from it, followed by bubbling red lava. Students' projects had certainly become more impressive over the years. I never remembered creating anything like that in my day.

We arrived in front of a room, and I stopped before we got to the doorway, taking a compact out of my purse and checking my make-up . . . just because.

Remy planted her hands on her hips. "What are you doing?"

"What?" I asked. "It's windy out. And I just sweated out a gallon of water going up those stairs. I want to make sure I look presentable. You know, make a good impression on your teachers."

"You mean one specific teacher. A certain ex-boyfriend of yours who's looking very dashing and very single these days?" Remy smirked. "Named Preston, maybe?"

I pointed at her. "It's Mr. Hammond to you." I finished touching up my makeup and snapped the compact shut. "And no, I am definitely not trying to make a good impression on Preston, specifically. Yes, he is objectively a very good-looking man. And yes, we have a history that I remember fondly. But that's exactly what it is, Remy—history."

Definitely was not interested in rekindling our romance, and all the drama that came with it.

"Clara, Remy."

I jumped about a foot in the air and spun to see Preston standing in the doorway, his muscled arms bulging beneath his striped button-up, tucked into black slacks. I would get down on my knees and pray to whatever gods I needed to right in that moment if it meant Preston didn't overhear that conversation.

"Why don't you both come in, and Remy, you can show your mom some of the projects you'll be working on this year. You'll also have to tell her about the senior float our class is building for the parade. I'll be around to check in with you in a little bit."

Remy smiled sweetly at him, but I didn't miss the scheming look on her face as she pulled me past him and into the classroom. "Thanks, Mr. H!"

I shot a glance behind me at Preston, who quickly averted his gaze as he walked over to a couple with their teenage daughter, all of them sitting at a desk, looking at something on her laptop.

"What parade?" I asked as we walked toward Remy's seat at the far end of the classroom, near the windows.

"The Autumn Equinox parade. The seniors get to create our school's float, and I'm on the committee that's helping plan it."

Ah. I'd totally forgotten that was happening in just a few short weeks. Autumn Equinox was one of the many special holidays witches celebrated throughout the year, and Whispering Willows threw a huge annual parade that drew in people from all over.

Remy sat down at her desk, and I pulled up a chair as she opened her laptop and typed in her password. Suddenly I was transported to over twenty years ago, sitting in this very same spot as my homeroom teacher droned on about some assembly we were attending later that day. But I hadn't been paying any attention to her. My gaze had strayed out the window to the soccer fields far below, where Preston Hammond ran with the other soccer players, doing knee kicks, jumping jacks, and stretches. Preston, a year older than me and the most popular boy in school, stretched his muscled arms overhead, showing a shock of pale skin that drew my eyes like a wand to its witch. Preston didn't even know I existed, of course. But he would. In time.

"Mom?" Remy asked, snapping me back to reality. "Is my English paper thesis that boring for you?"

My gaze focused on Remy's laptop, where she had a document pulled up titled Proposal, long lines of text underneath.

"No! Of course not. Sorry, hon. I was just getting lost in the past."

"Yeah, you do that a lot." Remy shook her head, her brown curly hair grazing her shoulders.

I pulled on my own stick-straight brown hair, twisting it around the end of a finger, hoping Remy had no idea I was, in fact, thinking about her homeroom teacher, who currently stood five feet away and looked better than he had any right to at the age of forty-one. He ran a hand over his buzzed hair, those piercing hazel eyes flicking to me before focusing back on the dad and son he was talking to.

I swallowed and shifted in my seat. "Okay, so tell me about this English paper you're writing."

"Well," Remy said. "We have to make an argument for or against the Council implementing the Law of 1922, which limited the ways supernaturals could use their gifts and strengths, and ultimately led to the demons becoming more powerful while also adding a much-needed system of checks and balances in the supernatural world."

"Wow," I said. "I remember having to write a paper about my favorite spell and why. That sounds complex, Remy." I had to admit, I was proud, looking at this document, at all Remy's notes, organized and typed up. "So what's your opinion on the matter?"

She donned a thoughtful expression, those green eyes rolling upward as she thought. "Well, my thesis is that the Council did the right thing in creating checks and balances because ultimately, it was like the Wild, Wild West of magic out here. Supernaturals could do whatever they wanted, and yes, that made it easier for them to fight against evil like demons, but it also created a lot of problems. Sure, the demon wars could've ended earlier if supernaturals were allowed to use their powers and strengths in any way they liked, but who knows what terrible things could've continued to happen if the supernatural community was left unchecked?"

I stared at her, in awe. When did this little girl of mine grow up? Become this whole human being with opinions and thoughts? Smart ones, too. One minute I was holding her wriggly tiny body in my arms and then I blinked and here she was: a woman.

"Remy, that's amazing. I think you're going to write a fantastic paper."

She glowed under my praise, and I wished I could bottle this moment up and keep it forever.

"That's what I told her," Preston said, standing over us. He dragged a chair up. "May I?"

"Yes, of course." I straightened in my seat as he slid into his.

He cleared his throat. "So as Remy's homeroom teacher, some of the main things I'll be overseeing—"

"When did you decide to become a teacher?" The question flew out of my mouth, and I clapped a hand over my lips in embarrassment.

"Mom, you just totally interrupted Mr. H."

"I'm so sorry," I said. "It's just, the last time I saw you, your dream was to join the police force in Whispering Willows. Create spells to help them catch the bad guys." I couldn't help but wonder what had led him on his path.

Preston looked down at his feet, his hands steepled together.

"You know what?" I said. "None of my business. So sorry I interrupted, please continue."

He cleared his throat. "So anyway, as Remy's homeroom teacher, I oversee her grades, help keep her on task, help her to problem solve if she's having trouble in any particular—"

"It's just, you always hated school," I said.

"Mom!" Remy's eyes bugged out of her head. "What is wrong with you?" she whispered.

Preston's jaw ticked, which meant he didn't want to talk about this. After all this time, I still knew his mannerisms so well.

"Right, no more interruptions, I promise." I sealed my lips.

He sighed heavily. "Things change, Clara. I'm not the same guy you left twenty-one years ago."

Well, that was a punch to the gut. Remy's gaze bounced between us, something calculating going on in those wide green eyes of hers.

She cleared her throat. "Mr. H, did I hear Mom just mention you wanted to be on the police force?"

"Lead spell detective," he said. "Dream job."

She smiled brightly. "Well, that's perfect, then."

I narrowed my gaze at her, her smile much too self-satisfied. "What's perfect, Remy?" I tried to keep the edge out of my voice, unsuccessfully.

Remy looked at Preston. "Mom needs help solving a mystery. And the last time she tried to solve a mystery, as you might have heard, it turned into a disaster."

She, of course, was referring to just a few weeks earlier, when I'd discovered the mayor was trying to get close to me so I'd sell him The Wish List, which he then planned on destroying because of a century-old grudge he had against my ancestors. He'd wanted to destroy my family's legacy, but I discovered his plan and stopped him before it was too late. That had also officially ended our relationship.

"She needs an expert," Remy continued.

Preston's eyebrows drew together. "A mystery?"

I pinched Remy under the table, but she didn't even flinch. "I'm sure Mr. . . . H has better things to do than help me with some—"

"What's the problem?" Preston leaned forward, elbows on his knees.

Oh, dear god.

Remy's gaze stayed locked on him. "Well, there's this golden lamp that Mom found while cleaning out the basement, and ever since she unearthed it, it's been causing problems. She even tried throwing it to the bottom of the ocean, and it appeared right back in The Wish List."

Preston leaned forward further. He was hooked, and I was in trouble. So, so much trouble. He always did love a good mystery.

"So my mom could really use the help of someone with an investigative mind. The rest of us are hopeless." Remy moved her finger in a circular motion by her head, really playing this up. "Please, Mr. H. This lamp is really stressing my mom out."

Oh, good god. Suddenly my daughter had turned into freaking Meryl Streep over here, giving the performance of her life.

His hardened features softened, and he ran a hand over his buzzed head. "Of course I'll help. I teach during the day, obviously—"

"How about tomorrow after school?" Remy asked. "Mom's got a lead she could use some help with. I was going to go with her, but I just have so much homework."

"Sure," Preston said, meeting my gaze. "I'll meet you at The Wish List?"

I didn't know what Remy was up to, but I did know I needed to stop her before she got too deep into something that she knew nothing about.

Remy and I walked in the cool California night air, a salty breeze sifting past us while palm trees rustled. After the disaster that was homeroom, the night had gone much more smoothly. We'd visited all Remy's classes, I'd met her teachers, put the Preston incident behind me, and been able to be fully present for my daughter, which was all I wanted. Remy's teachers praised her focus, her perseverance, and her creative problem-solving. Remy's teachers ranged from a spirited werewolf to an arrogant fae to a soft-spoken goblin—she'd have the best education possible, and I hoped she wouldn't come to regret this move.

"Okay," I said finally, after having some time to process the events of the night. "Now that we are done with Welcome Back Night, I have to ask: what in the hell were you thinking?"

Remy turned her wide, innocent eyes on me. "What are you talking about, Mom?"

I threw my hands up in the air as we continued along a sidewalk, entering the residential area where our house was. "The whole Preston thing, me needing someone to help with this investigation. You know I'm not planning on investigating anything."

"I didn't see you protesting too loudly when I asked for his help."

"Because you put me in an awkward position!" I said. "What was I supposed to do, say I had no interest in accepting help from Preston?"

Remy stuffed her hands in her jean pockets. "Why do you have no interest? Clearly you two have some history, and I see the way you've looked at him, and the way he looks at you."

I stopped. "You think he's looking at me?"

"Yeah, Mom," Remy said. "The minute you stepped foot in the classroom, he literally couldn't stop checking you out."

I sputtered. "Checking me out?" My body flushed warm at the thought.

"Mm-hmm." Remy did a little skip ahead, then spun around, walking backward. "I'm telling you, there's some unfinished business between you two."

I sighed. "It's so complicated, Remy. And I don't want any kind of drama right now. Life is good. Let's keep it that way."

Remy held up a finger, still walking backward on the sidewalk. "Mom, you just spent three months trying so hard to outrun your past that you almost lost us The Wish List, you basically got catfished, not to mention, you lied to me about who I really was."

I winced. Well, it sounded bad when she put it that way.

"Have you not learned your lesson?"

"I've faced my past," I said. "I opened The Wish List, I told you the truth about your heritage, I've been teaching you magic, granting wishes. This is not about running from the past. Preston and I are over. We had our closure. What more can I do?"

Remy stopped and I caught up to her. "Like you said, your past is complicated, and it includes a lot of different people and memories. Yes, you faced your fear of practicing magic, of becoming evil like Grandma, but you have a lot more to deal with. And that's gonna take some time, Mom."

She patted me.

"Why do I feel like I'm talking to an adult?" I asked.

"Well, I am almost eighteen, and I am pretty smart."

I flicked her in the arm.

"Besides," she said, "Mr. H is my homeroom teacher, and you're going to be interacting with him a lot this year. I need you two to get over whatever awkwardness is between you and at least learn how to be civil to each other. Maybe him helping you out on this one little mission will be a step toward that."

We arrived in front of our house with its pointed black peaks and black-tiled roof. The black paint covering the outside was in the process of being painted a forest green—Remy's idea. The bright yellow door beckoned us, and I roped an arm around her. "Fine, I'll let Preston help me with this one thing."

"That's all I ask," Remy said.

Chapter Nine

Preston stood next to me on the outcropping of rocks. We peered at a large cave that sat in front of us. Ocean water splashed around, misting our skin, our hair. The salt of the sea clung to me, and I licked a droplet of water off my upper lip.

"So you think the mermaids will know something else about this lamp, something that can help you get rid of it?"

"I think it's my best shot right now," I said, peering into Cave of Echoes, a well-known place where mermaids lounged during the day.

"Did you try the library?" Preston also squinted into the cave. "You know Edna keeps that place well-stocked. I can't imagine she wouldn't have a book about golden lamps and genies."

What was with everyone and the library?

I scuffed a toe on the rock where I stood. "You know Edna and I don't exactly get along. I'd rather take my chances with the mermaids. Aiden seemed to have a lot of knowledge about these golden lamps, and you know out of everyone in Whispering Willows, mermaids are the most well-traveled."

Preston scratched his jaw. His very well-sculpted jaw. "I'm sure Edna's gotten over your history."

I snorted. "Really? Because she banned me from the library two months ago, and it took a lot of begging to get back into her good graces."

Preston chuckled softly. "She's still upset that we dared desecrate her precious reading nook."

My cheeks heated at the memory. Shortly after we started dating, Preston and I had gone to the library to study but ended up studying each other's mouths more than the books. Edna had come upon us, raging, and of course, blamed me, not the golden boy of Whispering Willows whom everyone loved.

I cleared my throat. "Let's just see what the mermaids have to say first." I glanced at the satchel strung over my back, which held the golden lamp.

All of a sudden, a giant wave crashed against the rock where I stood, causing me to lose my footing. I slipped and stumbled forward toward the cold blue waters, but a hand shot out and grabbed my arm. Preston yanked me back, and the force of his pull slammed me straight into his hard chest, where he cradled me instinctively. I stilled in his arms, remembering all too well what it felt like to be held by him, pressed to him, completely consumed by him. I quickly stepped from his grasp.

"Thank you," I said, "for saving me."

Sharp spindles stuck out of the sea below us, no doubt waiting for some unlucky person to slip and fall straight to their death.

"Yeah, well, I couldn't let my favorite student's mom die. Bad form and all."

"Remy is your favorite?"

He stepped forward toward another rock, and I followed him. "She's smart, kind, inquisitive. She has this zest for life that, well . . ." He swallowed. "Reminds me of you. Or you when you were her age."

Ah.

"She's a good kid, and one of the ones who makes my job easy. Reminds me why I love what I do."

"Thank you," I said. "It's hard being a parent, feeling like I'm failing half the time, but comments like that make me think maybe I'm doing something right."

Preston looked straight ahead at the cave, hopping onto another rock. "You are. Trust me. You're a great mom. Anyone can see that by just spending an hour with your daughter."

Must not cry. Must not cry. Must not cry.

Afraid my voice would come out all wobbly, I swallowed back my tears and smiled.

Preston hopped off the last rock onto the pebbled shore that spread out in front of the Cave of Echoes, and I followed suit, landing beside him, seashells and rocks crunching underfoot.

Water washed in and out of the cave, covering the bottom of our feet, soaking my shoes so that they squelched every time I took a step.

We stepped inside, light filtering in through holes in the ceiling, shining down on tritons and sirens who lay in various positions: some on long flat rocks, some in the shallow pool of water gathered in the middle of the cave, others on the sandy beach surrounding the water.

Their eyes all moved toward us as Preston and I approached. A familiar siren sat up from her rock, a frown curving her lips.

"Karissa," I said, studying her shimmery purple scales, purple hair, purple lips.

She glared at me and crossed her arms. "You said you'd take care of the criminal who cut the coral from the bottom of the sea."

Oh, right. About that. I'd forgotten the promise I made to Karissa what felt like ages ago but was actually just one month earlier.

Someone had snuck to the bottom of the ocean and cut a piece of precious coral from the reef. The mermaids hadn't known who'd done it, no one had, but they made me promise if I found out, I'd bring the perpetrator to justice. Shortly after, I'd discovered the mayor, the very popular mayor, had been responsible. He'd needed the coral for his twisted, lengthy plot to ultimately burn down The Wish List. Luckily I'd stopped him, figured out his plan before he had a chance to act. Well, mostly before. But I didn't exactly bring him to justice—he was still the mayor, after all.

"Um," I said.

Karissa crossed her arms, all the mermaids glaring at us from behind her.

"Well, it's complicated?"

She pointed a long purple nail at me. "It's because he's your boyfriend, isn't it?"

I held up a finger. "Ex-boyfriend!" Preston shot me a side glance. "That's an important distinguishing factor, there."

The sirens and tritons behind Karissa didn't seem impressed by my argument.

I shifted the satchel on my back, feeling the lamp tumble to its side. "Listen, what do you want me to say? Daniel fake dated me so that he could get me to sell my family shop to him so that he could then destroy it in an attempt to get revenge on my great-great-aunt who denied him a really important wish that he needed to save his late wife's life."

At that point everyone's mouths were open, except Preston, who stared at me with an indecipherable look. I couldn't tell if he was angry or disappointed or completely freaked. Probably the last one. I would be. I was a hot mess, and I wouldn't get involved with someone like me if I had the chance.

"So you just forgave him?" Karissa asked. "You promised that if you found the person who cut away our coral, almost caused its destruction, that you would bring them to justice."

I sighed heavily. "Everything isn't so black and white, Karissa. Daniel did a lot of bad things, things that were inexcusable, but his actions came from a place of deep pain. He lost his wife, lost his entire world because of my great-great-aunt, and it drove him to revenge. He'd been to hell and back already. There was nothing I could've done to him that was worse than losing his wife and spending a hundred years of his life trying to destroy The Wish List, to destroy my great-great-aunt's legacy. But I helped him to see the error of his ways, and I really think he wants to turn things around, not live for revenge anymore." Karissa's frown softened just the tiniest amount, and I knew I was getting through to her. "I found who cut the coral, and now you have that closure. You know that he did it from a place of deep suffering, not out of malicious intent, and that it won't ever happen again."

Karissa looked back to the other sirens and tritons, some of whom were nodding along, like they agreed with my assessment of the situation. She turned, her tail splashing in the water, bits of light from above catching on her scales and splashing the color against the cave walls. "You did find the thief, and for that we're grateful."

My body went slack from relief, all the tension leaking out. They were going to help us. Preston's firm hand wrapped around my arm, steadying me.

The mermaids didn't make any move to kick us out, so I unslung the satchel from my shoulder and lay it gently on the floor, like a peace offering. The lamp hopped from inside the satchel, making everyone jump.

"What's inside?" one of the tritons said from behind Karissa.

I kicked at it. "Something that's been causing a lot of mischief, and I thought maybe you would be able to help."

I picked up the satchel and dumped the lamp out. Everyone gasped upon seeing the shiny golden object.

"I threw it in the ocean yesterday and then it appeared right back in my shop this morning. I clearly won't be able to get rid of it, so I need to destroy it."

Karissa shimmied from the rock where she lounged and pulled herself across the shallow water toward her clan, where the rest of the mermaids joined her. They huddled together, frantic whispers rising from their group.

"Hey," Preston whispered. "I'm pretty sure that triton, the skinny one with the red scales, knows something. When you just revealed the lamp, his eyes were shifting like he was uncomfortable, and he kept fidgeting with his hands. Something seems off with him."

I looked at the triton Preston had pointed out, an older man with thick white hair, a sheen of sweat across his skin, and his face seeming paler than normal. I shot a side glance at Preston.

Maybe Remy was right and I did need his investigative skills. I hadn't even noticed that triton, my attention solely focused on Karissa, but he was definitely acting cagey about this whole ordeal, his eyes flicking to the lamp every few seconds.

The group stopped conferring, and Karissa turned back toward us. "Aidan told you all we know about golden lamps such as these. If this one appeared back in your shop, then dark magic is underfoot that is not typical of a golden lamp. Someone cursed this lamp, and we want nothing to do with it."

My head hung. Not what I wanted to hear.

"Clara, be careful," Karissa said. "A golden lamp like this one ruined the life of a mermaid in our clan. She became consumed by it, and because of the lamp she's trapped . . ." Karissa's eyes welled with tears. "Well, it doesn't matter. She made her choices, bad ones."

"So what happened?" I asked, staring down at the lamp on the ground.

Karissa swallowed. "It doesn't matter. It was a long time ago, and she paid the price for her selfish deeds, for stealing a lamp, becoming bound to it."

My head snapped up at that. "Bound? How do you get bound to a lamp?" Karissa might've said Aiden told us everything we needed to know, but she sure was revealing a lot of new information.

"Once you summon a genie, the lamp is bound to you until you finish making your wishes. No one will be able to take it from your possession."

"So this siren bound herself to the lamp, made the wishes?"

Karissa swallowed. "It destroyed her. That's all you need to know."

She clearly didn't want to say anymore on that matter. How sad. Questions began to slither into my mind, unwanted and obtrusive: was this the same lamp that belonged to that siren? Was there a genie in this lamp? Could I summon the genie and make actual wishes? I pulled a barrier down, stopping the questions, stopping my racing thoughts. No. No. I didn't want to ask more questions. All I'd wanted to know was if the lamp could be destroyed, and Karissa didn't seem willing to answer that question. But she had further confirmed that this lamp was nothing but trouble. Exactly why it needed to be destroyed.

Karissa flipped her long black hair over her shoulder. "Also, tell Martin to call me."

I wanted to tell her to get in line because it seemed like Aiden also had unfinished business with the imp, but I nodded instead. The clan stared at me expectantly, my feet having a hard time moving. I couldn't let this be a dead end. I needed to destroy this lamp before it hurt anyone else. My feet wouldn't cooperate with my brain. Preston's hand gripped mine, and before I knew it, he was leading me out of the cave. I tried to tug, to protest, but he ignored me, gently pulling me out into the fresh air, sun shining down, blue skies overhead.

I huffed, crossing my arms over my chest. "Why did you do that? I wasn't done with them."

"No, but they were done with you. Besides, we got a lead now."

"What, the old triton?" I asked. "I don't even know his name, and I have no idea how to find him. What am I supposed to do, go for a swim?" I was acting like a brat, I knew it. Taking out my frustrations on Preston, which wasn't fair. But I so badly wanted this to be over, and I'd really thought the mermaids would give us some answers, not just fill me with more questions.

Preston crossed his arms over his chest. "I have bad news and good news."

I pursed my lips, waiting for him to reveal what he knew. "Go on, then."

"The good news is I have a plan; the bad news is we are, in fact, going for a swim."

Chapter Ten

"Ohhhhhh, this is freezing, this is freezing, this is freezing." Half a lifetime living in the seaside town of Whispering Willows still hadn't prepared me for the shocking cold of the Pacific Ocean. The water seeped into my bones, my veins, my very blood, icing every part of me.

The sun sank lower in the sky, and if we were going to find the older triton, then we needed to hurry, but Preston still hadn't given me the details of this little mission.

Water lapped around us, up to our waists now.

"Oh, c'mon." Preston nudged me. "How many moonlight dips did we take when we were eighteen?"

My cheeks flushed. What he didn't mention was that we loved to skinny dip, specifically. Not just the two of us, but often groups of us, wild teens without a care in the world. Me, Preston, Emerson, her other best friend Cruz, and others from school joined us.

"That's the point. We were eighteen. I'm forty now, and all I want are naps and hot tea and a bedtime at nine p.m."

Preston chuckled, the sound low and rumbly. "I bet you'd still enjoy a moonlight dip with me, even if it's after nine p.m."

His words conjured an image that sent tingles down my body. This conversation was entering dangerous territory. I needed to change course. "Hey, you still haven't told me where we're going."

"I thought you liked surprises," he said from beside me as we waded deeper, my toes barely skimming the sand.

I cut him a look. "I like surprises when they're jewelry or a fun date, not swims out in the freezing ocean chasing down a triton for information about a lamp."

A lamp that we'd left on shore. I wasn't too worried about someone taking it since the damned thing seemed determined to find its way back to The Wish List no matter what.

Preston stroked his jaw. "Okay, okay. So I noticed a few things about the triton."

"Other than the fidgeting and nervousness?"

Preston nodded, and my feet officially lifted off the sea floor. I pumped my arms and kicked my legs as we swam around the Cave of Echoes and toward a series of jagged and pointy rocks sitting in front of a low cliff jutting over the ocean.

"He kept looking at the lamp while you held it, a weird kind of possessiveness in his gaze. He licked his lips, his hands twitching like he wanted to reach out for it. He almost couldn't keep his eyes off of it, and when you stashed it back into your satchel, his eyes bulged a bit, and he swallowed a few times, like he was having trouble keep control."

Holy bejeezus. I hadn't expected that level of detail. "Okay?"

"So you know how I told you to leave the satchel back on the beach?"

I looked behind me, but we were already around the bend of the cave and the satchel was no longer in sight.

"Yes . . ."

"Well, I think a certain triton might just try and steal the lamp."

I gasped. "You're luring him into a trap."

"Yes."

I continued to swim, keeping pace with Preston, even though my legs and arms were beginning to burn.

"And you wanted us to be out of sight so he'd take the bait?"

"Yes."

"And we're going to catch him in the act and then demand answers."

Preston grinned. "Yes."

"Preston! Why are you a high school teacher?"

I didn't press when he ignored my question, just grinning at him. "I'm starting to think you're an evil genius."

"Just a wannabe cop. Well, former wannabe."

His face sobered as we neared the rocks, and Preston pulled himself up, then offered a hand out to me. "You coming? We need to get out of here before we hear the siren's song."

My ears popped, as if responding to Preston's words. "Siren?"

"Rumor has it, she's here, ready to lure unsuspecting people to their deaths on her rocky beach."

I scoffed. "We've been hearing that rumor since we were kids. I'm pretty positive it's a bedtime story parents having been repeating for years, trying to scare us into not sneaking out to the beach to make out."

Every mermaid was a siren or triton, depending on their gender, but none of them chose to use their siren song for evil, and I'd never come in contact with any siren who sang to lure people to their deaths. It was just a silly story passed from generation to generation. Actually, I might tell it to Remy if I got any inclination that she wanted to sneak out here to make out with that vampire crush of hers.

In the distance, a wail echoed over the waves.

Preston grimaced. "What is that sound?"

I cocked my head, listening intently. "That would be a seagull who now sings show tunes."

"Come again?" Preston stretched his arms, swimming faster.

"The lamp put a spell on a seagull the last time we were out here so that it could sing."

"That's not singing." Preston winced. "That's torture for my ears."

"I think it might be a song from *Oklahoma!*."

"Forget a siren, that seagull is gonna cause a lot of deaths from its awful singing."

I just shook my head as the singing slowly faded away into the distance.

We climbed the rocks, my feet slipping on the slick surface, and from there, we jumped onto a little grassy patch of land that led back around to the beach. We'd be able to come up on the backend of the shore, where the triton surely wouldn't be expecting us. My feet pressed into the grass, soft and steady after being in the rocky waves. I shivered as the sun sank lower in the sky, the cool September breeze pushing past us.

Preston pressed a finger to his lips, and we crouched down, the beach in sight as we circled around back to it.

Sure enough, the older triton swam from the splashing waves and shifted to his human form, clothes rippling over his body as his tail disappeared. From this distance, I could see his head turning to look around as he tiptoed toward the satchel we'd left on the beach outside the cave.

"I can't believe you were right," I whispered to Preston. "I mean seriously, you had him pegged."

Preston grinned, his smile cocky and sure. I always loved that about him: how sure he was of himself. Preston always knew what he wanted and went after it. It was the shock of a lifetime when I'd finally realized what Mr. Popular himself wanted was me. He'd set my world on fire, and it never stopped burning, not the entire time we were together.

The triton lifted the satchel, soaking wet with ocean water that dripped from it.

I glanced over at Preston, and he nodded and lifted a hand, raising his fingers in a one . . . two . . . three motion.

When he got to three, we both jumped up and sprinted toward the beach.

"Drop it," Preston yelled in a voice so authoritative it made me want to stop and listen.

The triton dropped the satchel, and it made a resounding thud in the sand. He tried to dive back into the water, shifting as he did, his tail flopping on the ground, sand flying up in our faces. But before he could escape into the sea, Preston dove, tackling the triton to the ground and bending his arms behind his back.

"Why did you try to steal that lamp?" Preston asked.

I stopped short, breath heaving, a stitch in my side, but all that fell in the background as I watched Preston tackle this guy and go complete Boss Man on him. It was kind of a turn-on. No, it was definitely a turn-on.

"Please, let me go! I'm sorry, okay? I shouldn't have tried to steal the lamp. Don't arrest me!"

Preston stayed straddled over the triton, twisting his hands further behind his back.

The triton lifted his sand-crusted face from the ground. "I swear, I've never committed a crime before in my life."

"Relax, I'm not arresting you," Preston growled, leaving out the very important fact that he wasn't a cop and couldn't arrest the triton if he tried. "Now, if I let you go, will you promise to answer our questions?"

The triton nodded miserably.

Preston shot me a glance, then he slowly released the triton's hands from his grip. The triton pushed himself up to a sitting position, tail flopping on the ground as foamy dark water washed up around him.

Preston stood, and I grabbed the lamp and came to a stand beside him.

"First," I said, trying my own hand at playing cop. "Why did you want this?" I held up the lamp, which I then dropped safely into the satchel and secured the bag around my back.

The triton sighed. "I just wanted a wish. One wish from a golden lamp."

I gave him a pointed stare. "Which is illegal."

He shrugged. "When has that ever stopped anyone?"

Well, good point.

"I've seen a lamp before. Once. Brought by a far-off clan. We were all naturally curious about the lamp, so they answered our questions, told us everything we wanted to know. They claimed the Witch Granters trapped inside were criminals, witches who had done dark deeds and didn't deserve to walk free."

It sounded to me like mermaids who were trying to justify their own terrible actions. If the Witch Granters that had been trapped were evil, then that would make it okay in their minds to make wishes. It was all so twisted.

"The leader of the clan wanted to make an alliance with us, and as a show of good faith, he gave our leader one wish from his rare and precious lamp. He said some sort of summoning spell and, poof, there floated a genie, ready to grant whatever wish our leader wanted." He held up a finger. "But you want to know the interesting thing about the golden lamp? It pays the price for you. No need to give a piece of your soul."

My mouth dropped open. I hadn't known that part. No wonder trapping Witch Granters in a lamp was so appealing. You got the wish but without the steep price. All you had to do was take a person's freedom and trap them in one of the cruelest ways imaginable.

"Can you make as many wishes as you'd like?" Preston asked.

The triton shook his head. "No, no, there's a limit of three wishes. I don't know why, but that's what one of the sirens from the clan told me."

I wondered what happened after three wishes, but it didn't seem this triton knew anything about that.

The triton's thin shoulders slumped. "I knew it wasn't right, okay? I shouldn't have tried to steal the lamp, but well, I've been wanting a wish for a while." He met my gaze. "Can't afford the cost. Too much money for a triton like me."

"So you thought stealing was the answer? You don't even know if there's a genie in this lamp. You don't know what's inside. None of us do."

He bit his lip, looking down at his fidgeting tail, and my stomach turned to stone. I knew that look. The look of someone who had information.

"Unless you know something about this lamp, specifically?" I prodded.

Preston and I waited, both silent, biding our time before the triton spilled all his secrets. I had a feeling he was about to burst.

He twisted his hands together. "I saw your mother with this very lamp." He met my gaze. "Long, long ago, when she was sixteen, seventeen, maybe?"

My breath caught in my throat, and my entire body tensed. Preston grabbed my hand, squeezing it.

The triton pointed at the satchel. "I'd recognize that bent spout anywhere. And she was performing magic. Dark magic."

I shook my head. "No, she didn't turn evil until later in life. Way later. She wouldn't—couldn't—not at such a young age."

"What did you see, exactly?" Preston asked in a gentle voice.

"It was the middle of the night. I'd been out for a midnight swim."

He gestured to the distance. "There she was. Standing on a rocky little beach tucked in between cliffs that she could've only accessed by flying to."

My stomach hardened more.

"So I watched from afar as your mother lifted the stopper off the top of the lamp and poured some vial of pitch-black liquid over it. That's when I heard a scream, worse than any scream I'd ever heard before, split the silent night. I saw others with her, blurry figures that I couldn't make out from the distance. It scared me, and I ducked underwater before I could see the rest. That was the last time I'd seen that lamp."

"So you think she was trapping another Witch Granter in there?" I asked, pinching the bridge of my nose with one hand, squeezing Preston's hand tighter with the other. Everything always came back to my mother somehow. Every time I thought I'd conquered my past, faced my fears, moved on, boom, one of my mother's dark dealings came rearing back to remind me I could never escape her.

"Just a guess," the triton said. "If you say the summoning spell, the genie should appear. Every golden lamp in existence is spelled by an ancient magic to react to specific words."

"Do you know the spell?" I asked.

The triton shook his head. "I don't. I was planning on taking the lamp and then trying to figure out the summoning spell so I could get my wish. These lamps might be rare, but if you know the right people, you'll find the answers you seek."

I'd gotten a lot more information than I'd wanted, and not the specific answers I was seeking. "So you don't know of a way to destroy the lamps?"

The triton paused at that. "No one wants to destroy these. The Council banned making new ones long ago."

That I already knew.

"But they didn't know how to destroy them, as far as I know, so they worked to collect them, hide them away. Still, because these lamps are so rare and powerful, there are supernaturals willing to go to great lengths to find them and use them for their own dark purposes."

Supernaturals like my mother, who'd somehow gotten a lamp in her possession. At such a young age too.

"So—" I started.

But the triton dove back into the waves, his tail flapping before disappearing completely underwater.

I met Preston's gaze. I didn't want to perform this summoning spell, didn't want to risk letting out whatever my mother had trapped in here so long ago. It was starting to feel like I might not have a choice.

Chapter Eleven

Preston and I walked on the beach, the sun now gone from the sky, the moon taking its place. Stars twinkled above, nothing but the sound of crashing waves between us.

Preston carried the satchel with the lamp tucked inside, like he knew it might be a heavy burden I couldn't handle. Not tonight.

Finally, after walking in silence, he spoke: "So do you want to talk about it or do you want a silent companion?"

The silent companion. That's the term we used with each other to gauge if we should push a topic or just let it lie. The memory floodgates had burst open tonight.

I did want to talk about it. I just didn't know where to start. My thoughts were all over the place. I always thought my mother hadn't started using dark magic until later in life, when she'd gotten addicted to the high that came with granting wishes, got addicted to the power. But no. If what this triton said was true, she'd started using dark magic much earlier in life, when she was just a teenager—younger than Remy was right now. And she'd potentially trapped another Witch Granter inside that lamp. The one Preston carried over his shoulder. I didn't know how to process any of that. Plan Destroy the Lamp was not going well.

So I started with a question. "Do you think I should release whatever is in that lamp?"

Preston blew a big breath out, his cheeks puffing. "That's a loaded question, Clara. So let me ask you one in return: do you think your mother trapped something evil in there, did whatever she did for the common good, or do you think she trapped something in there for her own selfish reasons?"

I mulled over that. I hadn't actually thought about it. Hope fluttered in me like butterfly that just gained its wings. Maybe my mother had been trying to do some good, after all. Maybe she'd stumbled upon someone evil, someone who abused their witch-granting powers, and she had no choice but to trap them in the lamp. Then she would've hidden the lamp in our shop and spelled it so that if anyone tried to touch it, they'd forget about it. Exactly like what happened to me and Remy. If all that were true, my mother would be a hero, not a villain.

A voice whispered there were other, better ways to deal with evil than trapping it, but I ignored that voice in the moment.

"I don't know," I admitted. "My mother never was much of a team player." I'd learned that from a young age.

"Do you remember when you first started dating me?" Preston asked. "What your mother said to you?"

I chewed the inside of my cheek. I did. It had been a terrible day. I'd come home from school practically floating on a cloud. Mother had said I was glowing, asked what had happened. I told her, and her face had fallen. She told me Preston would only distract me from my goals, from my studies, that if I wanted to be a powerful witch, if I wanted to be a serious Witch Granter, I didn't have time for trivial flings. I wanted to tell her that Preston wasn't just a fling, that I felt like he could be the one, but of course I didn't. I listened to her. Like I always did. It had almost destroyed my and Preston's relationship before it could begin. But our love was stronger than my mother's warning, and it won out in the end.

My stomach sank. "I think she trapped someone in there for her own selfish reasons."

"Then I don't even think you need my answer. You already know what you should do."

I sighed heavily as a wave crested up and washed over our feet. The pebbled sand crunched underfoot, my feet hardened and used to the roughened path after years spent walking it with Preston.

"I guess I'm going to have to pay the Serpent another visit," I said. "If anyone knows about this summoning spell, it will be him."

"Whoa, whoa, whoa." Preston reared his head back. "I'm all for releasing whatever is in this lamp, but do you have a plan? In case what's inside is evil? In case it wants to kill you? Or destroy our entire town? You're going to need some backup. You're a great witch, Clara, but I don't want you taking this on by yourself."

I didn't know if I was going to release what was inside. A stubborn part of me still believed destroying the lamp could be for the best. Let whatever my mother was tangled up with die once and for all. It didn't have to be my problem.

"I'm not going to risk anyone else's life," I said firmly.

Preston shook his head. "You have a lot of people on your side, people who want to see you succeed. People like me."

A lump formed in my throat. I couldn't go down this path again. Not when it had lead to so much heartache the first time around.

"Preston, please—"

He held up his hand. "I'm not a boy anymore, Clara." His voice was low, and he stepped closer to me, my knees going weak. "I'm a man, a grown man, and I make my own decisions."

I looked up into his eyes, right now a darker shade of greens and yellows. "O-okay."

He leaned down, his lips close enough to graze mine, and there he hovered, his warm breath mingling with my own. I wanted to step away. Or maybe I didn't. Maybe I wanted to lean in, close the distance. It would be so easy. But so wrong. Inviting drama that I didn't need. No rocking the boat.

He leaned in just a little closer, lips millimeters from mine now. I swallowed, wondering what else had changed in the twenty years we'd been apart, how the taste of his kiss might have changed. My gaze flicked to his lips, and I licked my own.

He gave a devilish smile and firm nod, stepping away. "Glad we got that settled." And with that, he stalked ahead without another word.

Oh, I was in so, so much trouble. And I wasn't talking about the lamp.

Chapter Twelve

The lamp sat on the coffee table, staring me down with its bent spout and dinged golden shell. I wanted to pick it up and shake it, ask the thing what it was hiding inside, how my mother had gotten ahold of it, why she'd cursed something to live an existence so horrible.

I'd finally gotten my perfect life, my dream job, living in the town I'd always envisioned I would, and I was not going to let this lamp and its mischievous magic ruin that. I hadn't been able to grant wishes for three days now. After twenty years of not being able to do what I loved, I'd just started granting wishes again only to have it ripped away from me.

The bell over the shop jingled.

"I'm sorry, we're closed," I said, then looked up, and my eyes widened in surprise.

Dara stood there. Dara Charles. Emerson's mother.

Lanky gray hair hung past her shoulders, and she twisted her hands in front of her, worrying at her lip.

"Dara," I said, standing and gesturing to the purple chair sitting adjacent to the couch. "Come in."

Now guilt riddled me. I'd completely forgotten I told her to come back so we could figure out a solution to her destroyed wish. A solution I didn't have.

I was officially the worst.

Dara walked toward the chair, sinking down into it, her friendly demeanor gone. I couldn't blame her for being upset—what happened had been truly awful.

"Can I get you anything to drink? Water, tea, coffee?"

Dara just shook her head.

I couldn't imagine how she felt right now. I didn't know her well, to be honest, despite being Emerson's best friend once upon a time. When Emerson and I met, she'd come around to my house a lot, always making excuses why we couldn't go to hers. One day, Emerson had left one of her textbooks in my room after a study session. Even though she went to the public school in town and I went to the Academy, we still studied together often. I figured she'd need the book, so I performed a basic tracking spell on it, and it had led me to her house. I could tell Emerson was embarrassed when I'd arrived at her front door, even though she had nothing to be ashamed of. The house needed care, broken shingles, cracked windows, more dirt than grass in the front, and a chain-link fence surrounding the property that leaned sideways, but I didn't care about any of that. I just wanted to give my friend her book.

She'd invited me in, and then I smelled it: the dark fairy dust. Her mom stumbled into the kitchen, some guy on her arm, both of them high out of their minds. They began to float into the air—literally. Dark fairy dust elicited some crazy side effects. All the while they laughed and laughed, while Emerson's cheeks flushed a bright red. I never asked to come to her house again, realizing that she had her own reasons for not inviting me.

I looked up at Dara, who was staring down at her hands, currently twined together in her lap. Her cheeks were flushed red, the only sign she might be angry over what had happened the other day.

She and Emerson had a complicated relationship, much like myself and my own mother. I wondered if they'd talked at all over the last twenty years or if Emerson had shut out Dara like she did everyone in Whispering Willows when she ran away. From what little Dara had told me, it seemed like the latter.

"What can I do for you, Dara?" I asked in a gentle voice.

She tucked a piece of hair behind an ear, looking at me with her blue eyes, creased at the edges. "You're going to help me."

I shook my head. "Dara, I'm so sorry, I haven't come up with a solution yet. But I will. I'm going to figure out how to get you that wish—"

"We don't have time for that."

I had a feeling I wasn't going to like where this was going, but I braced myself.

"Emerson is arriving in just a few days, for her Aunt Kathy's funeral."

Emerson idolized her aunt Kathy. I'd only ever met the older witch once, but with her big sunglasses, expensive jewelry, and larger-than-life personality, she'd been a force to be reckoned with. She'd ran away from Whispering Willows at the young age of eighteen, chasing after riches and experiences this small town couldn't give her. I often wondered if Kathy's journey had been what inspired Emerson's sudden departure from our hometown.

Tears welled in Dara's eyes. Kathy was her sister, after all, and I'm sure this was hard on her. I reached over and patted her hand.

"I don't see how I can help you if I can't grant you that wish. My resources are limited."

"You can be there for Emerson," Dara said.

I practically fell off the couch. "Come again?"

Dara leaned forward. "You and Emerson were best friends. So use that. Get close with her while she's here, break down her walls. Get her to stay. Please. I just want my daughter back, and she's so angry with me. She won't listen to anything I have to say. But you, maybe . . ."

Not this. Not more drama. All I was trying to do was live my life, but it seemed that I'd become a magnet for trouble and not just my own. I wanted nothing to do with any of it. "I don't know if that's a good idea. I mean, what if Emerson is truly happy with her life in Los Angeles? I don't want to impede on that."

A night of Facebook stalking a few years ago had led me down the rabbit hole that was Emerson's life: parties, red carpets, night clubs, glittery dresses, hot men, bright drinks, and shiny jewelry. It had definitely been a far cry from my suburban life. It seemed like she had everything she ever wanted.

"You were going to grant me that wish! What's the difference between that and this?" Dara yelled, raising her voice for the first time.

"That's because wishes are smart, discerning," I said calmly. "You wished she would be happy, and that's exactly what the wish would give Emerson. It wouldn't take her away from LA if that wasn't the right thing to do. I don't have that same kind of power as a wish. I don't want to manipulate Emerson into staying if that's not what's best for her."

Selfishly, I also didn't want to get involved because of me, because of what I wanted for myself. Which was not to rekindle an old friendship with someone who'd basically abandoned me.

Dara reached out and grabbed both my hands, holding them tight. "Clara, you have to trust me. Just talk to Emerson. One time. You'll see. She isn't living her best life right now. Something's wrong. I don't know what, but I know that she needs help. I can see it every time I look at her Instagram or Facebook. With her aunt Kathy gone, she has no one to guide her."

I squeezed my eyes shut. I knew this was a bad idea. I didn't need to take anything else on my plate right now. But I owed Dara after that wish got destroyed. Besides, I didn't have to do a lot. It's not like I needed to roll out the red carpet and throw Emerson a party or tell her I wanted to be best friends again. I could just talk to her once, tell Dara I'd done my part, and then wash my hands of the whole thing. Then after I got rid of the lamp, maybe I could reach out to fellow Witch Granters and see if there was something I could do about Dara's wish.

"Be there for Emerson?" Dara asked again, looking at me hopefully. "I thought twenty years of distance might soften the edges of our rough relationship, but I know she still blames me for everything, blames me for why she ran away, why she never came back home. She hates me." Dara's voice wobbled.

"Oh Dara. I'm sure she doesn't hate you."

"No, she does," Dara said. "And I get it. I was an awful mother. After her father died, I didn't know how to cope with my grief, and I made bad choices. But I'm not that person anymore. I just wish Emerson could see that."

I thought about my own mother. If she were still alive and repentant, would I want a second chance at our relationship?

"Okay," I said. "I'll do it. I'll talk to Emerson."

Just once. No rocking the boat.

Dara looked at me. "Come to the funeral? That'll be your chance," she said. "Emerson's probably planning to leave right after, but maybe if you two start talking, reminiscing, she'll realize what she's been missing all these years."

I bit my lip. I highly doubted that. "Just . . . don't get your hopes up, okay?"

"Listen," Dara said. "If you could just get her to stay, I know I can turn things around, rebuild our relationship. I need a little help reminding Emerson of all the good things she left behind."

My gaze flicked to the lamp. I straightened in my seat. "When's the funeral?"

Dara smiled brightly. "Saturday. Ten a.m. at the Whispering Bluffs."

"Okay, I'll be there."

Which meant I needed to get this lamp dealt with before I tackled Project Emerson. Time to talk to the Serpent, and I'd either be summoning whatever was inside the lamp, or destroying it once and for all.

Chapter Thirteen

Stars twinkled above in the dark night, skies clear without a cloud in sight, the faint and distant sound of ocean waves echoing through the town. Myrtle stalked next to me in her wolf form, and Helen walked on the other side of me, black army boots, black pants, and leather jacket hugging her form.

"I can't believe we have to talk to a demon," I mumbled. "I thought demons couldn't even talk."

A lot of things had changed over the last twenty years.

"Demons have evolved," Helen said, as if that answer explained it all.

We crossed through dark alleyways, brick buildings rising up on either side of us.

A stench floated from an overflowing dumpster that was pushed up against the wall of a building.

"They're smarter, faster, stronger, and they talk back now," Myrtle growled from the other side of me.

We emerged onto an empty street and crossed the road, coming to a little square, empty and in disrepair. Old shops lined the square, all of them with broken windows and chipped paint. Old iron chairs and tables were overturned around the courtyard and faded blood stains spattered the cobblestone ground. In the middle of the square sat a dried-out fountain, the statue in the middle missing its head, which had been lopped off long before I was born.

I glanced around. "The mayor needs to make this place his new project. Revitalize the old downtown square."

"Oh yeah, that's a grand idea," Myrtle said, snout pressed to the ground as she sniffed. "Come have a coffee in the Old Square, and oh, while you're at it, enjoy a nice little view into the portal to Hell."

Helen guffawed, and my cheeks flushed. Okay, that wasn't my brightest idea.

I peeked into the fountain, bubbling red lava filling the bottom, a black hole smack in the middle where the lava dropped into. The last time I'd been here, over twenty years ago, that black hole had been so wide it almost encompassed the entire bottom of the fountain. But with Helen's arrival as Demon Slayer, the hole had closed up, almost like demons knew of her presence, knew they'd better not try and cross over to earth and test the Demon Slayer's abilities.

"Is it just me, or is the hole a little bigger?" I asked, eyeing it.

Helen waved her hand. "It fluctuates over the years, opening and closing and opening again, but I've always been able to keep the portal in check. You don't have to worry, Clara. I got this."

I believed her. Helen was more than capable, and she'd even recruited the local wolf pack to help her patrol at night. The pack had been more than willing, creating schedules, taking shifts, happy to be of service to the Demon Slayer. Even though Myrtle never officially joined the local pack, she loved patrolling with Helen, and I knew she came most nights. I didn't know if she patrolled because of the thrill or because she wanted to look out for Helen. Though the old werewolf would never admit it, I suspected the latter.

"I smell fresh meat," Myrtle said, baring her teeth, and sure enough, from the fountain crawled a demon like a little spider scuttling in the night. It stuck out its black tongue, licking dry and cracked lips. It whipped its misshapen head around, eyes a solid black. Fun times. So glad this was what Gene suggested I do to find the summoning spell. There was probably a better way, but I had a suspicion the vampire was punishing me for yet again dragging his wife into my "drama."

"Oh good, I was getting bored," Helen said as a glowing golden sword appeared in her hand.

"You got this one, then?" Myrtle said. "Just promise me I'll get a snack after you're done."

Helen smiled as she stalked toward the demon, and I wasn't quite sure what the plan was, here.

I raised a finger. "Um, before you kill that thing, are we going to interrogate it?"

"We don't interrogate to start," Helen said.

"We don't?" I asked. "But I need to know the summoning spell."

"And you'll get it, after we rough him up a bit."

I gulped. "Oh, okay. Well, I'll just be over here"—I jabbed my thumb at an old rusted table—"while you take care of that part."

The demon now crouched on all fours on the edge of the fountain, staring at me with its soulless black eyes. Helen flipped her sword in her hand, whipping it around so fast it was dizzying. The demon's eyes snapped to her, and it grinned wide, revealing a set of sharp and pointed black teeth.

"Do your worst," it croaked out.

Nope. Definitely did not like that.

Myrtle just laughed from beside me. "Idiot."

Helen stopped twirling her sword. "Oh, I will."

With that she leaped high in the air, her spiked blonde hair gleaming in the moonlight as she brought the sword down and drove it straight. The demon was too fast, though, jumping away from Helen as her sword hit the hard stone of the fountain. The demon scampered toward us, and Myrtle stepped in front of me, baring her teeth while I cowered and cried like a witch who'd lost her wand. I thought of myself as a strong, independent woman, but I was strong in an emotional way, not in a fight-a-demon way. Myrtle and Helen could handle the fighting. I liked my head attached to my body, thank you very much.

"Um, so how are we using this demon to get answers?" I asked.

The demon scampered back from Myrtle's sharp bite just as Helen stalked up behind it, sword raised. It swiped at her with its long black talons and knocked the sword from her hand.

She just rolled her eyes. "So you wanna delay the inevitable, huh? That's fine, demon. I got all night."

"Okay, but we don't actually have all night." I laughed nervously. "I mean, Remy is home alone, and she's seventeen and capable of taking care of herself. I left her pizza and told her she wasn't allowed to leave the house, but I'd still like to be back at a reasonable hour—"

"She's rambling," Myrtle said. "She only rambles when she's nervous."

The demon jumped on top of Helen's back just as she was about to pick up her sword.

"You're kind of ruining my vibe," Helen said, and I wasn't sure if she was speaking to the demon or me.

"Can she handle that?" I asked Myrtle.

"She's got it under control." Myrtle pawed at her own snout. "Trust me. I've watched the Demon Slayer kill hundreds of demons over the years. She's a pro."

Helen whipped around, demon on her back as it swiped at her short bob, so far opposite from what she'd looked like when she arrived in Whispering Willows twenty years ago as a forty-five-year-old divorcee. "Just trust me, Clara." She thrashed from side to side, attempting to get the demon out of her hair, literally. She flipped it onto its back, the creature now on the ground.

Well, this was certainly more complicated than I imagined it would be.

She straddled the demon and punched it in the nose, so hard its head made a dent in the cobblestone. My eyes widened as I watched her work. Damn she was a boss.

Myrtle just snorted in appreciation. The demon, now unconscious, stilled, and Helen wiped at the sweat on her brow.

"Are you gonna kill that thing?" I shouted. "I mean, you should probably kill that thing, right? I'm sure we can find the summoning spell from someone else. Yeah, we should definitely kill it and go home and never talk about this again."

At this point, I was veering Team Destroy the Lamp, so I honestly wasn't even sure I wanted the summoning spell.

Helen looked at me. "We're getting answers." She walked over to what looked like an old ice cream storefront, where some frayed rope lay, and picked up one of the chairs, dragging it over to the demon. It scraped across the cobblestone, a sound that pierced my eardrums.

Helen hefted the demon up onto the chair, tying its hands and feet to the legs.

"Are you sure this thing is going to be able to answer our questions?"

"I told you demons can talk now, and word is they've been very interested in finding any golden lamps still in existence."

"Oh great, so demons are in on this now. I thought the Council made this whole lamp thing illegal?"

Helen finished tying the demon to the chair. "Yes, because demons who are spawned in hell care very much about the law."

Myrtle padded over to the demon, sniffing him, and Helen wagged a finger at the wolf. "Do not even think about it. You don't get to eat our lead."

Myrtle sniffed. "But it looks tasty."

Helen just rolled her eyes.

I took a few cautious steps toward the trio, not sure how close I wanted to get.

"Myrtle, you're gonna have to find something else to snack on tonight," Helen said. "We're using this demon's life as leverage. It answers our questions, I don't kill it."

Myrtle huffed. "How about it answers our questions because we make it, and then I still get to eat it?" Helen just glared at the old wolf, and she lay down on the ground, resigned. "Fine, but you're going to have to find another demon for my dinner, then. I was promised food, and I'm going to get hangry very soon."

I shook my head, still processing what Helen had said about the demon. "So you're telling me there's enough demand for golden lamps out there that demons are actually trying to get hold of them?"

Helen ran a hand through her gelled hair. "The spell for trapping a Witch Granter in one of these things is so old, no one even knows it anymore. The Council hunted down any grimoires containing the spell and burned them with a special, dark magic long, long ago. The only way you can even trap a Witch Granter is by getting a hold of one of the already-spelled magical lamps, which are very, very rare, as you know. Only a few still exist today. And you happen to have one of them."

"If it's rare and powerful, of course the demons are going to want it," Myrtle said. "Everyone's going to want it."

And apparently the mermaids had another. I couldn't help but wonder how many were in existence, how many poor Witch Granters were trapped, forced to grant wishes until what? Did they just live forever in the lamp? Did they eventually die after three wishes were granted, paying the price for this powerful magic? I curled my fists in frustration, more questions than answers continuing to plague me.

It didn't matter, I reminded myself. I was not investigating.

"How do you know all of this?" I asked Helen.

Helen slapped the demon, trying to wake it up. "Well, since you stubbornly refused to go to the library, I went myself and did a little digging, with Edna's help."

"Oh." I swallowed. Right. The library. Which multiple people told me to go visit, and I completely ignored their advice. "That sounds very smart of you."

"Uh-huh." Helen stomped over to an old hose and gestured to it. "Will you help me with this? Just hold it and point it toward Spike Head over there."

I grabbed it and did as Helen directed while she twisted the knob connected to a crumbling wall. It squeaked as she turned and turned it, the water gushing out full force and straight toward the demon's face. Its head lolled, and it coughed a few times until its eyes blinked open.

Helen turned off the hose and stomped over. "Listen, Crater Face, here's the deal: we have some questions about a summoning spell used on a golden lamp."

The demon's eyes widened at the mention of a lamp.

"It's simple," Helen said. "Tell us the spell you need to summon a genie, and I'll let you go back to that portal where you came from."

Myrtle lifted her head from the ground. "Just so you know, I voted to eat you and got vetoed. But I'm still willing to do that if you won't give up the spell."

The demon growled at Myrtle, and she growled back, hers much more terrifying. The demon shrank back.

"That's what I thought," she said in her Irish accent, now thick with annoyance.

"No. Talk." The demon spat in Helen's face, a big ball of green slime that hit her right in the cheek. She swiped it off with a single finger, not even flinching.

"Well, that's a good way to piss off the Demon Slayer," Myrtle mumbled.

Helen used the hilt of her sword to thunk the demon on the head. It hissed at her, and she hissed right back.

"That's it, I'm eating it," Myrtle said, rising up and opening her large mouth, pointy teeth inches from the demon's face.

"Okay," it burst out. "Talk. I talk."

I crossed my arms. This was getting ridiculous.

Helen pointed her sword at the demon, the tip pushing into its throat, which bobbed under the pressure. "Now, I've heard from very solid sources"—aka her husband—"that the demons almost got their hands on one of these rare magical lamps and the summoning spell that came with it."

The demon's black eyes flicked between Helen, Myrtle, and me. "So what?"

"So we need to know the spell."

"I want wish," the demon said. "Promise me wish from lamp, and I tell you what I know."

"No, absolutely not." I stepped forward.

I might not have known exactly who or what my mother trapped in that lamp, but I did know that no one should be forced to pay the price of magic, especially not the heavy price that came with a wish.

"No wish, no deal."

"Meal time," Myrtle growled, and I rolled my eyes.

"Enough!" I was done with this. I was tired. Tired of this lamp. Tired of the mischievous spells it cast, tired of the trouble it had gotten me into, forcing me to reconnect with an old friend I had no interest in, an old flame I wanted to forget, forcing me away from a daughter waiting for me at home, away from a business I desperately wanted back open, a life I wanted to live. I. Was. Done.

I got close to the demon's face. "You're not getting a wish. Not now. Not ever. You are getting your life. That's what you win if you tell us the spell. Otherwise, the Demon Slayer is going to do her job and run that glowing golden sword straight through your thick head, and then wolfy over here is going to devour your entrails. So if you want to be able to slink back through that portal to Hell, then you better tell us the damn spell."

The demon's eyes were wide, mirroring the looks on Helen's and Myrtle's faces.

"Wow," Helen said. "Are you okay?"

"Anything you want to talk about?" Myrtle asked.

"Okay, I talk, I talk," the demon said. "Every spell different. Depends on lamp."

"So how do we know?"

"Rub lamp" was the response.

My eyebrows furrowed together. "I rub the lamp and the spell will be revealed?"

The demon nodded as Helen pressed the sword deeper into its throat. "You better not be lying," she said. "I've been to Hell before, and I'm not afraid to go back and hunt you down if what you've told us isn't true."

"Give the lamp a good rub now," Myrtle said. "See if he's lying."

I shook my head. I couldn't even if I'd wanted to. I left the lamp at home with Remy, afraid to bring it anywhere near the portal to Hell.

Besides, I was not ready to do the summoning spell now. A small part of me still hoped I could destroy this thing and be done with it, not have to summon anything. Though that hope was fading fast. "The lamp is at home, Myrtle."

"Let me go." The demon squirmed underneath the ropes. "Now. Now. Now."

Helen rolled her eyes and brought the sword down with a strike. It split right through the ropes, and the demon sprang free, scampering across the ground and toward the fountain. It jumped up onto the ledge, and with one backward glance, flung itself into the portal, out of sight.

Helen smiled bright. "Okay, so we got our answers! Now who's hungry?"

Leave it to the werewolf and the Demon Slayer to be starving after one of the most terrifying nights of my life.

Myrtle licked her fingers as we sat squished into a booth at the diner. "Love me a good raw steak."

I stared at her, my appetite unsurprisingly absent after watching her devour half of the practically still-mooing steak.

Helen pushed away her sandwich, half-eaten, patting her belly. "I have to admit, that was delicious. I can't believe you didn't eat." She nudged me. "What's wrong with you lately?"

I shifted in my seat. "Nothing. I'm fine."

I thought about my visit earlier with Dara, her request. About Preston and our weird interactions. I just wanted everything to go back to normal.

"You're more tense than usual," Helen said, and Myrtle nodded as blood dribbled down her chin.

"Well, I do have a golden lamp sitting back at my house, possibly full of dark magic."

Helen shook her head, frowning. "Don't do that. Don't deflect."

"You do that a lot," Myrtle added.

"What is this?" I asked. "An intervention?"

They looked at each other, then back at me.

"Oh my god. I was kidding," I said. "I don't need an intervention!"

"We just want to know what's bothering you." Helen said it so gently, laying her hand on my arm, and I studied the two women, really studied them. Helen had stepped into the gaping hole my mother had left when I'd discovered she was evil. And no, Helen couldn't replace my mother, hadn't tried to, but she was there for me in the darkest of times. So was Myrtle, who'd always been like the grandmother I never had. Now they both looked at me with so much concern and care in their gazes.

A fairy flitted past us with a heavy pot of coffee, the dark liquid sloshing back and forth in the glass carafe. She set it down on the long bar in the back, then flew to the pastry case and began refilling it with cookies and tarts.

I closed my eyes, and suddenly, the words were spilling out of me. About Dara, the destroyed wish, Emerson coming back to town, about Preston, how we'd fallen right back in step, like we hadn't spent the last twenty years apart. Piece by piece, I told them in excruciating detail about these blasts from the past that I didn't want.

"Huh" was all Myrtle said when I was done.

Helen stayed silent.

"Well?" I asked. "Go ahead. Tell me all the ways I'm being crazy."

"The thing is . . ." Helen tapped her chin. "I think you already know."

"Know what?" I asked.

"That you're being crazy," she said.

"I do not! Why is it crazy to not want to invite drama back into my life? Don't you think I've had enough of that already?" I looked at both of them, waiting for them to agree with my sage words. But neither did.

"Clara, sometimes the risk outweighs the benefit." Helen shifted in her seat. "And sometimes the benefit outweighs the risk. But you don't know until you dive in. What I'm saying is you don't have to ask Preston to marry you. You two can be friends, you know. Start off with something solid that doesn't involve any drama."

"Friends?" I echoed.

"Why not?" Helen said.

I hadn't thought about that. I just assumed we couldn't be friends. But the other day, well, we did work well together to get answers from the mermaids. And Preston had helped me, no drama between us. Maybe a little heat, but that was okay. Helen might be right. Maybe there was a way to have him in my life without ruining the delicate balance Remy and I currently had.

"And as for Emerson," Helen said. "Well, I can't tell you what to do, but it sounds like whether or not the wish getting ruined was your fault, you owe Dara. And again, just because you go talk to Emerson, it doesn't mean you're inviting drama into your life. You could even get some closure. It sounds like it really hurt you the way she left."

"Mmm," Myrtle said, staring at the bloody plate in front of her. "Closure."

I wasn't even sure she was listening.

Closure would be nice. Maybe Helen was right again and talking to Emerson wouldn't be so bad. Especially not if it meant I could get some answers about why she left, why she just cut me out of her life like I meant nothing. Besides, Emerson wasn't going to leave her rich, luxurious LA life for this little quaint one in Whispering Willows. Talking to her for a few minutes would fulfill my promise to Dara while allowing me to move on once and for all.

I bit my lip, mulling it all over, when the floor beneath us began to vibrate.

We all looked down at once.

Myrtle sniffed the air. "You smell that?"

"Smell what . . . ?" I started.

Then the stench hit me like a hard punch. Rot, decay, like fish that had been left to bake in the sun for a week. Bile rose in my throat, and I looked at Helen and Myrtle. "What is that?"

"Only one thing could smell like that," Helen said, and I looked down to see a glowing golden sword appear in her hand.

That's when I saw it: the dark wave of bodies marching through the night. Spikes, claws, scales, jagged wings. Demons. So many demons. And they were headed straight for my neighborhood.

Chapter Fourteen

Helen, Myrtle, and I broke into a run, racing through yards, jumping over bushes, scaling a fence, Myrtle once again in her wolf form. Turned out when an army of demons was about to ambush your house, your body went into turbo mode.

We'd been such idiots. I couldn't believe we told that demon we had a lamp and then just let it go. Of course it was going to scamper off and tell all the other demons about it.

And now they were coming to take it from me.

"The lamp," I said. "They're going to try and take it, and—"

Oh my god. Remy had no idea what was coming. She was alone. With the lamp. I pushed myself to go faster.

"C'mon." Helen grabbed my arm as Myrtle raced up ahead. "I know a shortcut."

She took the lead and raced through someone's backyard, then cut in-between two houses. I followed just as we burst out onto my street, and there sat my house: half of it painted green, the other half still black. The demon army marched at the end of the street, a huge wave of disfigured bodies coming toward us.

Oh, this was bad. This was bad. This was bad. This. Was. BAD. And it was my fault. I didn't listen to anyone. If I hadn't tried to ignore the problem, the whole thing might be solved right now. I shot a glance at Helen, remembering her words at the diner. I ignored a lot of things I shouldn't have.

We arrived at my house, Myrtle already there, pacing and readying herself for a fight. Helen got out her phone and shot off a series of text messages just as Gene arrived. Remy poked her head out her bedroom window.

"Hey, Mom, it looks like there's a whole demon army coming to our house? I think Aunt Helen's got it covered, though. Also, I already sent out an SOS to the whole town. Everyone should be coming to help fight."

"Nice to see you too, hon," I shouted up to her, stopping in front of Helen, out of breath and shaky.

"I also called for backup," Gene said from beside me, fangs sprouting from his mouth. "We have a fight on our hands, and it's going to be a big one."

I squeezed my eyes shut, guilt rattling me. "Do you have anything useful we can use against the demons?" he asked.

I thought for a moment. "Actually . . ."

I looked back to Remy high up above. "Remy, go to the attic and find as many weapons as you can."

"Weapons?" Gene echoed.

"My mom kept a lot of dangerous artifacts in the attic. And she spelled a lot of them to do some morally questionable things." Like the knife that always found its target. Or the candlestick that clubbed its victims. Why my mother needed to spell all these objects, I didn't know. Didn't want to know. But thank god I hadn't gotten rid of them yet, like I very much intended to do.

The demons marched closer, about three houses away now. There were too many to count, but if I had to guess, I'd say about a hundred of them were about to descend upon our house. A knife flew past my head and shot straight to the ground.

"Oops," Remy called from above. "Bad aim."

I shot her a glare. "Maybe don't throw the knife without warning?"

"Incoming," she called as a javelin dropped to the ground. My mother had a freaking javelin. Didn't want to know.

Gene grabbed the javelin, just as a pack of wolves emerged from the shadows.

"We're here to help," one of them said and nodded to Helen.

A group of vampires emerged next, and Gene tilted his head in their direction.

"Bones, you idiot!" a voice called. "How am I supposed to fight demons when you're secreting that terrible smell? How much garlic did you eat at dinner?"

Martin rounded a corner, his green skin flushed with anger as he flicked Bones's arm. The half-giant didn't even react.

"Martin?" I asked Helen. "You called the imp?"

"He can conjure fire," Helen said. "That's gonna come in handy." She gestured at Bones, who towered over all of us, cracking his knuckles, each bigger than my entire hand. "And I think we're gonna want the giant's help here."

The ground vibrated under our feet, the demons getting closer and closer, bearing down on us, their stench growing stronger.

"Ugh, god. They smell worse than you do, Bones," Martin said, pinching his nose.

Bones just cuffed the imp on the head.

"Are you ready for this?" Gene asked, raising the javelin in the air, his fangs sprouting longer from under his top lip.

Helen stood in front of everyone, sword poised for attack. She looked behind her. "Listen, just stun the demons until I can kill them with my sword."

Technically, anyone could kill a demon, but it was much harder without the Demon's Slayer's sword. Just one nick from that glowing golden weapon, and a demon would die.

"Mom, your stance is kind of weak," Remy yelled from the window above. "Make sure you really plant those feet in the ground."

"Thanks, Remy," I shouted back to her.

"Well, she has a point," Martin said from behind me, ball of fire floating above his green hand, lighting up his face and thick silver-streaked hair.

Bones punched his fist in his hand.

"Want the lamp," one of the demons croaked.

Well, if I hadn't already guessed that's what the demons wanted, it was clearer than ever now. I shot a glance behind me at the living room, where I'd left the lamp.

Helen pointed her sword at the army. "Charge!"

She ran headfirst into the demons, sword swinging and slashing.

"Mom, watch it!" Remy's voice blared over the sounds of yelling and bodies thudding together.

Next to me, a wolf tore a demon's arm from its torso. That was going to be burned into my brain forever.

"Mom, duck!"

I bent over, and my back cracked, but I somehow managed to not fall flat on my face and straightened just in time to shove a knife up into a demon's gut.

"Go, Mom! That's badass!"

Up ahead, Helen slashed demon after demon, whirling around, swinging her sword in big arcs. Her movements looked like poetry while mine looked like a toddler just learning to walk.

I stumbled back as a demon smacked me in the face.

"Oh, ouch. That looks like it hurts," Remy said.

I sighed. "Remy, maybe dial back the commentary while I'm fighting for my life?"

"Right, got it! I'll just silently make comments about what you're doing."

The demon punched me in the gut. Ow. Ow. Ow. This was not at all like they made it look in the movies. I was almost positive I was going to vomit. Bile rose up in my throat. Yep, definitely going to vomit any minute now.

I looked up, the contents of my stomach spewing all over the demon in front of me. "Sorry." I coughed, wiping my mouth. "So sorry."

Wait, why was I apologizing? I shook my head and drove the knife into the demon's neck. Green slimed oozed out as the demon grunted, then I wrenched the knife back, the metal squelching as it released the flesh.

I looked around me, at everyone fighting against these evil creatures who were closing in on the house. Helen was surrounded, slaying demon after demon, but there were too many. More and more coming in from the dark.

I couldn't do this anymore. This was my fault and I had to fix it. Fix everything. I remembered what Karissa said about the lamp being bound to whoever summoned the genie. That was the answer, the only way I could stave off these demons. If the lamp was bound to me, then they'd have no reason to stay and fight for it.

It was time. I was going to have to summon whatever was in this lamp, whether I wanted to or not. I breathed in a deep breath and took off toward the house at a run.

I burst through the front door and ran into the living room, my gaze catching on the lamp, sitting there so innocently, like it wasn't the cause of all this trouble to begin with. No, that wasn't completely fair. I was to blame too. I'd been stubborn, wanted to ignore everything happening around me. But I couldn't. Not anymore.

I heard the stomp of feet on the stairs and whirled around to see Remy, breathless.

I held up my hand. "Stay where you are, Remy. I have to do this myself."

"You're going to release it? Whatever's in there?"

I nodded. "It's the only way now."

"Oh, um." Remy pointed behind her, and I turned to see a demon standing there, window open behind it, curtains fluttering in the breeze, and in its hand . . . was the lamp.

"Wait, wait, wait," I said, slowly approaching, knife trembling in my grip. "Could you please set that down?" I smiled sweetly.

"I don't think demons respond to 'please' and 'thank you.' They're literally spawned in hell."

Ugh, good point. I was going to have to fight this thing.

"Okay, no more Ms. Nice Witch." I lunged forward and brought up my leg, higher than I ever thought it could go, kicking the lamp from the demon's grasp.

Its yellow eyes widened as Remy broke out into a cheer. "Yay, look at you! You can't even touch your toes, but you totally just did a high kick."

The demon growled, prowling around me, jabbing at me with its long and curled talons. Foam gathered at the corners of its mouth, and I shuddered, knife clutched tight in my hand. And that's when the demon spotted Remy behind me.

"Remy." My eyes locked on the demon. "Go to your room. Now."

"I'm not leaving you." The teasing tone was gone from her voice, a determination in its place.

The demon pushed past me and toward Remy. No. No way in hell was I letting that thing near my daughter. I looked at the knife, remembering it was spelled by mother to hit its target. I let it fly from my hand and with precision, the knife embedded itself right into the demon's head. It fell forward onto the stairs with a thud. Remy made a face and stepped over it, running straight into my arms.

"No more staying up late watching demon fights for you," I said into her head, pressing kisses against her soft brown hair.

"Mom, just get the lamp before another demon tries to claim it."

"Right."

My whole body clenched in anticipation as I approached the golden object and picked it up.

Here goes nothing.

I rubbed it in slow, circular motions, the metal cool and rough against my hand. The lamp started vibrating, rattling loudly.

"Look," Remy breathed, leaning in closer and studying as a series of words appeared on the side of the lamp. Through the window, I could see Bones picking up a demon and throwing it across the street like it was a rag doll. Meanwhile, Martin threw fireball after fireball at approaching demons.

I squinted at the words. It was time. I had to say the summoning spell and stop this madness.

"Rise, rise from within
Your time has come
To show yourself
Grant me a wish
And pay the price
Thrice, Thrice"

Smoke poured from the spout, a dark blue with shimmers of purple and pink. It filled the room until I couldn't even see Remy.

"Mom?" she said.

"I'm here," I responded, finding her hands and pulling her to me.

"What's happening?" a rumbling noise almost drowned out her words.

"I'm not sure," I murmured, smoking still encompassing the room.

All of a sudden, the rumbling stopped, and the fighting outside had quieted.

"Well, hello, there," a voice said. "I've been waiting a very long time for you."

Chapter Fifteen

The voice was an unfamiliar one, and I squinted, trying to see through the thinning smoke at the figure floating in the air. The figure started singing, and my instinct was to cover my ears and hope it wasn't trying to cast some spell on me. I didn't know what kind of powers this creature had.

Instead, I cocked my head and looked at Remy.

"Is that a Christina Aguilera song? I remember you making me listen to this when I was younger."

I went through a Britney and Christina phase and would listen to all their songs with Remy, having dance parties in our kitchen, Remy giggling and me shimmying my hips to the beat of the music.

The smoke dissipated further, though the genie was still covered in its blue haze. Yes, it was definitely singing a Christina Aguilera song, one of my favorites: "Genie in a Bottle."

What in the freaking hell? A male figure started to emerge as the smoke continued to thin out.

"He can carry a tune," Remy said, impressed.

He really could. He was hitting all the notes, pitch perfect.

Finally the smoke cleared, revealing a man with thick red hair, green eyes, freckles spread across his nose, belting out a song about a genie in a bottle. He hit the final notes, raising a finger in the air and closing his eyes, very Christina-like.

Both my and Remy's mouths dropped open.

He floated in front of us, blue smoke connecting his feet to the lamp like a tether as he adjusted his very chic white sweater and form-fitting jeans.

He stretched his back, cracking his neck from side to side before pinning his gaze on us. "My back is killing me. I'm going to need a masseuse, preferably one who specializes in deep tissue massage. I'd also like a heat pack, a foam memory mattress, and if you could get me a mai tai, that would be great. Thanks so much."

I had no idea how a genie trapped in lamp for as long as he'd been knew about these things, but I also had about a million other questions I wanted to ask first. We'd get to his education on pop culture and memory foam mattresses later. He floated down to the couch, sitting with his legs crossed, staring at us expectantly.

"Who are you?" I blurted out.

"Aren't you supposed to work for us?" Remy said.

He stared like he was seeing us for the first time and blinked slowly. "Wow, you've aged poorly." He looked me up and down. "I mean last time I saw you, you were like sixteen, but my god." He leaned forward, squinting. "Those eye bags. I'm not a fan of that hair cut with your face shape. You could do better. Also some highlights wouldn't kill you—"

"Enough," I said. "How did you get trapped in that lamp? And who are you? And what do you mean I've aged? I don't know you."

Right then, a demon crashed through the window, and we all screamed, including the genie, as Helen jumped in after it, driving her golden sword straight through its heart.

Oh, right. There was still a huge fight happening right outside out house.

I held up a finger. "We're going to continue this conversation in a moment. I have to do something first."

I grabbed the lamp and dashed out onto the lawn as the genie floated after me, still attached to the object.

"Hey! Where are you taking me?" he said. "Unless I'm losing my mind, I remember requesting a masseuse and a mai tai, in that order."

I ignored him, holding up the lamp while he floated behind me.

Slowly, everyone stopped fighting, their eyes turning to the lamp and the genie attached to it.

"Oh, ew," he said. "You guys need to learn how to dress because that is not it, honey." He pointed to a vampire wearing whitewashed jeans with a white tank top.

I shook my head and waved my arms. "You all can go home now. I rubbed the lamp. Summoned the . . ." I gestured back toward the floating figure. Well, I wasn't sure what I had summoned, but I was going to figure it out. "Thing," I finished lamely.

"Excuse you," the genie said behind me. "That's rude. I'm right here. I can hear you, you know. No manners," he mumbled.

The demons grunted and turned, slowly shuffling back through the neighborhood streets and presumably to the portal to Hell. Everyone else stared, tired, bloodied, scratched, and overly unimpressed by whoever floated behind me.

"Um, thanks everyone?" I said. "Really appreciate your help. Went ahead and summoned whatever was in the golden lamp and . . . ta da!" I gestured weakly at the genie floating behind me.

He cringed. "That was a terrible introduction."

I shot him a glare as everyone dispersed, mumbling and muttering while emptying our street. Neighbors who had been peeking out their curtains disappeared, lights winking out. Helen, Gene, Martin, Bones, and Myrtle, back in human form, came to a stand beside me.

"That's your trapped Witch Granter, then?" Myrtle asked. "What the feck do you know about him?"

The genie pointed at Myrtle. "Love the frames. Gonna need to know where you got them, and I'm actually okay with the whole tracksuit thing you have going on. I never thought I'd love a tracksuit, but you really pull it off."

Myrtle shook her head. "Oh god. Another quirky, cutesy little character-type coming to town. Perfect. I'm off." She shifted back to her wolf form and ran away.

Martin glared at the genie. "I can already tell you're extra. So let me give you some advice: this town only has room for one dramatic diva, so don't you dare try to upstage me." He grabbed Bones's hand. "Let's go Bones. We still need to get breakfast ready for our guests tomorrow morning." He did a hair flip and walked away while Bones just shook his head, grunted, and followed.

"Do you need anything?" Helen asked, turning to me.

"Please say no." Gene's fangs retreated back into his gums.

Helen elbowed Gene. "We can stay if you want?"

"I'm not a serial killer," the genie said, studying his nails with increasing interest. "Do you have nail primer or cuticle oil? I prefer the Hermes de la Rouche, but I suppose if you have another brand I can make that work on short notice."

I stared at him for a minute, mouth open, before turning back to Helen and Gene. "I think I've got this. Go home, and I'll fill you in tomorrow. Maybe." I shot a glance back at the genie, who was now studying his nails with increasing horror. "I'll be fine."

"Okay," Helen said, eyeing the genie. "This is gonna be interesting."

Gene slung his arm around her shoulder, and they disappeared from view. I held the lamp in my hand and marched back into the house, feeling the tug of the genie behind me.

"Excuse me!" he called. "I'd really appreciate if you could let me know before you just yank me around like a dog on a leash."

I ignored him and stomped in the house, slamming the door behind me, right over the smoke tether. Something banged against the door, and I winced, opening it as the genie rubbed his forehead.

"Sorry, I didn't mean to slam the door on you. I thought maybe you could float through it or something."

The genie stared back at the door like he was contemplating what I'd said. "Do I look like a ghost?" His face drew back in horror. "Is my skin that white? Oh god. I need some sun. We're hitting the beach tomorrow."

Remy sat at the bottom of the stairs, chin propped in her hands, and she popped up when she saw us enter, following me and the genie into the living room. We sat on the couch, and I placed the lamp in front of me on the table while the genie floated in front of us, hands on hips.

"Oh my gosh," he said, bringing his hands to his cheeks. "Here I am making all these demands, and I realized I haven't even introduced myself. Hi, I'm Isaac. I'm a Sagittarius, I love true crime podcasts, I'm a vegetarian, and I don't wear anything off the rack." He looked at my clothes in disgust. "Anyway, now I'm ready for my masseuse."

"Enough with the masseuse!" I yelled. "We're not meeting any of your crazy demands until you explain what's going on. Who are you?"

He let out a laugh. "Okay, Isabella. You can play dumb all you want, but you're the one who trapped me in here, and now it sounds like you have to deal with the consequences."

Isabella. My mother. He thought I was my mother.

"I'm not Isabella," I said. "My name is Clara. I'm her daughter."

"Oh god," he muttered. "She spawned."

"Hey!" I said.

He just rolled his eyes. "So where is Isabella? She's got a lot of explaining to do, and she better free me from this lamp pronto." He held up his hand. "Look at these nails. They haven't had a manicure in . . ." He threw up his arms. "I don't even know how long."

"Isabella is dead," I said, Remy stiffening next to me.

Now Isaac's face really did drain of color, his skin white, translucent. "Dead? But I never even got to know her."

It was the first time his voice showed even a hint of vulnerability. He looked so familiar as I studied him, but I couldn't figure out why.

"Who are you to Isabella?" I asked.

Isaac's gaze flitted up to me in annoyance. "I'm her twin brother."

Chapter Sixteen

The floor rocked underneath me, and I had to place a hand on Remy's shoulder to steady myself. Remy stayed silent beside me, but I could feel the tension in her bunched shoulders.

"That—that can't be true," I said, even though I knew it was. Now that he'd said it, I couldn't unsee it. He looked exactly like my mom, down to the way his eyes crinkled in confusion, the way his lips pursed in annoyance. Oh my god. *Oh my god.*

"Oh my god," Isaac said, looking around as if just for the first time noticing his surroundings. "This room, it's . . . horrible. Please tell me you're not going for farmhouse chic. That's so overdone now."

"Can we focus?" I snapped my fingers in front of his face. "How is it possible my mom had a twin brother that she never told me about?"

He snorted. "Well, that's easy. She didn't want anyone to know about me."

"You're going to need to start from the beginning," Remy said gently. "Start with your and Isabella's relationship, then why and how she trapped you in that lamp."

Isaac huffed, crossing his arms. "I can't believe I have to explain myself like this. Isabella isn't even here to answer for her actions. Just stuffed me away like some ugly doll she was ashamed of. If I were a doll, let's be honest, I'd be one of the American Doll ones."

Remy and I both gave him the look, the one I'd perfected over the years and had passed onto Remy.

Isaac threw up his hands. "Fine, fine. Your mom didn't know about me until she was sixteen years old, okay? We were separated at birth. I was kidnapped by a witch named Greta. She took me right out of the hospital, far away from Whispering Willows, and she raised me as her own, without magic. Never told me about it. Not a freaking peep."

"Oh, Isaac, I'm so sorry." I couldn't even imagine the pain of knowing the woman who'd raised you wasn't your real mother, had taken you from your birth mother.

He sniffed. "Well, it wasn't all so bad. Greta loved me, and she was a good mom. Minus the kidnapping, obviously."

"Why would Great-Grandma not look for you?" Remy asked.

Isaac shrugged. "I don't know. Maybe I was a really ugly baby or something and she couldn't stand the sight of me."

"No, that can't be true." But I didn't actually know. My grandma had died when I was young, a toddler, so I never had the chance to get to know her or my grandfather, whom my mom had cut out of her life as soon as she was able to. He died when I was a teenager, but we didn't go to his funeral, the rift between him and my mother too great.

"Whatever," Isaac said. "Either way, she didn't come for me. When I was sixteen, I learned the truth after some sparks started shooting out of my freaking hands. Mother—Greta—admitted what she'd done: I was a witch and she stole me from my family in Whispering Willows. So I left. Ran away to Whispering Willows, and when I got here, it was so eerie. Like I just knew where to go. Right to this little shop called The Wish List. That's when I saw *her*."

I held a hand to my chest, heart beating fast. I couldn't believe this. Poor Isaac. What an awful thing to find out. That your entire life was a lie. I glanced over to Remy, wondering if she saw any parallels between herself and Isaac. I had lied to her about who she was, what she was, her entire life. She'd only found out she was a witch a few months ago. But she forgave me. So maybe there was hope for Isaac and this Greta, whoever the woman was.

Isaac continued, "She stood over the cauldron tucked away in the corner, working on a spell. She'd had squid ink all over her arms, her face, her red hair wild, as she scribbled and scratched away on a paper while throwing ingredient after ingredient into the cauldron." Isaac stared into the distance, like he was reliving the memory. "The moment I laid eyes on her, I recognized her: my twin. I just felt it, and I was so excited. A sister. I'd always wanted a sibling."

Wind fluttered in through the opened window, and Remy rushed over to close it as the curtains billowed.

"But she didn't react the way I expected." Isaac huffed. "I thought we were going to have some kind of cool Parent Trap reunion, minus the whole trying to get our parents back together, and she was thinking it was more of a Lion King reunion."

Remy and I shot each other questioning glances, and Isaac just sighed dramatically.

"*The Lion King*, where one lion shoves his brother off a cliff?"

"Yes, okay, we get it," I said, motioning for him to keep going.

"I told her what I'd discovered, and she told me I must be mistaken, that there was no way I had the Westfold blood running through my veins. I could tell, though, that she knew. Deep down, she knew I was telling the truth."

"So what happened?" Remy asked, leaning forward.

"She hit me over the head with a vase."

My eyes bulged out of my head, and Isaac nodded.

"Rude, right? Next thing I knew, I was waking up on some rocky beach, Isabella standing over me with a golden lamp in her hand, performing a spell. She told me I was a Witch Granter, that she was sorry but she had to do this before anyone found out about me." He shrugged. "That's the last thing I remember before I woke up trapped in the lamp."

Oh god. I felt so bad for him.

"Now here I am, floating above the ground, staring at your blotchy complexion and giant eye bags."

Not as bad as I could, though.

"Why would my own twin sister want to do something like that to me?"

I bit my lip. He really didn't know my mom. "She had a problem with competition," I said. "And her long-lost twin brother showing up out of nowhere? Someone else to compete with her for control of The Wish List? To compete with her powers?"

Isaac pursed his lips. "Well, that's kind of bitchy."

Remy snorted a laugh.

Isaac twirled his hands in the air. "How long have I been trapped in this lamp for? Time is really wonky in there."

Oh boy. "Well, if you and Mom were sixteen, that would've been—" I counted on fingers. "Approximately forty-nine years ago?"

Isaac's mouth dropped open in horror and he cradled his face in his hands. "Oh my god, I'm old. Get me a mirror, get me a mirror. Get. Me. A. Mirror. Do I have wrinkles?" He gasped. "Please tell me I don't have wrinkles."

"Wrinkles aren't the end of the world, you know," I said, tracing a line over some of mine. I actually kind of liked them now. Gave me some character.

He scrunched his nose at me.

Remy raised a finger. "You don't look that old. Maybe being in that lamp slowed down your aging?"

I cocked my head. Now that I thought about it, Remy was right. He was supposed to be sixty-six, but he looked like he was in his mid to late thirties.

Isaac breathed a deep breath. "Okay, but I'm going to need to do a face mask tonight, and you have to get me anti-aging cream ASAP."

I rolled my eyes. "A few wrinkles and some gray hair might do you good, you know. Aging is natural, nothing to be afraid of, Isaac."

He crossed his arms. "Oh, that's easy for you to say. I don't see you waking up after being trapped in a lamp for almost fifty years."

Fair point. I guess if my sixteen-years-old self woke up as an almost seventy-year-old, there might be some trauma attached to that.

"Well? What are you waiting for?" Isaac asked. "Release me from this thing."

Remy and I looked at each other, then at Isaac.

"What was that?" He squinted at us. "You two just had some silent conversation about me."

"Um," I said. "So about that . . . We don't exactly know how to release you."

"What?" He emphasized the T, practically spitting it out.

"We're going to figure this out," I said. "Don't panic. We will release you, Isaac. It might take some time and resources, but we won't stop until you're free and I can atone for my mom's past mistakes."

He floated to the ground, laying down and draping an arm over his eyes. "This is it. Rock bottom. Just please go get me the mai tai I requested, a few cucumbers, a face mask, and a suitable bed. And by suitable I mean memory foam with cooling springs that keep me from overheating in my extremely agitated state."

I cocked an eyebrow, about to tell him an emphatic *hell no*, but Remy nudged me. "What?" I whispered while Isaac whimpered from the ground.

"The guy just found out he's been trapped in a lamp for almost fifty years. Maybe we should honor his requests."

"I don't even know how to make a mai tai, and I am not going to go out and buy him some fancy memory foam bed. I don't even have that!" All I had was an old bed with springs that squeaked every time I laid down, and my back was paying the price.

Isaac let out a loud groan, and Remy widened her eyes at me.

I clenched my jaw. "Fine, I'll make him a damn mai tai."

But I was not doing anything more than that.

Chapter Seventeen

Everyone wanted to talk to the genie the next day. I flipped the sign to Closed to signal the end of another busy day at The Wish List and pressed myself against the front door, body aching and tired.

"Yes, girl. I'm telling you, some subtle caramel highlights would really bring out the green in your eyes."

Isaac talked with one of my clients in the corner, who had come for a wish but changed her mind after Isaac told her she didn't need one to fix her life. So now she was chatting with him animatedly like he was her life coach or something.

I clapped my hands loudly, making the girl jump. "Okay, well, thank you so much for coming in today, but unfortunately we're closing, so . . ." I gestured to the sign.

"Oh!" The girl's hands flew to her cheeks. "Right, sorry." She looked back at Isaac. "But you and I are not done talking."

Isaac swatted his hand at the air. "Go. You have got this, Amelia. Remember, this is the only life you have to live."

She walked past me, smile on her face. Once the door closed, I rounded on Isaac, who had an equally big smile on his face. "You cost me five clients today!"

Isaac floated to the middle of the room. "Oh, don't be so dramatic. Some of these people don't need wishes. They can fix their own lives."

"How do you know? Wishes help people, Isaac. I screen all my clients, and I take my role as a Witch Granter very seriously. I would never grant a wish if I thought it wasn't necessary. Not when it costs a piece of the soul."

Isaac's mouth dropped open. "You're telling me when someone wants a wish, they have to give up part of their soul for it?"

I shifted from foot to foot. "Well, yeah. You didn't know that?"

"What part of I didn't know magic existed until I was sixteen did you not understand from my story?"

"Right, sorry." I sank down onto the couch. "Yes, a wish costs a piece of the soul."

"What happens when a person loses a piece of their soul?" Isaac asked.

"Well, it depends. It affects everyone differently. Magic is unpredictable, finicky, and it's personal. Missing part of your soul might not affect you at all, but to another person it might mean a hobby they're no longer interested in, a person they no longer love, a passion they don't have anymore."

"Why hasn't anyone wished for like world peace or something?"

I laughed. "Wishes have their limits. That kind of wish would require so much magic beyond what a single Witch Granter could do. We can change the life of one person, not the entire world."

Isaac stared at the crystal balls on the shelf, a wistful look on his face. "You know, I think I might be able to do this. This whole Witch Granter thing. Once you free me, that is. I can see myself granting wishes like you did today. Making people so happy."

"One thing at a time," I reminded him. "First we have to free you."

Isaac's shoulders slumped, and I couldn't help but feel sorry for him—and maybe a little guilty over how grumpy I was being. Yes, he was a diva, even more of a diva than Martin, which I'd never thought was possible. And yes, he was annoying at times. And yes, he was ruining this whole perfect life I was trying to build. But none of that was his fault. If there was anyone to blame, it was my mother. And she wasn't here to answer for her crimes, so I had to step up.

"So how are *we* freeing *me* exactly?"

"I'm still working on that," I said. "But I promise I'm going to figure it out."

"I've only been trapped in this thing for fifty years." He floated closer to his lamp. "Take your time."

I glared at him. "I just released you yesterday!"

He squinted at me. "And exactly how long did you have the lamp before you summoned me?"

I stared at my feet, not wanting to answer that particular question.

"That's what I thought. I'm clearly not a priority."

I huffed. "Believe me, Isaac, freeing you is a priority. Until I do, I'm stuck with you and that lamp."

His voice grew louder. "Oh, I'm sorry *your* mother cursing me to an eternity living in a metal box is so inconvenient for you!"

"It's not a box," I shouted back. "If anything, it's more like a circular structure." I cocked my head, staring at the lamp. "Or an oval. Whatever, the point is that I'm doing the best I can. Life has been hard for a long time, and it was finally perfect, and then you show up, and—"

"Yeah." Isaac shook his head. "Right. I'm always the problem. Always the unwanted one."

My gaze softened. "That's not what I meant."

Remy burst in the door. "What is all the yelling? Everyone within a mile radius can hear you two."

I glanced out the door and sure enough, everyone in the street stared at my little shop. And it was a lot of people too, everyone here to start setting up for the big parade next week. Fairies flew, stringing lights between the trees, a half-giant carried a huge bench over his shoulder, planting it on the sidewalk, goblins filled potholes with fresh gravel. The Autumn Equinox parade would bring supernaturals from all over to Whispering Willows, which meant more clients, and I did not want Isaac here ruining it all.

My cheeks flushed at Remy's reprimand, but Isaac just gave me a pointed stare. "Blame her. She started it."

My mouth dropped open. "Excuse me. I did not!"

Remy dropped her backpack on the floor, walking over to a chair and plopping down. "Can you two start acting your age, please? I really don't like having to be the adult in this situation."

She was right. We were behaving childishly. "Remy's right. This fighting isn't going to get us anywhere. Let's just try and get along since we're going to be stuck—" I paused, weighing my words. "Since we're going to be spending a lot of time together."

Isaac looked slightly mollified. "Fine, sure."

"How about I make us some tea, and you can tell me and Remy a little more about your time in the lamp?"

Isaac raised his nose in the air, floating a little closer. "Tea sounds nice. As long as it's organic and fair trade."

I pressed my lips together while Remy tried to hide her smile.

"I'm sure I can find some organic, fair-trade tea," I gritted out.

"Then, I'm game." Isaac floated toward the coffee table while I got our tea ready.

Five minutes later I set three steaming cups on the coffee table, the calming scent of lavender floating up in the air. We settled into our chairs while Isaac assumed a cross-legged pose in the air, and I hoped this might be a way to connect with my uncle and get to know him better.

"So what did you do in the lamp, exactly?" I asked.

"Oh, lots of things. After Isabella trapped me in that thing, I spent a lot of time yelling, screaming, asking for help, but soon, it became clear no one was coming to save me."

How awful. I couldn't imagine knowing you were trapped in something with no clue if you'd ever get out.

"But one day, I was banging on the walls and hurt my knuckles. I started crying and yelled out that I just wanted some ice cream. My comfort food."

"Hey, that's your comfort food too, Mom," Remy said. "She likes butter pecan."

"Ew." Isaac wrinkled his nose. "No, when I yelled I wanted ice cream, I had this picture in my mind of organic basil lemon sorbet."

"That's not really ice cream," I mumbled, and Remy shot me a warning look. "That sounds nice," I amended. "Did the lamp give it to you?"

Isaac pushed a hand through his red hair. "And that's when I discovered I could get pretty much anything I wanted in the lamp. It was how I discovered reality TV. I've seen every Housewives episode. I also binge-watched *Friends*. They were totally on a break."

"So you know about current times?" I waved my arm around. "About smart phones and smart TVs and smart, well, everything."

Isaac nodded. "I've learned about everything through TV. I saw the world as it changed around me, though time worked differently. I thought I'd only been trapped for a few years, not fifty."

That was good, at least. I was glad to know he hadn't been trapped in a totally hellish existence, that he had some comforts to lean on, and that it hadn't actually felt like fifty years. I wasn't sure he'd still be sane if it had.

"I journaled a lot, read, exercised. Did everything I could to keep my mind off being trapped. But there were dark moments." He shrugged. "You know, questioning my entire existence and purpose on this earth kind of thing."

Remy took a sip of her tea. "Well, you don't have to question that anymore. We're going to figure out how to free you, and then you have family, a place where you belong."

Well, I wouldn't go that far. I mean, of course Isaac was welcome to stay if he wanted to, but, well, I was kind of hoping he'd choose to go live his life somewhere else so Remy and I could get back to our happily ever after.

Remy beamed at Isaac, and then turned her smile on me, and I gave her a tight one in return.

Isaac gasped. "Maybe you can show me how to cast a spell." He glanced at the cauldron, at our family grimoire that sat next to it, all the spells my ancestors created in that grimoire, as well as one that I'd written just a month ago.

Remy clapped her hands. "Yes, let's show Isaac how to make a spell!"

"Remy, we don't create magic with no purpose." I looked at Isaac. "We make spells in times of need. And yes, some of those times might be more trivial or silly, but we don't just do magic for the fun of it. That's a waste of ingredients, of time, of—"

"God, you're a buzzkill," Isaac said.

"Can we take him to the Witching Well?" Remy asked, bouncing in her seat. She looked at Isaac. "The Witching Well is where you get your wand. You step up to the well, drink the water, and it makes the perfect wand for you." She reached into her backpack and dug hers out, showing it to Isaac. "This is mine. I got it a few months ago when Mom took me." Her wand sparkled in the sunlight streaming through the windows, shiny oak wood with delicate blue ribbon and unicorn hair sprouting out at the end.

I shook my head. "Not until he's free from the lamp. I don't even know if the Witching Well could recognize him as a witch when he's trapped like this. It's better to wait."

Isaac let a long breath loose, his lips vibrating. "Can I do anything fun at all? Can't learn to grant wishes. Can't learn how to cast a spell. Can't go anywhere without you by my side. Might as well go back in the lamp and watch reruns of Housewives. They're way more interesting than this." He stared at the lamp glumly. "That thing is so grimy. Can we polish it or something? And how did it get all those dents? Honestly where did Isabella find that thing?"

I sat up straighter, my mind spinning at the question. The answer might be the key to freeing the genie.

∼

"Where did she find the lamp?" I echoed Isaac. "That's a really good question." I jumped up and ran to the grimoire, flipping through the pages. "If we can find out where she got it, who she got it from, maybe we could find answers about how to free you."

I stopped flipping, thinking about the kind of spell necessary for this, letting the book sense what I needed. It opened to page near the beginning, my great-great-great-grandfather's signature near the bottom, signaling he'd penned the spell.

"What is that thing?" Isaac asked. "It's all leathery and wrinkly. Please tell me it's—"

"It's not organic," I snapped. Dear lord, I was being tested.

"I wasn't going to ask if it's organic." Isaac scoffed. "Duh. Books can't be organic. I was just going to ask what it's made from."

Remy came to a stand next to me, patting the book proudly. "It's made from cow hide, and there's a star on the front, which is the Westfold family crest."

I slung an arm around her, pulling her into me. I had to admit, I loved how proud of her heritage Remy was.

Isaac eyed the book as he hung in the air behind us. "Well, it is kind of cool, I guess. Except for the cow hide part. They could've just used pleather or something." He leaned over. "So what's this spell you think could help?"

I pressed a finger to the page, tracing the lines of text with my fingers as I read it. "It can take us to the lamp's previous owner. The last person who this lamp belonged to."

"What if they're dead?" Isaac asked. "Or across the world?"

"If my mother got this lamp when she was sixteen, then I don't think they're across the world. The previous owner must've been here. In Whispering Willows. As for them being dead . . ." I studied the page. "Well, then it'll be another dead end."

I groaned at the complicated list of ingredients.

"Just go to Potions N' Things," Remy said.

"What?" Isaac looked between me and Remy. "What's wrong with that?"

"It's the local spell ingredient store run by Mom's ex's mother. She's afraid to go in."

"I am not!" I said.

"Oooh, that's juicy." Isaac rubbed his hands together. "Does she hate you? Did you spread a nasty rumor about her? Slap her in public? Ruin one of her parties by dressing nicer than her?" His hand fluttered to his throat. "Sleep with her husband?"

"What?" I turned to him. "No, none of those things. Where did you even come up with that stuff?"

"I told you I watch a lot of Housewives. So why does she hate you, then?"

I looked away.

"Mom broke her son's heart."

"Oooh, okay, that's good. I didn't think of that one."

I glared at the two of them. "Will you two please stop? It's fine. I will get the ingredients we need, okay?"

Isaac studied me. "You seem like you have an avoidance issue."

My mouth dropped open. "Excuse me?"

"You're an avoider," he said.

"You just met me yesterday!"

"Avoider," he coughed out.

I pointed at him. "Stop saying that."

A smug look formed on his face. "Then go to Potion N' Things and prove me wrong."

"No, I don't need to," I gritted out. "I can find the ingredients we need. And for your information, I am not avoiding things." I thought about my conversation at the diner last night with Helen and Myrtle. A conversation that now seemed like a lifetime ago. "I'm becoming friends with my ex."

"Really?" Remy asked, genuine surprise flashing across her face.

I nodded. "Yes, really. And I'm going to meet with an old friend from high school tomorrow." At least, I thought it was tomorrow. I double checked the calendar on my phone. "Yes, tomorrow," I confirmed. "Going to get closure."

"You're going to the funeral?" Remy asked. "I thought you didn't want anything to do with Emerson."

I raised my nose in the air. "I never said I didn't want anything to do with her. So yes, I'm going."

"Can I come? I thrive on awkward situations," Isaac said. "And this sounds like it's going to be very awkward."

"I would also like to come while you get this closure," Remy said.

"No and no." I looked at my daughter. "You're going to be at home, doing homework." I looked at Isaac. "And you're going to be . . . with . . ."

Martin burst in the door. "Hello, hello." He turned his glum expression on Isaac and nodded stiffly at what he apparently viewed as his competition for role of the town's diva. "Hello."

"With Martin!" I finished.

Isaac's eyes widened. "Huh?"

Martin mirrored him, his green skin flushing and his pointed ears wiggling. "I'm sorry?"

"I need you to watch Isaac for a few days so I can concentrate on getting this spell right." I nodded toward the grimoire. "I have a lot of ingredients to collect, and I'm going to need to make sure everything is perfect so we can trace where his lamp came from."

Martin crossed his arms. "Oh, well, in that case . . . No."

"Martin," I whined.

"Martin, did you know that Isaac loves Housewives?" Remy asked, a twinkle in her eye.

Martin stopped at that. "Well, I do like all the franchises, except for..."

"Orange County," Isaac finished for him, and they both locked gazes from across the room.

"Obviously," Martin said. "That's the worst one."

Remy clapped her hands and whispered to me, "They're going to be best friends."

"Okay, fine," Martin said. "He can come stay with me. Only for a few days."

"Thank you, thank you, thank you." I stuffed the lamp into its familiar satchel and handing it off to Martin. "You can tell him to go inside whenever he's annoying you."

"Rude," Isaac said.

I pushed Martin toward the door. "Okay, you two have fun together."

"But," Martin protested as I shoved him outside.

"Bye now!" I slammed the door shut and sank back down against it.

"Now what?" Remy asked.

I squeezed my eyes shut, feeling like I just ran a marathon. "First, I have a funeral to attend. And then, I'm going foraging."

Chapter Eighteen

The next morning came far too early. I'd tossed and turned all night long, thinking about seeing Emerson for the first time in over twenty years, until my alarm rang out loud and clear and I'd realized I'd barely gotten any sleep. Remy was still in bed—I swear that girl could sleep all day if I let her. She might as well. I wouldn't be home.

I sent off a quick text to Dara, just so she didn't have to worry about whether or not I'd show.

CLARA

> See you this morning. I'm so sorry for your loss.

I got dressed, donning a black knee-length frock that seemed appropriate for a funeral, then I put on my witch's hat and got out my broom, covered in dust, the ends brittle and old. We didn't fly on brooms much anymore. It wasn't practical, especially when we had cars and airplanes and trains. But anytime a witch died, it was tradition to wear your witch hat and fly on the broom to the burial rites.

The broom ride to Whispering Bluffs was uneventful, and from the sky I spotted a gathering crowd around a tall stack of hay bales. I steered my broom down to the bluff, where Kathy's body lay on top of the bales. She had definitely aged since I'd seen her, but she wore big thick bracelets on her slim wrists, shiny diamond earrings, and a pearl necklace. Her white hair was cut into a chic bob that grazed her cheekbones. A big sapphire wedding ring sparkled from her left finger, but as I searched the crowd I didn't see anyone whom I thought might be her husband.

I finally spotted Emerson, her blonde hair shining under the morning sun. I'd spot Emerson anywhere. She didn't fit in with the rest of us, not with those long, tanned legs, her beautiful blonde hair piled on top of her head, that effortless smooth skin. She could've been a supermodel. But as I got closer, I saw how she looked empty, completely drained of any happiness, any kind of energy. Dara was right. Something didn't seem right with her. Obviously I knew she must be in pain over the loss of her aunt, but there was something else, an odd aura about her that I couldn't quite put my finger on. I shook away the feeling and landed my broom in the back of the crowd, trying my best to blend in. Now wasn't the time to approach Emerson.

The burial rites went by in a blur. We chanted, sang, listened to a short sermon, and then the bales of hay were lit, a fire burning bright and encompassing Kathy. Smoke twisted up into the air, and slowly, everyone began departing, including Emerson, who shuffled down a path toward the beach, where I saw a white tent set up with tables, chairs, and a table of snacks and drinks.

I took a deep breath. Time to go catch up with my ex best friend.

Emerson sat alone at a white picnic table, apart from everyone else in the far back corner of the tent. The blue ocean spread out in front of us, but luckily the tent shielded us from the sun. The September air was cool and pleasant, and with no breeze, it was the perfect day to be at the beach. I approached Emerson, her blonde hair in an elegant bun, earrings dangling from her ears, her nails manicured and beautiful. Her beauty might not have changed, but now it was more curated. I wondered what kind of shields she had up as I approached her.

"Emerson?" I said cautiously.

She jumped in her seat, turning to assess me. Of course I couldn't tell what she was thinking with those big round sunglasses covering her eyes, frames lined in a shiny gold that told me they probably cost more than my entire outfit. When she didn't say anything, I slid into the seat next to her.

So I said the only thing that popped into my mind. "I never thought I'd see you again."

She stared at her impeccable French manicure. Mine were purple after Remy and I decided to stay up late and paint each other's nails, not nearly as perfect as Emerson's, but I loved them all the same. "Yeah, only took a funeral to lure me here," she said sarcastically.

Her voice, her demeanor, everything about the fun-loving, sweet girl I knew was so different. This woman sitting in front of me had no warmth radiating from her. Isaac's stupid words about me being an avoider echoed in my head. Clearly I wasn't an avoider. I was here. Talking to Emerson.

"I'm sorry about your aunt. I didn't know her that well."

"No one did." Her words came out sharp. "This funeral's all wrong."

I clasped my hands in my lap. "Yeah, well what do you expect?"

When she didn't say anything, I started talking faster, nervous for a reason that I couldn't place my finger on. "You know, when my mom died, I felt the same about her death rites. It had been a small ceremony, to honor the good she did in the world."

Which was mostly out shadowed by all the bad she did.

I still remembered when I got that invitation in the mail. My heart had stopped. I stood at the mailbox, frozen, staring at the piece of paper. It had been raining, just a fine mist when I'd left the house to walk to the mailbox, but by that point, the rain was pouring down, soaking me.

You are invited to Isabella Westfold's death rites.

I'd told Greg I wanted to take a weekend for myself, do some self-care. He believed me, probably because I never asked for anything for myself.

Only a few had attended, and I had a feeling they'd done it for me more than for my mom. It had been held in the place she died, where she'd fought to the very end.

Emerson just stared out at the ocean, still not speaking, as I came back from the memory.

"It was hard," I said gently, "seeing my mom like that, so vulnerable and still. It was also pretty hard not to focus on all the horrible things she'd done."

I almost didn't even believe she was dead, that it had all been some elaborate trick on her part to make us think she was gone. I don't think I truly believed it until the day I got the letter in the mail that The Wish List had passed to me. You couldn't fake magic as strong as that. If The Wish List was officially mine, then she was truly gone. That's when I'd lost it. Months after her burial rites had happened. Stood in my kitchen sobbing, the water running from the faucet, filling the sink as I stared at the stupid notice that The Wish List was mine. When the water had started to spill over the sides of the sink and onto the floor, I'd snapped out of it, wiped my tears, cleaned up the mess, and continued washing the dishes like nothing had happened.

"You know what I decided to do?" I asked Emerson.

Nothing, no response, so I continued on, "I treated her death rites like a party. I talked about my good memories of her. And shockingly, it made me feel better."

Emerson finally turned her head toward me, and I wondered if she'd heard anything I'd said at all.

"It's a funeral, Emerson," I said. "Not a wedding. If you think about it, they're never great. Her funeral sucked, so what? It's not about how she died, right? It's about how she lived." I tugged on a strand of my brown hair. "What matters is that you remember your Aunt Kathy and the way she lived her life, and you carry on with her spirit, keep it alive. If you're the one who knew her best, then that means you're her champion after she's left this world."

Tears leaked from behind her sunglasses, down her cheeks, and she quickly patted them away. Great. I'd made her cry. Exactly what I was supposed to be doing.

"So how's Los Angeles? Details now." Probably best to stop talking about her dead aunt and go for a lighter topic, especially since I was supposed to be bonding with her. A voice deep down said I wasn't trying very hard, but I ignored it. I was here. That was enough.

She gave a little shrug and stared at her nails. "Awesome."

This conversation was like pulling warts from a toad. "I figured," I said and snatched a cookie that sat on a plate in front of us, stuffing some of it in my mouth. Nervous eater. "I hear Witch Inc. pays their staff a lot of money to create those spells."

Emerson worked for a well-known company in the witching world that provided spells for powerful and rich clients. Spells that weren't illegal, but walked a very fine line between right and wrong. A politician might want their speech to inspire awe from an audience, a football team might want their running back to have extra confidence during a big game. At least, that's what the company claimed they did. Many thought they went further than that, but there was no proof. Witch Inc. was the first of its kind in the witch world, and I don't think the Council knew how to handle them just yet. Either way, they paid their witches boat loads of money.

"Yeah, something like that."

I noticed a tall figure at the other end of the tent, dark bronze skin, thick curly hair, tall, and huge. Emerson's other high school best friend. I'd only hung out with the werewolf a few times, but I'd always felt like I knew him so well because Emerson talked about him nonstop. "And have you talked to Cruz?" I asked, nodding toward his hulking figure.

"Yeah." She focused her attention on some faded crayon marks etched into the table. "Didn't go too well."

"Right." Batting zero for three, here. I swallowed another mouthful of cookie. "Well, I bet he missed you while you were gone. We all did."

I winced. That had come out wrong. Accusatory almost. I guess I had some anger I needed to unpack over how Emerson just up and disappeared.

She pulled her sunglasses off her face, anger flashing in those icy blue eyes, all warmth gone from them. "I don't owe anyone an apology, Clara."

Now, anger of my own surfaced. Here I was, trying to make nice after Emerson basically abandoned me without so much as a goodbye. "Maybe you don't, but it would be nice to hear one anyway. Imagine waking up one day, and the person who means the most to you is gone without an explanation. And when you try to call her, the number is disconnected."

Emerson just scoffed and rolled her eyes.

"You could've contacted us once you got a new phone."

She'd disappeared before the age of social media. No Facebook or Instagram to stalk her. That had come years later. I wiped a few stray cookie crumbs from my black dress.

Emerson tipped down her sunglasses and trained her cold, hard eyes on me. "Didn't you leave shortly after me? Up and ran? Left for twenty years before coming back? Sounds kind of hypocritical."

I leaned back like she'd slapped me. "That was different. I had to leave, and I didn't just disappear without a trace. I let the people I cared about know where I was going and why I had to go."

Emerson started to stand. "If you came here to lecture me, then you can—"

"I came over to say hi, Emerson. I didn't know if I'd get the chance."

I'd already lost her attention, though. Emerson's focus now trained on her mom, who stood with a small group of people laughing about something. "Yeah, Clara," she said, gaze stuck on them. "Thanks for saying hi, but I'm headed out, actually. I'll see you around."

I had a feeling she wouldn't but didn't say anything in response as she stalked away.

That had gone about as bad as it could have. Dara asked me to talk to Emerson, get her to stay, and all I'd done was push her away more. It wasn't my fault Emerson had turned into . . . this. I'd done what I could, and now I could wash my hands of this entire thing. I knew Dara desperately wanted her daughter to stay, but I couldn't make that happen. I couldn't compete with her life in LA. No one could. It would be better for Dara to just let her daughter go.

Besides, no rocking the boat.

Raised voices caught my attention, and I looked up to see Emerson screaming at her mom, at everyone. Oh no. I'd been so caught up in my own thoughts, I missed whatever set Emerson off. She stalked away from the group and Dara shot me a pleading glance.

Dammit.

I nodded at Dara and jumped out of my seat to follow her daughter. "Emerson, wait!"

I chased after her, not an easy feat in the sand. Emerson didn't slow down, stalking out of the tent and across the beach, fumbling with her phone, tapping at it frantically.

"Emerson," I said again, finally catching up to her. "What are you doing?"

"I'm leaving." Her voice was shaky, hands trembling. "I came for my aunt's funeral, and I need to go back to work. Okay?"

"Just calm down and take a deep breath," I said.

She shuddered like my words were the scariest thing imaginable. "No. I don't want to be here."

Forget it, then. I couldn't do this, no matter how much Dara wanted me to. I couldn't fix whatever was broken inside Emerson. "We understand. Loud and clear. You hate this place, but maybe you're meant—"

She punched in something on her phone. Without warning, the phone made a garbled noise and smoke erupted from it. Emerson and I shrieked, and she dropped the phone into the sand, jumping away from it as thick plumes rose into the air. We coughed and sputtered, waving away the massive dark clouds.

That looked an awful lot like dark magic. I shot Emerson a quizzical gaze, but she just stared at the phone, chest heaving, eyes wide.

"You've got to be kidding me," she said.

I cleared my throat. "Like I was saying, maybe this isn't the place you want to be, but it's the place you need to be."

Emerson's gaze flitted to a tangle of bushes gathered around a cliffside. Her face turned pale, and her hands fluttered to her neck, like she was seeing something that I wasn't.

"I've got to go," she said and fled before I had a chance to say anything else.

And for the second time in our lives, Emerson left me without saying so much as a goodbye.

Chapter Nineteen

After that disastrous morning, I needed a cleanser. Remy and I sat on the floor of our living room, glitter, papier mâché, glue, and streamers covering the hardwood floors around us. My mother would have a heart attack over this mess if she weren't already dead.

Growing up, my mother had taught me how to spell cleaning supplies to keep the house in perfect condition. Everything had a specific place. Walls were always a white or gray. Furniture navy or white. Very few pictures on the walls. Instead my mother liked priceless art and artifacts to decorate our house, things that had no meaning.

I looked around at the mess covering the living room. We'd bought some covers for the couches, bright and floral-print, that Isaac said made it look like we lived at the Rainforest Cafe—which I think was supposed to be an insult. We'd also been testing out different paint colors for the monochrome walls, so splashes of yellows, blues, and greens streaked across the walls. We hadn't decided on a color yet for the living room, or any other room in the house.

"Are you sure we can't just create a spell for this?" I asked Remy, lifting up a hand with newspaper and thick glue stuck to my skin.

"Yes!" Isaac said from where he floated above us.

Martin had dropped him off earlier this morning, saying he had gardening to do at the bed and breakfast, but he said he'd be back to pick up the genie later while I foraged for items for the tracing spell.

Which I was going to do later. For now, I needed to help my daughter with her school project. Remy wasn't going to come second to anything, not even a genie I desperately wanted out of my life.

My daughter scowled at me. "No, Mom. We're not doing a spell for this. Everyone in the senior class has to make a contribution to our float, and we're not allowed to use magic. I've told you that already."

Isaac flopped in the air, laying down, draping an arm over his eyes. "But this is so boring. Can't you guys at least entertain me like Martin does? He's very talented with the cello. And Bones is great with the drums. Martin also has the best gossip. Did you know that Myrtle once plotted to kill the Serpent?"

"I'm sorry we're so boring," I replied drily.

Isaac let his arm fall from his face, peeking over it at me. "Not forgiven."

I flapped my hand, trying to get the newspaper that was glued to it off. "Remy, I can't believe I'm saying this, but I'm with Isaac. It would be way easier if we could throw a few ingredients in the cauldron, wave our wands, and poof, we've got your contribution."

"Is that how spells work?" Isaac said, his eyes widening in excitement.

I kept forgetting that he knew nothing about magic.

I stood and walked over to the cauldron that sat in our hearth. "Okay, how about this? I won't create a spell for your contribution," I told Remy, "but I'll just create something that helps make it strong, indestructible."

Remy eyed me suspiciously as she squeezed a huge dollop of glue on a piece of paper. "I guess that would be fine."

"And that means I get to see how magic works." Isaac clapped his hands together and floated toward the cauldron, a long, blue smoky tether still connecting him to the lamp that sat on our coffee table.

I grabbed a piece of paper and a quill from a table in the entryway and dipped the quill in the fresh ink pot sitting on the table.

"What's she doing?" Isaac asked.

Remy was bent over her creation, curly hair curtaining her face.

"She's writing the spell down. In order for any spell to be enacted, it has to be written."

"Huh," Isaac said as I scratched out a spell and the ingredients I thought it might need. A strengthening spell was pretty basic magic, and I'd performed a variation of this spell many times over, so I felt confident about getting it right.

"I better not get in trouble for this," Remy said from behind me as I finished writing out the spell. "Mr. H doesn't like cheaters."

At that, I turned, paper clutched in my hand. "Preston is the one who gave you this assignment?"

"Ooooh, Mr. Ex?" Isaac said, and I made a face at him.

"Yeah." Remy started snipping at her creation. "Remember? You learned about it during Welcome Night? It's a homeroom project to celebrate Autumn Equinox." Remy paused as I walked toward the closet where we housed a few common ingredients needed for potions. I grabbed a piece of silver, diamond dust, bear fur, and then walked into the living room and nabbed a tube of glue.

Remy eyed me, mischievous smile on her face. "You never did tell me how your date with Mr. H went."

My head shot up at that, hand squeezing a little too hard on the glue, which spurted out onto the floor. "That was not a date, Remington."

Remy didn't even flinch at my use of her full name.

"It was a date, it was a date." Isaac floated above us, clapping gleefully.

I glared at him as I dropped all the ingredients into the cauldron. "You don't even know what she's talking about. You were still in the lamp when Preston and I went on our mission."

"Date," Isaac said, defiance shining bright in his eyes.

"He was helping me figure out how to find the summoning spell for the lamp," I explained to Isaac, "which Remy would know because she's the sneaky little one who orchestrated the whole thing."

"I thought you weren't avoiding him." Isaac studied his nails. "Seems like you and Preston haven't spent much time together since your little mission. Not very friendly, if you ask me."

"Do you want to learn magic or not?" I asked, and his mouth snapped shut.

Remy just smiled smugly and went back to work on her arts and crafts project for the parade.

"What are you making again?" Isaac asked, as if reading my mind while I stared at Remy's creation in confusion.

Remy methodically cut a line into an orange piece of paper. "Since Autumnal Equinox is a celebration of only one of two days a year when the length of day and night are exactly the same, our senior float is going to be a half moon, half sun, and every senior is contributing by making our own star, which we can take our creative liberties with."

"A lot of creative liberties," Isaac murmured, then his attention focused back on the cauldron. "Okay, okay, I'm ready. Teach me magic."

"I'm just showing you how a spell works," I said. "You can't do magic while you're trapped in that lamp."

At least I didn't think he could. I wasn't taking any chances. "Spells are all about the three c's," I said. "Collect, cultivate, create."

Isaac stared at me blankly.

"You have to collect the ingredients, cultivate them, and then create the spell. Now, this is a simple strengthening spell, so I focused on ingredients that I thought might work well together to make a strong bond for Remy's star, something that will make her star unbreakable."

Isaac peered at the ingredients in the cauldron. "And you had to write all that down on the paper?" He gestured toward the paper sitting next to me on a side table.

I nodded. "Yes, once the spell is written, it can officially be enacted. But just because it's written doesn't mean it will work. Spells can go wrong for a variety of reasons. Wrong ingredients, weak intentions, wrong wand movements. The more you practice magic, though, the easier it gets to know what a spell needs. It comes more naturally. Intuitively."

I thought about my intent with this spell, what I wanted from it, and waved my wand over the cauldron repeatedly as Isaac stared in fascination. As I moved my wand in a circle, shimmers of pink and purple magic swirled in the cauldron, gaining speed.

Isaac gasped.

I continued, the magic growing brighter, stronger, and I felt it filling my veins, like the adrenaline rush you get after riding a rollercoaster.

"Wow," Isaac breathed as he stared.

Finally, the magic grew so bright in color, it filled the whole room, washing it in shades of pink and purple. Then it snapped back into the cauldron, now filled with a dusky liquid that shimmered.

"Is that the strengthening spell?" Isaac asked in awe, and I nodded.

"Yep. Once Remy is done with her star, we can coat it in the magic, and it should remain indestructible." I arched my neck to look at Remy's progress. "You sure you don't need help with that?"

Her creation was looking less like a star and more like a bent rectangle at this point.

"Don't worry." Remy frowned at it. "I didn't really count on you helping. I figured you'd be more emotional support. I called for backup."

"Backup?" I did not like the sound of that.

The front door burst open from the hallway. "Help has arrived!"

Great. "You called Martin?"

"He had to come anyway to pick up Isaac," Remy said as Martin appeared in the opening of the living room, green skin bright and flushed from excitement, his pointy ears twitching.

He looked down his nose at me, to the bits of paper still sticking to my hand, cheeks covered in glitter, and just tutted. "Honestly, Remy, you should've just called me to begin with."

He fluttered over and sank down into a cross-legged seat on the floor.

Remy just smiled and shook her head. After staying at Martin's bed and breakfast for two months when we first came to Whispering Willows, I had to admit, Remy becoming friends with Martin and his half-giant assistant Bones had not been something I expected. For reasons I'd never understand, the three just clicked, and now they had a group chat and everything. I couldn't even imagine Bones texting with his ginormous thumbs.

"Oh, hi," Isaac said, briefly glancing up at Martin before turning his attention back to the shimmery potion bubbling in the cauldron. The pink of the magic reflected in his irises, and his gaze kept flicking to my wand with interest. As soon as we freed him from the lamp, I supposed I'd have to take him to the Witching Well to get his own wand. I was already teaching Remy magic, so I guessed I could teach Isaac as well.

"Now, what were we discussing before I arrived?" Martin asked as he grabbed a bunch of newspaper, scissors, and glue and started getting to work. Remy must've told him she needed to make a star for the float because he didn't ask any questions.

"How Clara is avoiding her ex," Isaac said, now floating back over to the floor and sinking down, his legs crossing as he tugged at his oversized black and white sweater, paired with skinny black jeans, that looked like it came straight off the runway. I wondered if every morning he just closed his eyes and, POOF, some amazing outfit appeared on him.

"That's not what we were talking about," I argued. "I was teaching Isaac the basics of casting a spell."

Remy snipped at her creation, still looking like a complete mess. "That's technically what we were talking about before you did the magic."

Traitor.

"Remember? I said you went on a date with Mr. H and then you said it wasn't a date and then Isaac called him Mr. Ex, which I really love—"

"Okay, yes, yes," I interrupted.

Martin concentrated on his project, currently folding the newspaper in impossibly complicated ways. It looked like origami. "Oh, Preston and Clara have such a dramatic relationship. If you think they're bad now, you should've seen them back in high school."

My head snapped to him as he started to cut the paper with his scissors, the blades working so fast I couldn't even tell what he was doing.

"Excuse you," I said.

Martin tilted his head. "Clara pines after Preston, who ignores her. Preston finally admits he has feelings for Clara. Isabella doesn't like Preston, so Clara lies and tells Preston she doesn't have feelings for him. Clara finally admits feelings for Preston. Preston is in a relationship. Preston breaks up with girlfriend. Preston and Clara finally get together. Then rinse, wash, repeat like six hundred times and you have a good idea of their relationship."

My mouth practically dropped open to the floor. That's what people thought of my and Preston's relationship? Like we were some soap opera, here to entertain others?

"Wow," Remy breathed, eyes wide. "You never told me any of that."

I hadn't remembered it like that, I supposed. Martin packaged our story up so neatly, as if it could fit in a box. But it hadn't felt like that when we went through it. I swallowed. He was right, though. The whole thing had been dramatic from the start. Tumultuous, full of trouble. Yes, we got together in the end, but at what cost? I ended up breaking his heart anyway, breaking my own heart. Exactly why I didn't want that kind of trouble now. I needed stability for me. For Remy.

"You know, I was wrong about you, Clara." Isaac propped his chin in his hands. "I thought you were kind of a downer, to be honest. Very boring, definitely no taste in clothes." He studied me. "Or hair. Or makeup. Or design—"

"Okay, Isaac. Get to the point," I said through clenched teeth.

"You're kind of interesting, after all."

My phone lit up with a text.

> **DARA**
>
> Emerson is still here. Her car broke down and she can't leave until it's fixed. We just got in a big fight, and I think she went to The Brewery with Cruz. Do you think you could meet her there and talk with her maybe?

Ugh, speaking of drama. No. No, absolutely not. I had done my part, gone to that funeral, and talked to Emerson. She had no interest in me or anyone one else here in Whispering Willows. It wasn't my job to keep her here. Hell, it wasn't even fair of me to try. She had a life in LA, and I was not interfering with that.

Dara sent another text.

> **DARA**
>
> Please, Clara. I think staying here might be really good for her, but she just can't see it.

I groaned again, and Remy wrinkled her nose.

"Who's texting you, Mom?"

"It's Emerson," Isaac said before I could answer, looking over my shoulder.

"Hey!" I brought the phone closer to my chest. "It's not Emerson, for your information."

"She wants Clara to go out tonight," Isaac said.

Martin snorted. "That's not gonna happen."

"What is that supposed to mean?" I asked.

"Ever since the whole mayor debacle, you've stayed in your little house and refused to go anywhere or do anything." Martin began piecing his project together. "Her past might be interesting, Isaac, but now, Clara is a boring old fart."

"I like boring," I said. "Boring is good. I've had enough drama for a lifetime, and I'm not planning on inviting any more into my life."

I rubbed my temples.

"I was right, I guess. You are an avoider," Isaac said cheerfully.

Martin finished cutting and now began dotting all his construction paper and newspaper with thick glue. "Ah, yes. An avoider. That fits."

Remy pressed her lips together, trying to hide a smile. God, everyone was so annoying. Did they have to be so annoying all the time? I stared hard at my phone, then before I could think more about it, shot off a text to Dara.

CLARA

I'll be there.

"What's got you looking so smug?" Isaac asked.

"I'm meeting Emerson at a bar. Tonight. Not avoiding," I said. "And I think I might be able to find an ingredient I need for the spell at The Brewery. It's a win-win."

"Okay, then," Isaac said, snapping his fingers in a zig-zag motion. "Go you." He looked me up and down. "Please let me dress you."

I rolled my eyes.

"There we go." Martin admired his work.

We all looked at him, and my mouth dropped open. He had four perfectly shaped stars sitting in front of him that he had somehow papier mâché'd.

"What in the hell . . .," Remy said, glancing at her own misshapen star.

Martin shrugged. "It could be a little neater, but I think it'll do as your contribution to the float." He handed her one of the stars, and Remy just stared at it in awe.

The imp stood. "Well, I have to get back to my Bed and Breakfast. Bones is probably serving our guests tea using our basic tea ware and not the fine china I bought. Like the heathen he is. I'm guessing I'm still your babysitter?"

"Yes," I said, as Isaac tried to protest loudly. "You are. Until I get all the ingredients for this spell. After tonight, I should have the first one, at least. And the less you two bother me, the quicker I can work." I sent a pointed glare Isaac's way.

"Okay, but not before I have a chance to pick out your outfit for tonight." The genie waggled his eyebrows.

I was about to protest, but Remy cut in. "Yes, Mom! Isaac has a good eye for this stuff."

"Fine, fine." I huffed and gestured up the stairway. "But I don't want anything that's going to make me stand out."

Chapter Twenty

I tugged at the hem of my short hot pink dress that kept riding up my thighs. I'd forgotten I even owned this thing. I'd bought it for some silly date night Greg had wanted to take me on when Remy was younger. He'd gotten a babysitter, a hotel, planned the whole night, and told me to wear something sexy. So I'd bought this, worn it once, and then never looked at it again. Now it clung to every curve of my body as I made my way through the bar.

The Brewery was packed, unsurprisingly since it was one of the only bars in town. I sat at the bar top, trailing my finger through a puddle of condensation, and gave my order. After a few minutes, the bartender scurried over with a bright pink drink in a glass shaped like a witch's hat, and I sipped from it, enjoying the fruity sweet taste. I'd looked for Emerson but hadn't been able to spot her so far in the darkened room, lit only by lanterns fixed to the wall.

The heavy black door to The Brewery burst open, bringing with it a chilly gust of wind that raised the hairs on my arms.

Emerson and Cruz entered the bar, Emerson eyeing me and running straight at me with something like relief in her eyes. Cruz sauntered off to another room, his thick mop of dark curly hair disappearing around a corner.

She threw her arms around my neck. "Clara, you're here."

After how cold she'd been at the funeral, I didn't expect her to care whether I was here or not.

I offered her my drink and she threw it back, chugging it like she was fighting her own demons tonight. I guess I wasn't the only one looking for an escape from reality. I got us two more drinks while Emerson stood in silence, surveying the room, probably watching for any familiar faces. The drinks came, and I took a sip of mine while Emerson once again threw her head back and gulped hers down.

"Whoa, you should probably slow down," I said. "Remember how strong witch's brew is?"

She ignored me, grabbing a shot off a tray floating throughout the room.

Good luck to her. I'd gotten drunk off witch's brew exactly one time, the night I'd met Emerson. I had been fifteen, stupid, and desperately trying to impress Preston at some beach bonfire party, except I didn't have the courage to face him without drinking . . . a lot. I'd ended up wandering away from the bonfire, drunk and crying after I'd tried to talk to him, only to completely embarrass myself. I hadn't realized I'd stumbled near the tide pools. I walked across a line of rocks separating the pools from the sea, something I'd done thousands of times, but a huge wave crashed into the rocks, knocking me off-balance. I'd have drowned, except out of nowhere a strong hand gripped my arm and dragged me to safety. A blonde witch, beautiful, someone I didn't recognize. But she'd saved me, sat with me on the beach until I sobered up, listened to me cry about Preston, how in love I was with him, how he'd never notice me.

She'd looked me straight in the face and said, "Time to make him notice you." And that had been that.

From then on, Emerson and I talked every day. We might not have gone to the same school or came from the same background, but we'd been each other's person.

That was a long time ago.

We weren't those people anymore, never would be.

Emerson had been silent, and it should've been weird, but it wasn't. As teens, we'd spend hours in the same room, doing our own thing, not talking, just there for each other. This didn't feel any different.

Before I could attempt to ask about her car, how long she planned to stay, Emerson grabbed my arm and dragged me toward a room off to the side where a raucous game of beer pong was being played.

"C'mon," Emerson said. "Let's go play."

"Beer pong?" I asked, tugging at my clingy pink dress.

"Yep." She flashed a winning smile. "Let's go."

We stepped in the room, and I immediately spotted Preston, my drink suddenly sticking to my throat. I had no idea he'd be here tonight. It wasn't that I didn't want to see Preston, but I wanted to be prepared. Every time I saw him, it was like getting a cold splash of water straight to the face. A shock to my entire system. Isaac's words echoed in my mind. Avoider. Well, I wouldn't be avoiding anything tonight. I was here with Emerson, with Preston. I would prove Preston and I could be friends. And as for Emerson, well, her and I didn't have to be friends because she would be leaving as soon as her car got fixed. She'd be gone soon enough, one less thing for me to have to worry about tipping the scales of my carefully balanced life.

Emerson eyed me, her gaze flitting between me and Preston, but she just pressed her red lips together and didn't say anything. I couldn't help but think she had a lot she wanted to say. She'd been the one who gave me the courage to finally talk to Preston. Then she'd helped me prepare for our first date. For our first kiss. Emerson had been there for it all, guiding me and helping me gain confidence in myself.

She hip-checked Preston, who'd just sunk another shot into his opponent's cup. He just flashed her one of his dazzling smiles, the kind that was so effortless but that made my breath catch in my throat.

"Our turn, boys," I heard Emerson say, though it was hard to pay attention to her when Preston was in the room, his presence so intoxicating, just like it had always been. Someone tried to argue with Emerson that it was their turn next, but she bull-dozed over them, like she tended to do with her big personality.

I hadn't played beer pong in a long time, and it was clear Emerson was drunk, too drunk. Still, once the game got going, we had fun. We threw shot after shot, sinking balls and forcing the other team to drink. Each shot we made, we squealed and high-fived. Emerson talked a little smack. Okay, a lot of smack. But that was Emerson. She was as competitive as they came. We won our first game, and Emerson hugged me tight, whooping and hollering.

"How you doing, Emerson?" Some guy sauntered into the room. He looked familiar with his green skin and pointy ears, narrow eyes, long, thin nose. I couldn't quite place him. "They treating you well in LA?" He came around the other side of the table and roped Emerson to him, squeezing her tighter than necessary against his leather jacket.

I wanted to throat punch him.

Emerson pushed out of his arms. "I'm doing great, Todd. Better than ever."

Todd. He bullied Emerson relentlessly in high school, giving her a hard time about her drug-addicted mom. I'd spent many a night plotting his fake death with Emerson just to make her laugh, hoping I could keep her from crying over his cruel comments.

"Good." Todd took to his spot opposite me and Emerson at the table. "Then I won't regret kicking your ass. You've probably forgotten how to play beer pong after spending so long at that fancy schmancy company of yours."

Emerson scoffed, and I hoped she wouldn't let Todd ruin our night. We'd been having fun, actually. I hadn't expected it, but it was nice, both of us working together, a team, like we'd always been.

Emerson straightened next to me. "Just shut up and throw the ball."

He launched the ball, and it bounced, wedging in between two cups before it floated up to me and Emerson for our turn.

Emerson nodded at me, and I couldn't help but feel Preston's heavy stare as I threw the ball. It dropped straight into a cup. We screamed and bumped hips. Todd shook his head, tipping the cup back. His partner, a goblin wearing gold chains, gold bracelets, and with a gold stud in his hooked nose, nudged Todd and whispered something. I think I heard the words "lucky" and "throws like a girl."

Oh no. Emerson wouldn't let that go. She pinned her gaze on the goblin. "I guess I'd be insecure, too, if I was the only guy here who couldn't get laid."

By the way his cheeks turned to a ripe tomato, I could tell Emerson had him pegged. She always did. She read people's vibes so easily, and as I learned, her assessments were usually correct.

The goblin started forward, but Todd held him and patted his back. "Don't worry about her, man."

She gave them both a little wave and a sickly sweet smile, and I wished she would just stop and play.

"Okay, let's all calm down and focus on the game." I nudged her, trying to distract her. "You know, you should come back more often. Bring your friends, and we'll show them how we do it, Whispering-Willows style."

Emerson didn't answer, just tipped her cup back, not taking a breath between gulps of the purple witch's brew sloshing inside.

"Damn," Todd said approvingly. "You haven't forgot how to throw 'em back, have you?"

Cruz walked into the parlor room, adding to our list of spectators. His hulking form towered over everyone, and his brows puckered in disapproval. Cruz had always been protective over Emerson, especially when she no longer had a mother or a father to look out for her.

"Emerson, you might want to slow it down," he warned. "I can't take you back to your mom's house completely wasted."

"Why? You're an adult and so am I. Stop being such a buzzkill, Cruz."

Oh, god. This was going downhill fast. Exactly the kind of drama I didn't want to be involved in.

"Wow," someone from the crowd said. "I didn't believe it when I heard about your fit at the funeral, but you really have changed, Emerson."

Emerson's gaze snapped to the person who made the comment.

Cruz cut a look through the crowd, leaning against the wall. Some blonde vampire sauntered into the parlor, pressing herself against his chest. I snuck a look at Emerson, but she didn't seem to notice, just studying her nails in that way she did when she wanted everyone to believe she was bored with them. I knew better. She wasn't bored, she was livid.

"Ignore them," I whispered.

But she'd never been good at ignoring or hiding her feelings. "If I've changed, then it's for the better," she shot back.

Todd missed another shot, but Emerson grabbed one of the cups and chugged anyway.

"Emerson," I said, no longer having fun. The air in the room shifted, tense now.

Emerson stumbled around the table, her gaze now stuck on Cruz and that blonde vampire. Todd snorted, noticing the way Emerson practically snarled at the blonde.

"Have you ever thought about the fact that maybe I've evolved?" She snatched someone's cup, shaped like a cauldron, from their hand and took a swig. "Kind of like monkeys and humans." She giggled, stumbling and snorting. "Like you guys are the monkeys that haven't evolved, and I'm the human."

My mouth dropped open. I turned to Cruz. "Did she seriously just . . .?"

Emerson pushed the blonde away and draped her arms over Cruz. "You get what I'm saying. You barely graduated high school, for chrissakes."

Cruz shrugged Emerson off of him. I attempted to grab her arm and de-escalate the situation. "Emerson, time to go. You've had too much to drink."

"Get off of me!" she yelled.

"Enough," Cruz said. He grabbed her arm with a tight grip impossible to wiggle loose from. "We're leaving now."

I never should've gone along with this whole beer pong charade. Never should've come to this bar in the first place. Look at the kind of trouble I'd gotten into with Emerson back in my life. She almost caused a huge fight to break out. Something was clearly wrong with my former friend, but it wasn't my battle to fight.

Cruz tugged Emerson toward the door, leaning over and whispering to me, "I've got her. Just enjoy your night."

And with that, he dragged a screaming Emerson from the bar.

After that, I wasn't in the mood to drink.

I left the bar, needing some fresh air.

"Clara, wait up!"

I stopped as Preston jogged up from behind.

"Are you okay?" He gestured back to The Brewery. "You looked a little shaken up back there."

I thought of Emerson, how angry she'd been when she started

yelling at everyone, at the little seed of guilt that was growing in my gut, telling me I should've done more.

I frisked my arms as we walked. "I don't know. I—" I sighed and told Preston the whole sordid story about Dara and her destroyed wish.

"Life is supposed to be good now," I said to Preston. "You know? No more money problems, I'm finally doing what I'm meant to, my daughter is happy. I don't want to invite more trouble."

"And you think Emerson is trouble?" Preston asked, tugging at his black jacket.

We started walking away from The Brewery and toward an alleyway that connected to Main Street.

"Have you seen Emerson?" I gestured back toward the bar. "She's a mess."

"Well, it looked like you two were having fun for a while. Sinking shot after shot, giggling, high-fiving. Reminded me a bit of our high school days. Like you two just picked up right where you left off."

I frowned. "It was fun . . . until . . ."

Preston scratched his head. "Yeah. Yeah, she went a little ballistic on everyone, didn't she?"

I sniffled. "I just don't know what's going on with her. She's nothing like the person I knew so long ago. It's like she's done a complete 180. She doesn't seem to care about anyone but herself, and the way she acted tonight, yelling at everyone like that." I huffed and drew my arms around myself. "But it's not my problem."

Preston nodded, eyes staring ahead as we left the alleyway and entered Main Street. Fairy lights hung from palm tree to palm tree, shops still open, their lights beaming out onto the little street. Big banners had been hung that read Autumn Equinox, and lights now covered the bases of the palm trees, all in preparation for the upcoming parade.

"Cut yourself some slack. You just moved back to Whispering Willows a few months ago. It's okay if everything isn't perfect. That's a lot of pressure to put on yourself."

"I guess that's the problem. I'm so tired of everything being hard," I said as we passed a packed ice cream shop, a line of people out the door and winding onto the sidewalk.

"Well, not everything's hard."

We stepped around the line, and my gaze shot to Preston. "What does that mean?"

He gestured between the two of us. "I thought . . ." He scratched his head. "I thought things had felt pretty easy between us."

That brought a smile to my face, even if I wasn't sure what to say. Was he hinting that he wanted things between us to go back to the way they were? But no. That would be messy. Complicated. Definitely not keeping the easy balance I needed, wanted, in my life. Besides, he was Remy's teacher. I couldn't do that to her. What if we got back together and then broke up? Remy would be stuck with him for the rest of the year. I shook my head. I was getting ahead of myself. Preston hadn't even said that's what he was thinking.

"Well," I said carefully. "I think we work well together, and we've matured. We handle ourselves, our relationship, better than we did when we were teenagers." I peered at him. "Do you think we were dramatic back then?"

He snorted. "God, yes."

"Really?" I asked.

His head swiveled in my direction. "Do you remember all the fights we got into? The make-up sessions afterward."

"A lot of sticky situations," I agreed, dodging his waggling eyebrows when he said "make-up," which brought back some very vivid images of his lips on mine, his body pressed to me.

"Very sticky," he said in mock seriousness. "The stickiest."

I laughed and gave him a little shove. "Stop it!"

"What? You're the one that had to use the word sticky."

"Well, it was what came to mind."

He grabbed me, then, and pressed me against a brick wall. My breath caught in my throat as he caged me with his arms. "You want to know what's coming to my mind right now?"

I swallowed. Yes. Yes, I did.

Except, no. No. We were friends.

That's what I'd decided I could handle from Preston. Nothing more. I could ignore the way my heart beat in my chest right now, the way my toes curled when his warm breath puffed on me, the way I wanted to lean in so badly and see where this could go.

I needed to focus on myself and Remy. And this damn spell I had to perform for Isaac. I gasped. The spell. The ingredients.

I groaned out.

Preston's mischievous smile vanished. "What's wrong?" He backed away, taking all his warmth and electricity with him.

He uncaged me, and I stepped out to face him, putting distance between us . . . and whatever heat had been sizzling the air.

"I was supposed to get an ingredient for the spell from the bar. You know those little mints they have?" I asked him. "I know for a fact the mints contain a special form of peppermint, which I happen to need for this spell, so I was going to grab a few—"

"You mean these mints?" Preston reached into his jacket pocket and pulled a few out, the fresh smell hitting me like a ton of bricks.

The smell was so familiar.

"You have them!" I exclaimed.

"Here, take them," he said.

"Oh my gosh." I threw my arms around his neck.

"It's not a big deal, Clara. I can always go back and get more."

I unwound my arms, realizing how easily our bodies just fit together, melded right into each other. His gaze traveled the length of my body, pupils dilating in a way that made me swallow several times.

"Thanks. I didn't really feel like making the trek back there. Everything with Emerson is so messy now, and I just . . ."

Preston kicked a pebble and it skittered across the street as we stood there in the dark. "I don't know. Sometimes messy is fun." Some of his playfulness returned as he looked up at me, grinning.

I swallowed, wanting to tread carefully. Friends. We could be friends. I didn't want to hurt him again. I had to make him understand this was what would be best for us.

So I tried to be playful in return. "I don't know, Emerson has a great life in LA that seems mess-free. Amazing job, boatloads of money, hot boyfriend. Sounds like that would be pretty hard to give up." I tried to keep my tone light.

"Is that what you want?" Preston shoved his hands in his pockets. "Because I gotta tell you, you're definitely in the wrong place for all of that." He paused. "Well, except for the hot boyfriend part." His tone turned gravelly. "I think we could make that part of your reality."

I took a deep breath. "Preston, um, the thing is . . ."

He took a step forward, his body close enough to send ripples of heat through me. The man didn't even have to touch me to set me on fire. Lord help me if he ever did. I might just combust.

He dipped his head down, lips inches from mine. "Just say the word, Clara."

I jumped back, shaking my head. "No, Preston, I'm sorry, but this is a bad idea. You're Remy's teacher. We broke up twenty years ago. We can't get into this again."

"Why?" Hurt shone in his eyes. "Why are you being so stubborn?" He grabbed my hands. "We're good together. Great, even. If you hadn't left Whispering Willows, we'd be—"

"But I did leave." I gently pulled my hands from his. "I left, and now I just need easy. Once I get rid of Isaac, Emerson leaves—everything will go back to normal and life will be good."

No rocking the boat.

"And being with me would mess that up?" He crossed his arms. "You know, I thought you'd learned your lesson after breaking up with me the first time."

"What lesson?" I asked. "I did what was necessary to survive."

And now I was doing what was necessary to live my best life, free of any complications.

A gust of wind pushed past us, the scent of salt riding on its tails.

Preston let out a quiet laugh. "You're scared. You're so scared of living."

Anger flared, hot and ready to lash out. "Are you kidding me? I faced my fears. I opened my mother's wish shop, I started practicing magic, I told my daughter about her heritage. I stopped the mayor in his evil plot to burn down my family's legacy. I am not scared."

"I better get going," Preston said. "Lots to do tomorrow to prepare for the work week."

"Right."

He began walking away.

"Thank you again," I called after him, and it was only after he'd disappeared into an alleyway that I realized why these mints smelled so familiar. Preston used to always suck on them right before he kissed me.

Chapter Twenty-One

The bell jingled over Potion & Things as I entered the store. Last night had been a wake-up call. Yes, I got the damn mints from Preston, but how much longer would it take to get all the other ingredients? I didn't have the time, especially not after Martin dumped Isaac at my doorstep early this morning, claiming he could no longer watch the genie. Isaac had even managed to annoy the imp, not an easy feat. With him back in my possession, I needed to have this figured out. So I put on my big girl panties and decided it was time to go visit Preston's mother.

The lamp hopped in my purse, and I whispered, "Cut it out. I told you not to make a sound in there. You are not here," I said. "You might as well be invisible. And if you don't listen, I'm taking away all those face masks I bought you."

He complained that every time he asked for a face mask in the lamp, all he got were the cheap ones. I'd been nice enough to actually spring for the good stuff, and I knew Isaac wanted it.

With that threat, the lamp stilled, and I glanced up, taking in the familiar shop that surrounded me.

Shelves lined the walls, each one full of ingredients, categorized by the type of spell you might want to cast: tracking spells, healing spells, kitchen spells, cleaning spells, and so on.

Jars of eyeballs, frog feet, rabbit fur, snake venom, fabrics, and so much more filled the shop. Everything a witch could possibly want to cast a spell.

"Well, well, well," Marjorie Hammond drawled, stepping out from behind the counter, all five-foot-one of her.

And so it had begun.

"You have a lot of nerve stepping in this shop after what you did to me."

I did a double take. What I'd done to her?

Red dotted her round cheeks, her gray hair short and wavy, hands planted on her curvy hips. She stared me down through the glasses that enlarged her eyes and always reminded me of an owl. "You know, I have a right to refuse service to anyone I choose."

"Marjorie." I put my hands up in a peace offering. "I'm sorry about disappearing like that, but you have to understand. I'd just found out my mother was evil. I had no choice but to leave."

She put a hand to her chest. "I treated you like my own daughter. Invited you into my home, cooked you dinners, let you into my heart."

Oh good god. Why were there so many dramatic people in this town? You'd think I'd stepped back into a soap opera when I moved back here.

"I had even started planning your wedding." She sniffed.

"I was nineteen!" I cried.

"I had your dress picked out," she continued like she hadn't heard me.

My dress. She thought she was going to pick out my own wedding dress?

"Had the menu planned. The venue was all sorted. I'd arranged everything. Even picked out a date for you two."

"You chose a date? For my wedding to your son that I didn't know was happening? We weren't even engaged."

She grabbed a tissue from the nearby counter and blew hard into it, a honking noise filling the room.

Great, now she was crying. This was why I hadn't wanted to come here. Marjorie was somehow always the victim. I wasn't even sure she remembered it was her son I'd left and not her.

"I truly am sorry about twenty years ago—"

"I'm not upset about that."

I pressed my lips together, taking a few cautious steps into the shop, letting my gaze roam covertly toward the ingredients I needed for this spell. "I think you might be just a little upset about that, Marjorie."

She dotted her eyes, then jabbed a finger at me. "It wasn't enough that you tore out my, um, his heart and stomped all over it. Now you're going to go and do it again. Preston told me you two have been spending some time together."

Oh good god.

"What are you talking about?"

She moved back behind the counter, straightening the business cards sitting in a neat stack by the cash register. "I thought now that you were back in town you and Preston could get the fairytale ending you both deserve. Preston was waiting for you, you know. He dated here and there, might have pretended he moved on, but he never could after you. And I thought you would come to your senses. But then you go and date the mayor."

She made a face.

I backed toward a shelf and reached behind me, snatching a hawk talon. I'd pay Marjorie back later. I needed these ingredients and foraging for them was not an option at this point.

"Yes, that was admittedly a mistake. What do you want me to say? Preston and I are ancient history. He's my daughter's teacher. I can't just go and date—"

"And then," Marjorie said, interrupting me, "you lead him on. Let him help you with your little missions, go on your adventures with you, let him fight a mermaid for you. Go on moonlight strolls."

She let out a wail and flopped her head into her arms on the counter, shoulders shaking. Good, that meant she had low visibility. I dashed to another shelf and grabbed an eyeball.

She lifted her head just as I dropped the eyeball into my bag.

"You're gonna go and break him for good this time. I saw him last night—"

I straightened. "You saw him last night?"

"He came to my house, a mess. Eyes all puffy and swollen. Wouldn't talk about it, but I knew. I knew it had to do with you." She spit out the last word like it was poison. Like I was the poison.

I didn't realize I'd hurt Preston that badly. I—I never wanted to hurt Preston, but surely he understood why we couldn't be a thing. He had to understand.

"Mom, that's enough." Preston stepped into the shop, and my throat tightened.

He gave me a look. "Clara has some items in her bag that she needs to purchase."

My cheeks flushed. Busted.

"Let her buy what she needs, and then let her go. She has important business to attend to."

His usual swagger, charm, had disappeared, and he was all business.

"Why aren't you at school?" I asked.

He cleared his throat. "Took a personal day. Needed to clear my head."

He watched as I took the items I needed to the cash register and let Marjorie ring them up, keeping my head down. Her glare weighed heavy on me the entire time, but she kept her mouth shut.

I thanked her profusely, and when I was done purchasing everything I needed, I turned to see Preston already gone. I had to make this right.

"Thank you again, Marjorie," I said, but she just turned her head, refusing to acknowledge me.

I sighed and chased after Preston out the door. "Preston, wait!" I busted out onto Main Street. "Are you okay? Did something happen with your job?"

His eyes crinkled. "My job?"

He was already two shops down, and I jogged after him, ingredients clanking with the golden lamp in my bag. "You said you took a personal day."

"Christ, Clara."

"Are you having second thoughts about this whole teacher thing? I know you still would make an amazing policeman. After how much you helped me with the mermaids—"

"Clara, I'm never going to be a policeman," he burst out, his jaw clenched tight.

I took a few steps back. "W-why not? It's never too late to chase your dreams."

He ran an agitated hand over his head. "That was my dream with you. Don't you get it? I was going to be the police chief. You were going to run The Wish List. We were going to buy a little house, right in that neighborhood over there." He pointed past Main Street, toward the ocean. "Two kids," he continued.

"One boy and one girl," I said quietly.

It had been dumb, planning it all out. It wasn't like that was something we could control. But we'd spend hours talking about our future together.

"When you left," he continued, "my dreams left with you. I had to start over. For me. So no, I didn't take a personal day because I'm rethinking my career. I think you know why I took a personal day, and for whatever goddamned reason, you can't admit it."

I shifted the heavy bag on my shoulder. "I hoped we could at least be friends."

"Friends?" His muscles tensed under his tight T-shirt. "I can't be friends with you. Don't you get that? It's all or nothing for me. I can't do some in-between thing." His hand fell from his head. "I'm not that guy. And I won't apologize for it."

I thought we could be friends, but now I realized how delusional that was. Preston and I could never be friends. If we weren't together, we weren't anything. The thought made me sad, even if I knew it was necessary.

"Oh." My voice came out small. "Okay, well, I understand. Um, goodbye, then."

I turned, not sure why my throat was closing up and my eyes were filling with tears. This was for the best. Preston and I were over, exactly the way it needed to be.

Chapter Twenty-Two

My feet ached and sharp pains shot through my back after another long day of wish granting. We'd been busier than usual today, probably because I'd had to close the shop for so long before I finally released Isaac. I was sore, but happy. Granting wishes, knowing I was making literal dreams come true, always made me happy. Even if it felt like everything else was falling apart.

I flipped the sign to Closed in the window that looked out on Main Street, then turned to the lamp. "You can come out now," I said to Isaac, who appeared, frowning, arms crossed.

He glared at me. "I'd like to point out that I am not a little pet to be put in a cage."

"And I'd like to point out that I am currently working as hard as I can to free you from said cage." I gestured to the cauldron, all the ingredients I'd bought that morning laid out next to it, the grimoire open to the page needed for the spell.

Isaac's eyes widened, his anger melting away as he floated over to the spell. "It's finally time?" he asked eagerly. "Oh, I can't wait to be free."

"I'm going to perform the spell, and it might lead us to the lamp's previous owner. That doesn't mean you're going to be free," I reminded him. "We might still be a long ways from that."

"Okay, Debbie Downer," he mumbled. "You know, no one likes a killjoy."

"Do you want me to do the spell or not?" I tapped my foot, agitated. "You're still supposed to be with Martin, and you somehow managed to screw that up."

I could've sworn Isaac's cheeks flushed, which would've been wildly out of character, because I didn't think anything could make the genie blush.

"That's not what happened," he said.

"Really? Then why did Martin dump you at my doorstep this morning at the crack of dawn and insist he couldn't watch you anymore?"

Isaac raised his nose in the air. "Ask him, not me."

"That's what I thought."

The bell over the door rang and Remy appeared, Myrtle behind her, the ancient werewolf with her usual scowl on her face. "Look who I found wandering the streets," Myrtle said, then jabbed her thumb over her shoulder to the white van sitting outside. "Thought I'd give the girl a ride home from school."

Remy's eyes were wide, her hair mussed, a dazed, and slightly horrified, look on her face.

I rubbed my temples and then pointed at the werewolf. "Myrtle, I thought I made it clear you weren't supposed to drive Remy in that thing, ever. It doesn't even have seatbelts!"

The one and only time I'd rode in Myrtle's van, she'd almost killed me. It was one of the most terrifying experiences of my life, which was saying a lot when you lived a mile away from the portal to Hell.

Remy walked to the couch and dropped her backpack. "I saw my life flash before my eyes," she said. "Like five different times."

Myrtle looked at us through her rectangle glasses, today a lavender shade that matched her sparkly lavender track suit and purple hair, which she'd finally been able to fix after the lamp had turned it green. "You two are so dramatic. I swear. I do a nice thing like give you a ride so you don't have to walk, and all you do is complain."

"Thank you for the ride, Myrtle," Remy murmured, then turned her gaze to me right as the bell over the shop rang again. This time, it was Helen who stepped inside.

"You look tired, hon, you okay?" I asked, walking over and running a gentle thumb under Remy's eyes.

"I'm fine. We had a sub today in homeroom and he made us spend the entire two hours going through all of our classes, our assignments, organizing due dates, projects, homework. Normally Mr. H just lets us use the time to unwind and work on what we feel we need. He doesn't micromanage us. He lets us decide what to do. I hope he's not sick."

Isaac coughed out, "He's not."

Helen squinted at me. "Weren't you at a bar with Preston last night?"

I scuffed my shoe on the floor.

Myrtle adjusted the glasses on her nose. "And didn't you make a trip to Potions & Things this morning and get in a small scuffle with Preston's mother?"

"Yes," Isaac coughed behind his fist.

"Stop coughing out your words!" I said to him.

"Just making sure we're all on the same page." He gave a cheeky smile that made me want to ban him back to the lamp.

"Yes, I was with Preston, and he tried to kiss me, or well, he wanted to kiss me, and I knew he wanted to kiss me, and he knew that I knew he wanted to kiss me, and instead of letting him, I told him now was not the right time to get in a relationship. Then we got in a fight and I told him I wanted to be friends, he shot me down, and now we're not speaking. Likely ever again. Happy?" I stomped back behind the counter.

Helen shook her head slowly. "Preston wanted to kiss you and you wouldn't let him?"

"Wow, Mr. H is such a boss," Remy said. "Good for him, going after what he wants like that."

"No, not good for him." I planted my hands on the cool marble counter. "I'm not ready to get into a relationship after I just got out of a fake one, in case you all are forgetting that it was literally a month ago that the mayor pretended to date me."

"Eh, she has a point," Myrtle said.

"It's not about timing," Helen protested, running a hand through her spiked blonde hair. "You think that my little trip with the Serpent down into the portal to Hell was a good time for us to get together?"

Remy's mouth dropped open. "Um, forget Mom and Mr. H. I want to hear that story!"

"Me too," Isaac said, leaning forward in the air with his legs crossed under him.

"No, you don't," Myrtle said. "Trust me, it's far too dramatic, and it involves a lot of kissing."

Helen raised her eyebrows in a challenge.

"Forget Housewives, you guys are all the entertainment I need."

I did a double take. Isaac now had a bowl full of popcorn and was munching on it while he watched this circus.

"I'm not dating Preston, okay? And he got upset about it, and I guess he needed to take a day for himself because of that. I thought we could maybe be friends, but we clearly can't. Which is probably for the best." I pointed to the ingredients on the counter. "Now we have some work to do, if you don't mind." I shot a glance at Helen, then Myrtle.

Thankfully, everyone dropped the subject, probably realizing that I was very close to losing it.

"Are you performing the spell, then?" Myrtle asked. "The one to free the genie over here." She jabbed a thumb at Isaac.

I sighed. "I'm going to stop texting everyone in our group chat if every time I tell you something you barge into my shop."

"Again, you're welcome for giving your daughter a ride home from school," Myrtle said.

Helen came to a stand beside the werewolf. "Sorry, not sorry. You're the one who came back to Whispering Willows, and now you have to deal with us."

Isaac just stared at Myrtle, his gaze moving from her feet up to the cloud of purple hair atop her head. "I really want to know how you make those tracksuits work for you. They shouldn't, but they just do. It's freaking me out."

I came to a stand in front of the ingredients I had laid out:

- a hawk talon
- a mint
- an eyeball, nerve endings and all dangling from it
- the object being traced
- the hands of a clock

"That is a weird assortment of objects," Isaac said as Remy approached, digging her wand out of her bag.

"What's she doing?" Isaac asked.

"She's the one performing the spell," I replied.

"That girl is one the best witches we have in Whispering Willows," Myrtle added proudly.

"Oh god, my future is dependent on a sixteen-year-old."

"I'm almost eighteen," Remy said. "And you're in very capable hands."

"Okay, then, do your thing." Isaac had discarded the popcorn at some point and now stood, tapping his foot in the air, the blue smoke tether wiggling with the movement.

Remy dropped each object in to the cauldron, then read from the page of the Westfold grimoire, waving her wand in a zigzag motion that the spell specified.

"Why is she twitching like that?" Isaac asked.

"She not twitching," I said. "She's following the spell. I told you each spell requires different movements, intentions, ingredients. All three have to work together for the spell to be cast."

"Huh. Weird."

As Remy continued with the motion of her wand, the cauldron grew brighter with color.

"She's so talented," Helen said. "I think she gets it from me."

I just rolled my eyes.

Soon the color expanded in the cauldron, and in one bright wink, flashed out. The lamp, still connected to Isaac's feet with that blue smoke tether, zoomed toward the front door of the shop.

"Looks liked the spell worked." I watched the lamp. "Now we need to chase that thing down."

"It's getting away!" Remy said, pointing her wand at it.

The lamp dragged Isaac along. "Hey, hello? Are you all gonna follow me or what?"

"You all stay here," I said to everyone. "I'll go."

"I'm not missing this," Remy said. "I'm the one who performed the spell, so I get to go."

"Me too," Helen echoed.

"Me three," Myrtle said.

"We can't all fit in my car!" I gestured to the clunker that sat outside. I needed an upgrade soon.

"I guess I'll have to drive, then," Myrtle offered, and we all looked at her white murder van. "Better get going before we lose the lamp and your genie.'

"Hello!" Isaac yelled from outside, already across the street as the lamp pulled him along.

"Ugh, fine." I shooed everyone out the door. "Let's get this over with, then."

Chapter Twenty-Three

Everyone collectively screamed as Myrtle wrenched the wheel and made a sharp turn to the left. I sat in the middle row, and my head banged against the window.

"Seriously, Myrtle?" I asked and she hit the pedal with her foot and accelerated.

"I fight demons for a living and this is the scariest situation I've ever been in." Helen sat in the front seat, her hands clutching the armrest so tight her knuckles were white. "I thought you both were just being dramatic, but she really is a bad driver."

"I might be three hundred years old, but I can hear you, you know," Myrtle said. "I get no thanks, do I? Just carting you all around on your ridiculous adventures, and all you do in return is complain about my driving."

"I wouldn't call this driving," I mumbled under my breath, and Myrtle's gaze snapped to mine in her rearview mirror. "Okay, sorry." I held up my hands. "Just maybe watch the road. I'd like to survive this trip to wherever we're going."

The lamp zoomed up ahead, zigzagging across the street, Isaac being pulled behind it, screeching with each jerky movement the lamp made.

"I'm going to get sick," he yelled. "Why did I eat all that popcorn?"

Remy leaned forward next to me. "I wonder where it's taking us. This is so exciting."

Exciting was not the word I'd use for this.

Terrifying? Yes. Most definitely.

I hoped this would be the lead we needed, but I had no idea what to expect. Who could've owned this lamp before my mom got a hold of it? And how did she get a hold of it? I wasn't sure I wanted to know the answers to those questions. Wasn't sure I could handle learning that my mother did yet another terrible thing, and way before she was supposed to be terrible. If she'd stolen that lamp from someone . . . Well, I didn't have to go down that road. Not yet. I needed to see where this lamp took us first, and then I could prepare myself for whatever was coming.

The lamp veered sharply off the road and onto a grassy spread of land.

"Buckle up," Myrtle yelled. "We're going off-roading!"

"Myrtle no!" I yelled, but I could barely get the words out before she took a sharp turn and we careened off the street and onto the grass.

All of us flew up in our seats, heads banging against the ceiling of the van as it plunked down onto the ground with a resounding crack.

Helen rubbed her head. "That did not sound good. When was the last time you got this thing serviced?"

"Oh please." Myrtle followed the lamp as it continued to fly through the air. "That's a scam."

I stared at her, horrified. "Getting your car serviced is not a scam! Myrtle, what in the hell?"

Helen turned to her. "Are you telling me you haven't ever gotten the brakes checked, the fluids topped off—nothing? How is this thing still running?"

"Because it's a good car, that's how. Don't need any of that other stuff." Myrtle looked over at her. "All you have is a motorcycle. You don't know how cars work."

"Yes, I very much do," Helen said. "Trust me, my husband happens to love them, which means I have to hear about them all the time."

"Well, you don't know how this one works!"

"Guys?" Remy asked.

"No, no, she's right, Helen," I said, staring at the both of them bickering. "You have to own a car to know that it needs to be serviced to keep it running. That's not common knowledge or anything."

"Are you being sarcastic?" Myrtle turned in her seat. "Because I don't much like your attitude right now."

"Guys!" Remy yelled.

"What?" I turned to her, her finger pointing.

Our gazes snapped forward as the murder van careened toward the edge of a cliff jutting out over the ocean. We all collectively screamed while Myrtle yelled, "Oh feck!" and wrenched the wheel to the left as hard as she possibly could.

I couldn't watch. I squeezed my eyes shut as the van skidded, every single bump throwing my body upward, seats and floor vibrating underneath me. The (most likely nonexistent) brakes squealed and screeched, while Remy's hand gripped my arm tight. I really didn't want this to be the way that I died. Not that there was a way I preferred to die. Well, maybe in my sleep. In old age. In peace. Definitely not in Myrtle's freaking murder van while trying to free a genie my mother trapped in a lamp.

Note to self: never accept a ride from Myrtle ever again.

And then gravity slammed me forward into the seat in front of me, everything growing still, not a sound coming from anyone in the car. I slowly peeked open one eye, and there we were, right on the edge of the cliff, teetering. The car let out an ominous creeeeaaaaak.

"Out, everyone out!" Helen yelled, and we all scrambled to the doors, wrenching them open and flinging ourselves out. I made sure Remy went in front of me. No way I was risking her going down in this thing.

I fell onto the grassy cliff, laying on my back, looking up at the sky, chest heaving. Remy landed next to me, then Helen, and finally Myrtle fell with a thud.

I turned my head to look at Remy, then turned it to look at Helen, and we all burst into laughter just as the van tipped and went crashing down into the sea below.

"What in the feck is so funny?" Myrtle asked, tugging at her tracksuit. "That's my precious van. Our ride home! And now it's gone."

That only made us laugh harder, so hard tears were streaming down my face. Remy's shoulders shook, and Helen was crunched over, knees in her stomach, none of us able to catch our breath.

Myrtle just stared, her eyebrows raised. "You've all lost it. Absolutely off your rockers, the lot of you."

"Helloooooo!" Isaac's voice echoed from somewhere in the distance.

I shot up at that, laughter fading as I ran toward the cliff.

"Be careful, Mom," Remy shouted after me. "You don't need to join the murder van down there."

"Murder van?" Myrtle asked. "Have some respect, for god sakes."

We all came to a stand as close to the edge as we dared, watching as the golden lamp flew down into a cluster of rocks far below and then disappeared into a little opening, not quite a cave, but something smaller, something that would be nearly impossible to get to by swimming or walking.

"Save me!" Isaac yelled before disappearing into the little crevice in the cliffs. From where we stood it was impossible to see where he'd gone. The waves crashed around the rocks, ocean water spraying in all directions. We'd lost him. I couldn't believe it.

"Well, Myrtle's van isn't gonna get us down there," Remy said.

I shook my head. No, for that we needed a boat, and I could only think of one person who could lend us a boat on such short notice.

Chapter Twenty-Four

"I'm coming with you," Remy yelled as we stood on the dock where Martin's boat floated in the water.

"You are absolutely not." I put my hands on her shoulders. "Listen, this is going to be dangerous. I am not risking anything happening to you. And you're not eighteen yet, so you still have to listen to me."

She just scoffed. "This is ridiculous. I should be able to go with you. To help."

"You're helping me by staying here, safe and sound. If I have to worry about you, that means I can't focus on finding Isaac."

"She's right, Remy," Helen said. "You're staying, but I'll watch after your mom."

I shook my head. "You're not coming either, Helen."

Her mouth dropped open. "Excuse me, I'm a full-blown adult, and I absolutely am."

"You're going to be too sick once we hit the water. You won't be of any help if you're barfing over the side of the boat. And those waves were vicious."

Helen's face fell. She knew I was right.

I turned my gaze to Myrtle, who held up her hands. "Don't worry. I have no interest in going with you. Sounds awful, truly. You go have fun with the imp."

I just rolled my eyes and looked at Martin, who was tapping his foot impatiently. "Oh good. So I get to go on the deadly mission out to sea, not only risking myself but my beautiful Ms. Peaches."

He gestured to the boat, which was anything but beautiful, but I needed it so I held my tongue and stepped in.

"Be careful," Remy said, a concerned look pasted across her face.

"I will be," Martin said, then looked between me and Remy. "Oh, were you talking to your mother? Right, that makes sense. Though I would appreciate a few well wishes since I am risking my life yet again for you all."

He stepped into the boat and Helen knelt down and pushed us away. "Don't do anything stupid," she called after us. "Nothing I wouldn't do!" Then she paused. "Wait, no, I do a lot of stupid things all the time. Just . . . be safe!"

I waved at them and turned to Martin as he rowed us out to sea. "When did you risk your life for us the first time?"

He sniffed. "Every time I row you all out to visit the mermaids, which has been twice now, in case you've forgotten."

"How has that been a risk? The mermaids are friendly!"

"Not if you've slept with half of them!" Martin yelled.

Oh good god. "Well, that's your fault. I think you might have some commitment issues."

"I do not!" Martin put a hand to his chest. "How dare you suggest that. Just because I can't spend more than one week in a relationship with someone doesn't mean that—" He stopped, his eyes widening. "Oh."

I just shook my head while we fell into a silence, the boat cradling us while waves tossed about. He rowed for what felt like an hour, though it must've been less than that, before I finally spoke out.

"Okay, row that way!" I pointed to the cropping of rocks we saw in the distance, nestled into a crevice between two tall cliffs, where waves crashed with a resounding boom.

"Over there?" Martin pointed an oar. "Are you insane? I'm not rowing my boat over there. Do you know anything about boats? It would never survive those kinds of waves, and we'd get smashed against those rocks. Splat! Like little bugs getting crushed under a shoe."

I threw out my hands. "Well, then, what are we going to do? I have to get over there!"

Martin just shook his head, green skin losing some of its color. "No, no, that is a terrible idea, and I don't want to die today. I just figured out I have commitment issues. I need therapy!"

I grabbed his shoulders. "Martin, snap out of it. We need to figure this out. Maybe just get me close enough so I can swim over to the rocks?"

Martin's eyes bugged out of his head. "Swim? You want to swim in that?" He gestured toward a giant swell of water that smashed so hard into a rock it broke a piece off.

"I don't ever row in this direction. It's called No Man's Land for a reason."

"There's a name for this area?" I asked.

Martin nodded solemnly. "Every seaman knows it well. You don't come near the rocks. Too many ships have met their end over there."

I stared helplessly at the rocks in the distance. I didn't know what I was going to do to get that lamp back, but I had to do something.

"Maybe I could fly in there on my broom?"

Martin cocked his head, then bobbed it from side to side. "I still think you'd go splat."

An awful thought popped into my head. Maybe the tracing spell would keep Isaac trapped in that little crevice, never to see the light of day again. It would solve all of my problems. I could have my life back. Pretend all of this never happened. Go on granting wishes, finally have some peace.

"Maybe you're right," I heard myself say. "Maybe that lamp, and Isaac, are lost for good."

"Isaac?" Martin snapped. "What are you talking about?"

I gestured toward the rocks. "The lamp, it's stuck somewhere over there."

Martin began rowing. "Why didn't you say that in the first place?"

"I thought you knew that's what this entire thing was about."

"Of course not!" Martin yelled over the roar of the sea. "We have to go after that lamp!"

My brows furrowed. "Why? What does it matter to you?"

Martin continued rowing with a fierceness I'd never seen. "I just know how important that lamp, and Isaac, are to your family, and how important it is to solve the mystery."

I crossed my arms as a swell of water crashed into the boat, pushing us sideways and momentarily off course. "You care about all of that?" I asked, growing suspicious. The imp was acting weird. Well, for weird for him.

Then, a voice floated through the air, hard to hear at first but growing louder.

"Do you hear that?" Martin started rowing faster. "What a voice."

The harmonic sound grew louder, singing in a language I didn't understand, but the melody was sorrowful, lilting, the most beautiful thing I'd ever heard. We needed to find the voice, to do everything we could to get to the source.

Suddenly, I had the urge to jump out of the boat, fling myself straight into the icy waters and swim as fast as I could toward that heart-wrenching sound. I'd gladly drown myself just to hear it a little longer. I inched toward the edge of the boat, watching eagerly as Martin rowed us closer and closer to the rocks, the choppy waves pouring over the sides, rocking us violently. I just clutched the wooden frame tighter.

Then another voice broke in: off-key and singing—was that *Singin' in the Rain?* Yes, the voice was definitely belting out the show tune, so loud I could barely hear the other beautiful voice.

"Moses supposes his toeses are Roses,

But Moses supposes Erroneously,

Moses he knows his toeses aren't roses,

As Moses supposes his toeses to be!"

The seagull plopped down in the distance, its mouth wide open as it continued to sing. I wanted to grab its beak and shut it up. I wanted the beautiful voice back.

I shook my head, surprised Martin hadn't said anything yet. Wait, why were we going toward the rocks?

Martin didn't seem to hear the seagull, his eyes glazed over as he rowed closer and closer to the deadly outcropping. Ocean water pounded against us, and I heard a crack somewhere beneath my feet. Oh no. I looked down at ocean water seeping through the floorboards. I'd gone from murder van to murder boat.

"Martin!" I snapped my fingers in his face. "Martin! Stop."

I tried to wrestle the oars from his hands, but the imp was surprisingly strong, keeping on course. The seagull continued to sing, now splashing its wings in the water to accompany the horrible sounds it made.

"Please, you have to snap out of it," I yelled at Martin just as a big wave propelled us up and straight toward the sharp rocks jutting out of the ocean. "What is wrong with you?"

I screamed, and Martin just smiled, a dopey dazed look pasted across his face.

Higher, higher, we went, the boat flying over the rocks and down into the crevice, tucked in between two towering cliffs. The boat crashed on sand, and Martin and I flew from it and onto the little beach. Pebbles and seashells broke my fall, scratching and scraping at my skin. I groaned, rolling over and slowly sitting up while I felt the sting of a thousand little cuts all over my hands, my arms, my face. I blinked a few times, my gaze focusing on a beautiful siren sitting on the sandy shore, singing her song. She closed her mouth and smiled, and that's when I noticed the lamp cradled in her hands.

Chapter Twenty-Five

The siren lay on the beach, big enough to maybe fit six people as the cliffs stretched high above us. Ocean water splashed onto the sand, but we were protected from the harsh waves by the outcropping of pointy rocks that had almost just killed us.

The siren held up the lamp. "Looking for this?" she asked in syrupy sweet voice.

"What . . ." I shook my head, then glared at Martin. "Did you sleep with her too? Seriously, Martin? Maybe choose a different supernatural to stick your penis into. Or, better yet, don't stick your penis into anyone ever again for a very long time."

Martin stared at the siren, wide-eyed, that glazed-over look disappearing from his eyes as he came back to himself. "I have not slept with her, thank you very much." His eyes darted to the lamp, and he addressed the siren. "Now, just kindly give that to us, and we'll be on our way."

The siren brought it closer to her chest. "I haven't seen this in so long. Too long." Tears slipped down her scaled cheeks, the tears leaving streaks of glitter on her shimmery blue and green scales.

That's when it hit me. The rumors about the siren's song, Karissa's story about the mermaid who'd been consumed by a lamp, who'd been banished by her own clan. I'd assumed the siren Karissa told us about had died, but she was here, very much alive. It had to be her.

Martin stepped closer. "It seems like you have some kind of attachment to the lamp, but I'm going to need it back now, if you don't mind—"

She hissed at him and held it tighter.

Martin moved back. "Okay, she's a tough one. Your turn."

I focused on the siren. "What's your name?" I asked. "I'm Clara, and this is Martin." I gestured toward the lamp. "And inside that lamp is Isaac."

"Yes, and I'd like to come out now." Isaac's voice echoed around us.

Martin reached toward the lamp, and I swatted his hand away. "Will you knock it off? Why do you want the lamp so bad?" I shook my head at him. He was acting crazed over this whole situation.

"I'm Alisandra," the siren said, sharp teeth poking out over her blue lips. She flipped her long black hair over her shoulder. "And this was my lamp. Once upon a time."

I sensed a story coming on and sat down on the squishy sand while Martin leaned against the cliff side, crossing his arms. Might as well get comfortable.

"Why don't you tell us about the lamp, how you got it, what it means to you?"

If I'd learned anything after being fake-dated by the mayor, it was that talking to people, listening, was sometimes all they needed to let go of something they were holding onto. Both figuratively and literally, in this case.

"Simple," Alisandra said. "I got the lamp the same way I got you. By singing my siren song. I've always liked to sing to bring people to me, to hear their stories, to talk to them about their travels, their lives. They hear my voice, they come to me, and I make new friends. One day, I saw a ship out at sea and called to it like I always did, but tragedy struck." She pointed to the rocks. "Drove their ship straight into those sharpened points. I tried saving the sailors but couldn't. My clan found out, and I got banned to this beach as punishment for it. They wouldn't even hear my side of the story."

So that was why Alisandra's clan banned her. It was illegal to use a siren song for evil. The Council had made that into a law nearly thirty years ago. It sounded like an accident, though. Surely there had to be exceptions for situations like that.

"But it didn't matter," she said. "Because in the wreckage of that ship, I got something priceless: this lamp."

Alisandra cradled the lamp so tenderly that I didn't think she was talking about the wishes or the power, but something else that had drawn her in.

"I thought I was going to make a wish, maybe for a new life, somewhere far away from this beach. Find a new clan to accept me. Find a place where I could sing my song and people would appreciate it instead of fearing it. But this lamp granted me something so much more powerful than a wish. Love."

She ran a finger along the gold metal.

"Stop, that tickles." Isaac giggled from inside.

"You fell in love with a genie?" I asked.

Alisandra nodded. "She was so beautiful, so perfect. We spent hours talking, day after day, and soon, I realized I didn't want her wishes. I just wanted her. The only problem was that I didn't know how to free her. I was afraid to wish for her freedom, hearing horror stories about how genies paid the price for wishes made. I didn't want my precious Vi paying any kind of price."

She stared at the lamp so lovingly. Her and this Vi must've had a special kind of love, one that only came around once in a lifetime.

"So what happened?" Martin burst out. "What happened to your genie?"

Alisandra's chin dipped toward her chest, and her tail swished back and forth in the sand. "I thought maybe I could find answers from the local Witch Granters who lived in town."

My mother. It had to be. "And?" I prompted.

"I couldn't leave the beach because of my banishment, but I was able to get a note to Isabella Westfold, the Witch Granter. I told her about my dilemma, what I needed. I waited weeks for her response. Finally I got a note back that devastated me. She said there wasn't anything she could do. That the only way a genie could be free was to right a past wrong. Vi and I had no idea how we could make that happen."

Martin pushed off the cliff at that, standing straighter, pointy ears perked up.

My nose wrinkled, and I wasn't sure I'd heard her right. "To right a past wrong?"

Alisandra nodded. "Redemption has power."

"And Vi couldn't think of any way to do that?" I asked, already knowing what the answer must've been. After all, Alisandra lay here, alone, still singing her siren song.

"She wanted to." Alisandra's tail flopped against the ground. "S-she wanted to be better, just like me. But her home was so far away, and I couldn't leave the little beach I'd been banned to. Couldn't leave Whispering Willows. We were afraid if I let that lamp go, it would get into the wrong hands, that someone would force Vi to grant wishes that she'd have to pay the price for."

"So what happened?" I asked.

"Out of the blue, Isabella appeared on this very beach one night, said she'd found a solution to my problem."

My stomach hardened. If I knew my mother, she was about to trick the siren, do something that would inevitably ruin someone's life. I steeled myself for what Alisandra was about to say.

"She told me she'd done some digging and discovered that a genie could only grant three wishes. And after those three wishes were granted, the genie died."

I gasped. That was the price. The genie's life.

"But she also told me she'd discovered something else. A genie couldn't be freed by a simple wish. The magic trapping them inside the lamp was too powerful for that, but a genie could be freed in exchange for another genie's entrapment. That if Vi wasn't able to right a wrong, I could make a wish to exchange her imprisonment for another's." Alisandra smiled through her tears. "That's when I saw the boy laying in the sand, unconscious."

Isaac. That had to be Isaac.

"I didn't pay him mind, only caring about Vi and how close we were to getting our happily ever after."

I held my breath, needing to hear every word of this story, to know exactly what my mother did.

"Isabella gestured to the boy, said he was evil, that he was trying to take away everything she loved, and that he was also a Witch Granter. She told me he deserved to be stuck in that lamp. That way he could do no more harm. That's when Isabella brought out a potion. A vial full of dark liquid. It looked like tar." Alisandra's voice wobbled. "She said it was a spell she'd concocted and that it would free Vi and trap the boy. She tipped the vial over, and that's when I heard the boy scream, still unconscious, but he must've been in terrible pain."

I sent a furtive glance at the lamp, wondering if Isaac was listening to this story, if he remembered any of this happening to him. It sounded terrible.

"But something miraculous happened. There Vi stood, right in front of me, so close I could touch her. The boy disappeared into the lamp, and I forgot about him almost instantly."

My shoulders sagged in relief. Not because of what my mother did to Isaac, but because of the good she did for Alisandra. I'd been expecting the worst. But she helped true love prevail. It shouldn't have mattered so much to me, but somehow it did, knowing that Alisandra got her happy love story because of my mother.

"Vi and I lived out our days on this little beach. I stopped singing my song while she was here with me because I didn't need it. We were happy, so happy." Tears welled in her eyes. "Life couldn't stay perfect forever. Sirens live long, long lives. Far longer than that of witches. Vi grew old, and I didn't." She gave a small shrug. "After she died, I starting singing my song again, still banned to this little beach, all alone, like I had been before Vi came along."

Martin choked back a sob, my own eyes welling with tears.

"Did anyone else focus on the part of the story where I could literally die?" Isaac yelled from inside the lamp. "Three wishes and I'm a goner?"

Martin's face grew pale.

"No one is dying! Just calm down." I wished I felt as confident as I pretended to be.

Alisandra stared at the lamp, as if just now realizing someone was inside. "Is that . . . is that the boy who took Vi's place?"

I nodded. "It is," I said.

"I'm sorry for what I did, for agreeing to let him switch places with Vi like that."

"You should be!" Isaac yelled.

"You didn't know," I assured the siren. "Isabella told you to make the wish, convinced you it was the right thing to do. I think she thought it was the right thing to do too. In her own twisted way." I reached out toward Alisandra. "But I do need the lamp back."

Alisandra clutched it tighter. "It's all I have left of my precious Vi. Please. I've missed her so much over the years."

"Okay, okay." Martin stepped forward with both hands raised. "Let's not be so hasty. What if Clara could return it to you once she's done with it?"

My head snapped to him, and I widened my eyes to say, *What are you doing*? I had no idea if I could make something like that happen, when I could make it happen. It could be years before I figured this out. Lord help me, I hoped not. Still, I didn't want to give the siren false hope.

"You'll give it back to me? Once you've freed the genie?" she asked.

Once Isaac figured out how to right a wrong. "Yes," I said. I could make that promise, at the very least.

I hesitated. "Alisandra, maybe the lamp isn't what you really need, though?"

Her eyebrows furrowed. "What do you mean?"

"Maybe it's time to try and reunite with your clan. I know they banned you to this beach, but that doesn't mean you have to stay here for the rest of your life."

Banishment was a powerful form of magic, but it could be undone with the blessing of a clan, with a majority vote. I thought of Karissa's face when she spoke of the siren who had been banned, who had been consumed by this lamp. The way her eyes welled with tears telling the story. Alisandra's clan got it so wrong. She wasn't consumed by the lamp's power. She'd been in love. That wasn't a crime. Surely they'd understand, want her back.

"I don't want to." Alisandra shook her head. "There's nothing for me out there but more heartache. At least now I know life is safe. Maybe not amazing, but I'm happy here on my little beach."

"Right," I said, not knowing how to respond to that. I couldn't disagree with her assessment. This was likely the safest place for her. "If you're sure."

She narrowed her eyes at me. "Just promise you'll bring back the lamp."

I nodded but raised a finger. "No more luring sailors to their deaths."

She stuck out her bottom lip. "I didn't do that on purpose! I just like to have people to talk to."

"Okay, but just . . . take a break from potentially . . . killing people."

She crossed her arms and huffed. "Fine, fine."

"Okay, great." Martin clapped his hands together, making us both jump. He strode forward and grabbed the lamp, cradling it to his chest, much like Alisandra had just moments ago. "Well, we should really get going now. You know. Errands to run. A genie to free. Normal things."

He gestured toward his boat, which I feared might not get us back, and I turned to Alisandra. "I promise I will bring the lamp back to you."

She studied me for a minute with those large blue eyes, then said, "I believe you. You remind me of that other Witch Granter, Isabella. You'll help me like she helped me."

I'd gotten past the trauma attached to my mother, but still, it was so odd hearing someone speak praise about her. For once, someone remembered her for something good she did instead of something evil.

I was my mother's daughter, in some ways. In all the ways that mattered.

Chapter Twenty-Six

I stood back at The Wish List the next day after another terrible night's sleep. After our harrowing trip out to sea, I'd had to assure Martin several times that Isaac was safe with me for now, and I'd work on figuring out how to help him right a past wrong so he could be free. Though, in truth, I had absolutely no idea how I'd go about doing that. Could it be any past wrong? A specific one? What if it involved a person or thing that was no longer around? Then what? Was he just stuck forever? I couldn't handle that thought. And if I made three wishes, he'd die. Or I could go my mother's route and find an evil Witch Granter, perform some spell to switch their place with Isaac's. I shook my head at the frustrating turn of events.

Outside, supernaturals were already beginning to gather for the parade. I had to get my mind right, ready for a busy day of wish granting. Thousands of people would be packed onto Main Street, ready to celebrate Autumn Equinox, and many of those people would want to stop by The Wish List for the opportunity to get a wish granted. Most towns didn't have Witch Granters, so The Wish List had a bit of a reputation on the West Coast. The streets were cleared of all vehicles, orange and yellow caution tape hung from orange cones that spelled out NO CARS. I took a deep breath, steadying my racing pulse. It had started racing last night after our trip to the beach and felt like it hadn't stopped since.

Luckily Remy was at school today, preparing for the Autumn Equinox parade. I'd sent a text to our group chat to let Helen and Myrtle know I was handling things. Handling being a very generous term for what I was doing.

"You can come out now," I called to Isaac, and he appeared, frowning at me.

"The only reason I'm not mad at you right now is because I found a new show to binge about couples who get put on an island together and can't leave until they either decide to commit to each other and get married or break up. One guy is falling in love with another guy, and their girlfriends don't realize they're gay. I don't think they realize it either, but trust me. My gaydar is strong—"

"Isaac, focus." I snapped my fingers. "Did you hear what Alisandra said, about righting a past wrong?"

He tapped his chin with a finger. "Mm, I kind of remember something about that, but it was right when James was telling Melissa that she has morning breath and it's a dealbreaker for him. Can you imagine? I mean how bad does her breath have to be?"

I pinched the bridge of my nose. "Okay, Isaac, listen, in order for you to get out of this lamp, you have to right a past wrong."

He scrunched up his face. "I'm sorry, what?"

"A past wrong. Something you've done to wrong someone." I waved my hands in the air. "I don't know, but that's the deal, so figure out some wrong you did and let's fix it."

And get you out of this lamp so I don't have to deal with you anymore.

"But I haven't done anything wrong. I'm the one who was wronged!" He jabbed a finger at me. "By your mother!"

"Yes, I remember. But it's not like you're some angel. No one is perfect, Isaac. There has to be something you can think of. What about with your mother—Greta, right? I mean you just up and left her, no explanations. Surely you regret that."

Isaac crossed his arms. "Oh no. She kidnapped me, lied to me about my entire upbringing. She's in my past, and my new life outside of this lamp is not going to involve her."

"But it could?" I hedged.

I was reaching now, and I knew it. But maybe his past wrong had to do with Greta.

"I don't even know if she's still alive," Isaac said, and I detected the smallest hint of sadness in his voice. "Don't know if she's still in the same place. If she ever came looking for me."

"Well, there's only one way to find out." I tried to keep the eagerness from my words and tempered my expression. "We could put feelers out. If you want."

He squinted at me. "Are you trying to get rid of me?"

"No."

He just stared at me.

"No! I'm not! I'm trying to help free you from this lamp. I thought that was what you wanted."

"So you can kick me to the curb, like everyone else in my life!" He stuck out his bottom lip.

I gritted my teeth. "I am literally putting my life on hold to right the wrongs my mother committed. Everything was perfect before you showed up, and ever since you've arrived, it feels like nothing in my life is going the way I want it to!"

I thought of Preston and our fight, Emerson and the way she'd ruined our night out at the bar.

Isaac scoffed. "Your life wasn't perfect."

"Excuse me?"

"Guess what, Clara?" Isaac threw out his arms, floating above me. "Life isn't perfect! It's never going to be perfect, and the more you try to make it perfect, the worse you're making it. I didn't have to show up. You're wrecking your life all on your own."

I stepped back like he'd slapped me. "That's not true."

"Yes, it is. That's why you're pushing away a perfectly good man who clearly loves you." A self-satisfied smile formed on his face like he'd just made a winning argument to a jury.

"You know nothing about me and Preston."

"I hear everything from inside that lamp," he said, "and I've heard enough to know that you're scared. Your life isn't perfect. It's safe. Just like Alisandra on her little beach, accidentally luring sailors to their deaths. You told her to take risks, and you're not even willing to take your own advice!"

"Shut up," I said, my voice raising. "Just shut up. God, you're so frustrating. I can see why my mom put you in that lamp!"

"And I can see why she left you all the time!" Isaac shouted back.

I let out a squeak, tears welling in my eyes as he glared at me, as I glared back. We stared at each other like that, chests heaving.

Just then someone knocked on the door, and I ran to it and opened it wide. "Happy Autumn Equin—" I stopped, arms falling by my sides when I saw Emerson standing there, red rimming her eyes. "Oh. I thought you'd be halfway back to LA by now."

I couldn't believe she was still here. Surely her car should've been fixed by now, and after that awful night at the bar, I didn't think she'd want to show her face here. Why wasn't she back in LA with her amazing job and amazing boyfriend and—I shook my head, not comprehending what I was seeing.

"That's the thing," Emerson said. "I decided not to drive back to LA, not to go back to LA at all, actually."

"But your life in LA is perfect." I had to be missing something.

Emerson scoffed. "Perfect is overrated, Clara. Listen, it's a long story, and one I will tell you at some point, but right now I need to find Cruz. Do you know where he lives?"

"Of course," I said slowly, not liking where this was going. Everyone knew that Cruz was in love with Emerson. Everyone but Emerson, who still thought of him as her childhood friend.

Isaac coughed behind me. "Avoider."

My temper flared. At him. At Preston for not just being my friend and making things easy. At Emerson for still being here, still causing all kinds of drama.

Relief flooded Emerson's face at my answer. "Awesome. You think you could text him and tell him we're coming over?"

"We?" I asked, anger simmering. It wasn't enough that Isaac had to come and upend my life, but now Emerson thought she could do the same to her mom, to Cruz? It was wrong, and someone needed to say something to her. If it had to be me, then so be it.

"Please?" Emerson pressed her hands together. "I need your help, Clara, and I'm hopeless with directions. Go with me to Cruz's, hang out in the car while I talk to him, and then I'll bring you back here in time for the big parade."

I stepped back inside my shop, mind spinning. She just expected me to get wrapped up in her problems? After what a terrible friend she'd been to me. I doubted she knew I had a freaking genie in my shop, doubted she'd even care.

"Wait a minute." I straightened my shoulders. "Why do you need to see Cruz?"

"Because I think I'm in love with him," Emerson blurted out.

My mouth dropped open for a second before I snapped it shut. Well I hadn't been expecting that, but no, that wasn't good enough. I shook my head. "I don't think so."

Emerson's mouth dropped open. "What?"

"Emerson, you might be the only person on the planet who doesn't realize this, but Cruz has been in love with you his entire life."

She gave me a "duh" look, and I wondered when she'd figured it out. "I know. Which is why I need to tell him how I feel."

"So you can hurt him again? Don't be selfish. Think of other people, for once. Love isn't some fairytale with grand declarations and big, amazing reunions. It's messy and hard and there's not some guaranteed happily ever after."

I prepared myself for a battle, for Emerson to hurl some snarky comment at me, but her expression softened. She grabbed my shoulders and gripped them tight. "Listen, Clara. I'm not going to break Cruz's heart. I want to be with him. I want to make this work, but I need to tell him the truth."

She seemed sincere enough . . . maybe I could . . . Isaac coughed behind me, bringing me back to reality. Right. I had a genie to deal with and a parade I was not going to miss. Then I saw something behind Emerson, a flash of black, a face underneath a hood. Something I couldn't explain.

"What?" Emerson's face drained of color. "What did you see?"

"Nothing," I murmured. "I thought I saw something, but . . ."

"Hello?" Isaac yelled from inside the shop. "Am I just chopped liver now?"

I whipped around. "I will deal with you in a minute, okay? I'm a little busy right now."

"Sure, already forgetting about your promise to help me," he whined.

"I'm not forgetting anything, believe me," I gritted out, but when I turned around, Emerson was already gone, her car peeling away from where it sat on the sidewalk, driving through the caution tape that had been put up to prevent any kind of vehicle on the parade route. Parade volunteers yelled at her as her car revved off into the distance, disappearing from sight.

Regret immediately filled me. I did that. I made her run away.

No.

I turned slowly, pinning my gaze on Isaac. No I didn't. He did. This was all his fault. If it weren't for him, for that lamp, I wouldn't be unraveling like this. I'd lost my temper on Emerson because Isaac had set me on edge. Now she was driving away in an emotional state to god knows where. I gasped. Maybe I forced her back to LA. That's where she was going. I groaned. She was trying to tell me she loved Cruz, asking for my help, and I let my own issues get in the way. I glared at Isaac. I couldn't do this anymore.

"Well, you really messed that up," Isaac said. "Just like you messed things up with Preston."

I screeched and threw my hands up in the air. "That's it! You're going back into the lamp now. I can't handle this anymore. I can't handle *you* anymore. Until I figure out how free you from this stupid lamp. I don't want to see your face."

Isaac snorted. "Yeah, right. I have a beautiful face. It's very symmetrical."

I pointed at his golden home. "Back to the lamp. Now."

He rolled his eyes. "Fine. I'm ready for a nap anyway. Buh-eye."

With that, the blue smoke twisted and curled, sucking Isaac in until I could no longer see him. I picked up the lamp and eyed the basement door, walking toward it with purpose. The genie was going back where he came from.

Chapter Twenty-Seven

The stairs to the basement creaked with each step I took. I marched down the steps and into the dark, dank space. My hand fumbled until it finally found the light switch and flicked it on, illuminating the little room, still filled with boxes and clutter from a few weeks ago, when this entire mess started.

There in the back wall was the little hole where my mother had hidden the lamp.

"Hey!" Isaac yelled from inside the lamp, banging against it. The lamp vibrated in my hands. "I changed my mind. I'm not ready for a nap." I ignored him. "Hey! You let me out right now. I'm getting claustrophobic. Now that I've tasted freedom, you can't just trap me back in here."

"It's not forever," I said back. "But I need some space, okay? So you're going back in the basement until I get things sorted."

"This isn't the answer." Isaac's muted voice floated from the lamp's spout. "You know deep down this is wrong, that you're not really mad at me. You're mad at yourself."

"No, I'm pretty sure I'm mad at you, and if I need a therapy session, I'll call my therapist, thanks."

"Oh please. Don't pretend like you have a therapist. You're not nearly well-adjusted enough for someone in therapy."

I yelled out in frustration and shook the lamp.

"He-e-e-e-y. You're making me dizzy. Quit it!"

I gripped the lamp tighter as I approached the back wall, picking my way over vases, picture frames, articles of clothing, and other random artifacts that had fallen from the boxes. I remembered how just weeks ago I'd told Helen I wanted to fix this place up for Remy's birthday. The birthday that was quickly approaching, and there was no way I would have time to get this place renovated like I'd wanted to.

Just another way everything was going wrong.

A dusty old cauldron sat in the corner of the basement, and I wondered for a minute if I could spruce that up and give it to Remy to use to practice her spells. I shook my head. One thing at a time. I'd already taken on too much, and that was part of the problem.

"I'm sulking, you know," Isaac said. "You can't see me, but I'm giving you major stink eye right now."

I ignored him as I faced the little hole in the wall where the lamp had been hidden. I lifted the lamp, then hesitated, wondering if I was doing the right thing by putting it back. It's not like I was planning on just leaving Isaac here to rot. I was still going to fix this. I just needed a breather. There was nothing wrong with that. He'd said a lot of hurtful things, untrue things. I hadn't ruined things with Preston or Emerson. I'd done the right thing by not allowing either of them back into my life. That was my choice to make. No one else's. And Alisandra and I were nothing alike. She wanted to stay on an isolated beach by herself. How was that the same as what I was doing? It wasn't. Isaac just knew how to push my buttons.

A wail erupted from the lamp, making me jump in shock at the loud sound. My feet tangled together, and I tripped over a box, the lamp flying from my hands. I watched it sail through the air, Isaac's wail growing louder as the lamp collided with a vial of liquid sitting on a shelf, some old potion. Both fell together into the ancient cauldron. Light exploded in front of me, colors shooting in every direction, twisting, turning, forming a picture.

I shook my head, not sure what was happening, what the cauldron had just triggered. Then it hit me: it wasn't the cauldron, it was that vial, that potion. It must've been a memory spell, and now that spell had been cast on the lamp, showing me a memory of it. I stepped closer. The vision in front of me became clear, and that's when I saw *her*.

My mother.

My breath caught in my throat at seeing her. She and Remy were almost twins, apart from my mother's red, straight hair. She was young, so young, so full of life, her edges soft. Life hadn't hardened them yet. She stood at the cauldron in The Wish List, and I realized it was this same cauldron.

I barely wanted to take a breath, didn't want to miss anything. I studied her as she methodically dropped ingredients into the cauldron, then waved her wand over it. Oh, Mom. I wanted so badly to reach out and touch her, to talk with her, to ask her what I should do. Once upon a time, she was my moral compass. And yes, she'd turned out to be evil, but still, there was a time I trusted her with everything I had.

The door to The Wish List burst open, a boy standing there, red hair, freckles, vibrant green eyes. Isaac. He and my mother stared at each other, twin expressions of shock on their faces.

"Wow, so it's real," Isaac breathed, his eyes widening. "Magic is real."

"Of course it's real," my mother said matter-of-factly, then cocked her head. "You have magic. I can sense it. So why does this surprise you?"

Isaac took a few more steps forward, gaze roaming around the shop.

"Who are you?" my mother asked, curiosity in her voice. No animosity or hate like I might have expected based on what she'd done to Isaac.

"I think I'm your twin."

Isaac had been right, my mother's face didn't show any kind of shock at the news. In fact, I swore I saw the slightest hint of excitement flash in her green eyes.

"I always knew something was missing," she murmured. "Deep down, I felt like I should have a sibling. How odd. So you don't know about magic, then?"

Isaac shook his head, running his fingers along the crystal balls on the shelves.

"Oh, don't touch those," my mother said gently. "They're very delicate."

"What are they for?" Isaac asked.

"To grant wishes." My mother set her wand down, the cauldron now bubbling with plumes of a glittery maroon smoke rising into the air.

Isaac's eyes widened. "I'm sorry, did you say—"

My mother put her hand on his arm. "You better sit down for this." She gestured to the purple couch sitting in the shop, the very same one that was still up there.

And then my mother told Isaac everything: how we were Witch Granters, a rare breed of witch who could grant wishes, how receiving a wish cost a person a piece of their soul, how great a responsibility we had on our shoulders. It sounded almost exactly like the speech I'd given Remy when she found out magic was real. I sensed no ill will in my mother. None at all.

"I'll teach you if you like," my mother said. "I can teach you everything you need to know about magic, and you can come back home with me." She frowned. "Mother never told me about you, but I sense she didn't know, that something foul is at play."

Isaac nodded. "I was taken by a woman named Greta who raised me as her own. I recently found out the truth about magic. Greta hid it, hid my identity from me. She told me my parents didn't want me, gave me to her, but I had to come see for myself."

I could sense the pain in Isaac's words, the deep-rooted sorrow, but my mother didn't seem to have that same thought, because she didn't lean forward with a hug or a gentle touch to his arm. Nothing.

She just continued on, all business. "No, that can't be right. Mother would never give up her own son. She loves being a mother. But my father." Her voice darkened. "He was behind this, I'm sure of it. He's an awful man." She shuddered. "I can take you to meet Mother, if you'd like."

Isaac scooted back, away from my mother. My gut churned. Something wasn't right. Something wasn't adding up about Isaac's story and what I was seeing.

"She's not my mother," Isaac said, voice full of scorn. "Not really. She won't even know me."

My mother popped up, bustling around, paying no attention to the hurt lacing Isaac's words. "She can get to know you. We all can. You know, one day, this shop will be mine. Right now, it belongs to my mother, but when she dies, it goes to next of kin. I can let you work for me, if you want."

"Work for you?" He spit out the words like they were the ultimate insult. He stood and prowled around the room, toward my mother. "Why?"

She walked behind the counter and picked up her wand, stirring her potion. "Why what?"

"Why did you get all of this, and I got nothing? Why did they want you, but not me? Why?"

She shrugged. "I don't know, but I'm sure we can figure it out."

I wanted to scream at her to run, that something wasn't right. But my mother didn't even notice.

"No," Isaac snarled. "No, I don't want to figure it out. I want this life that I deserved. I deserved it, not you. And I'm going to take it back."

"What does that mean?" my mother asked, her gaze finally snapping to him.

"I'm going to take it, take everything from you, from *your mother*."

"No, you won't." She widened her stance. "I won't let you."

"You won't have a choice."

Isaac stalked forward, and my mother pressed herself against the shelf behind the cauldron. "What are you doing?"

"I'm taking what's mine. The Wish List isn't going to pass to you. It's going to pass to me, right after I get rid of you and your mother."

"You mean kill us?" my mother asked.

"Well, maybe I won't kill you," Isaac sputtered at the use of the word, some of his bravado cracking.

Isaac continued, "But I can get rid of you."

My mother's entire demeanor changed. Her eyes flashed. She bared her teeth, every muscle in her body tensed. She was ready for a fight, ready to defend this life she loved.

My mouth dropped open. Isaac hadn't told us about any of this. Of course he hadn't. He'd threatened to kill my mother, his twin sister, to take everything she loved away from her.

Isaac grasped for her, and I had no idea what he planned to do, but my mother was quick. She reached behind her and grabbed a heavy vase, then whacked Isaac right over the head with it.

He crumpled to the ground, and my mother stood over him, visibly shaking.

"I can't let that happen," she said. "No one can know about you. If Mother finds out you're alive, she'll want to try and redeem you. She won't understand that we can't take that kind of risk. You could ruin our lives, and I can't save you. So I have to find a way to trap you," she murmured to herself. "Some kind of object strong enough to keep you inside forever."

The vision slowly dissipated, color disappearing from it until nothing was left but a haze.

I stood, staring at the space, unable to move. My mother hadn't been evil, after all. She wanted to bring Isaac into the family and teach him magic. He'd been the one who ruined it.

"Isaac, get out here." My voice shook as Isaac appeared.

"Okay, I know that looked bad," he said, worrying at his lip.

"Shut up." My entire body trembled from rage. "Shut up. I'm binding you back to this spot." I pointed at the wall behind him, the little space where my mother had hidden him. "You're going back there, and everyone is going to forget about you."

His face paled. "You can't do that. You said you'd set me free."

"So you can take The Wish List from me? Take away this life I just got back? So you can hurt me or Remy?"

"You're being dramatic," Isaac said.

"No. Don't do that. Don't act like I'm the crazy one."

I spun on my heel and stomped up the stairs, Isaac following me, the scrape of the lamp against the cement basement floor the only sound between us.

"What are you doing?" Isaac asked.

"I already told you." I burst out of the basement and into my shop. "I'm creating a spell, and I'm putting you back in that wall."

"No, no, please." For the first time, his voice held a hint of fear.

I wrenched open the door to the backroom and ran inside, grabbing ingredients off the shelves that I kept stocked.

Superglue

Rope

Amethyst dust

And . . . I stepped out of the backroom, arms full of ingredients . . . the lamp.

"W-wait. Can we talk about this?"

I got a piece of paper and started scribbling out the spell I wanted to create.

Isaac stretched his neck out. "Seriously, please stop."

"No. I'm writing out a spell, and you're going bye-bye." My vision blurred, and I pawed at the tears trying to escape. Isaac had fooled me. He fooled all of us.

"I thought you said magic was a lot of trial and error. How do you even know what you're doing?"

"We'll find out," I murmured, barely paying attention to him as I continued writing. It was sloppy, but I didn't care. As long as it got the job done.

Outside, I thought I heard the crack of a firework. The parade would be starting soon, and I was going to end this now. Isaac didn't deserve to be here, ruining my life all because of his greed.

I finished writing out the spell—a binding spell, a strong one, I hoped, and tossed each ingredient into the cauldron.

"Stop," Isaac said. "Just think this through before you cast some spell. I mean, are you even a good witch? Didn't you say you just started practicing magic again like a month ago?"

"Two months," I said, marching toward the lamp and snatching it.

"Oh my god," Isaac said. "I'm going to die."

"No, you're not. But you are not my problem anymore. I'm going to get my life back."

"You sound a little deranged," Isaac said. "Maybe we should call Remy—"

"Remy's busy." I dropped the lamp into the cauldron, then picked up my wand.

"Clara, c'mon, I was just an angry kid. People make mistakes."

I waved my wand around the cauldron as it glowed, brighter, brighter, brighter while I thought of my intention: *bind the lamp, bind the lamp, bind the lamp.*

Blue swirls of magic filled the cauldron, the color glowing brighter and brighter.

"I don't like this," Isaac said, breaking my train of thought.

I shook my head and continued with the spell until the color grew so bright it filled the entire shop, just like I expected it would.

Something loud popped, and I squeezed my eyes shut as a blinding white light flashed in front of my eyes. Everything went still, silent, and I slowly opened my eyes, hoping the spell had done what I meant it to. Isaac would be back in that wall, this time for good.

My gaze focused. Isaac floated in front of me, but . . . I looked around at the floor, covered in a colorful bohemian rug, a little bed, a chair—golden walls, a golden ceiling.

"Congratulations," Isaac said, "looks like you just bound yourself to this lamp."

Chapter Twenty-Eight

"No," I said and banged against the walls of the lamp. "No, no, no. Help," I called out. "Please, someone help!"

Isaac crossed his arms, his feet firmly planted on the bottom of the lamp. It was so odd seeing him just standing before me instead of floating. "Yeah, that doesn't work."

He snapped his fingers and a bag of Cheetos appeared in his hand. He held it out toward me. "Cheese poof?"

"Seriously?" I pushed the bag away as my panic rose. "How am I going to get out of here?"

"No idea. You got yourself into this, and now you have to get yourself out of it." He shot me a far too smug smile.

"I'm going to miss the parade," I said, sinking against the cold metal wall of the lamp.

"The parade?" Isaac asked, his brows wrinkling. "You just trapped yourself inside a lamp for possibly all of eternity and you're worried about missing a parade?"

I banged my fist against the wall and, OH MY GOD OW. Right. Metal walls. Metal prison. I lifted my fist to my mouth as sharp pains shot through it and reverberated up my arm.

Isaac waited, not saying anything.

Finally, after the radiating pain faded, I spoke. "I haven't been there for Remy like I should've been since her father died, almost two years ago now. This was supposed to be our fresh start. Things were supposed to be easy, not complicated. Perfect."

"But that hasn't been the case," Isaac said knowingly. "I mean, I could've told you that wasn't gonna happen. Who do you know that has an easy, uncomplicated life?"

I rubbed my temples. "Emerson." And she was going to throw it all away.

"The blonde chick that you yelled at like an hour ago?"

I gave him a look, and he just pursed his lips. "You know she's totally cursed, right?"

I stopped at that, blinking. "I'm sorry, what?"

"Yeah, your friend is cursed with a capital C."

My mouth dropped open. "How do you know that?"

"It takes one to know one. I can spot a curse from a mile away."

Oh my god. It made so much sense now. Why Emerson looked so tired and haggard all the time, why she was so jumpy and jittery and on edge. Why she was being so terrible. Of course she was cursed. I gasped. Was that why she ran away from The Wish List like she had? Or drove away? Now I felt even worse. She was cursed and I'd yelled at her. I let my head thud against the lamp. I was an idiot.

"She'll be okay," Isaac said. "I have a feeling she's gonna get herself out of it."

I hoped so; otherwise, I didn't want to know the alternative.

"Anyway, the point is, Emerson's life is definitely not easy," Isaac said.

"I have to get out of here." I looked around helplessly, then spotted a hole, probably the one that led to the spout. I ran toward it . . . and hit some kind of barrier that bounced me straight back onto my butt.

"You don't think I've tried that like a million times?"

In the distance, I heard a familiar bell tinkling. My head snapped up. "Someone's come in the shop. Help," I yelled as loud as I could. "I'm trapped in here, help me, please!"

No one responded.

"Can you stop with the screaming?" Isaac sat on his bed. "You're voice is like a screechy little hyena."

"Ugh." I groaned. "No one's going to know what happened to me!"

"I mean, they're gonna find out you're in here." Isaac rolled his eyes. "And if for some reason they can't hear your piercing voice, I can tell them."

"I don't trust you. All you want is The Wish List, power. You're just as bad as my mother."

"Isaac?" a voice called from outside the lamp, and I tilted my head at the familiarity of it.

I paused and narrowed my eyes at the genie. "Why is Martin calling your name?"

Isaac looked away, his cheeks turning pink.

"Okay," Martin said. "Here goes nothing: I'm sorry I freaked out the other day. We had a moment, and instead of embracing it, I grabbed the lamp and dropped you back off at Clara's house. Because I was afraid. Afraid of what that moment meant. I know we haven't spent a lot of time together, but, well, the time we have spent together has been . . . meaningful."

His words took a minute to sink in. Meaningful. What did that—I sucked in a breath and hissed out, "Seriously? You and Martin?" I shook my head. "The genie and the imp?" I felt faint. "What is happening?"

Isaac's cheeks flushed a deep red, but he shushed me and pressed his ear against the wall of the lamp.

"The thing is," Martin continued. "I don't have the best reputation when it comes to romantic relationships. So there is a chance I might break your heart, but I started therapy recently, and I think I learned that I tend to push people away before they can leave me. And, well, given that you're stuck in a lamp, I don't think you're going anywhere. At least not for a while."

Isaac's eyes welled with tears. "I wouldn't leave you anyway," he said, but Martin didn't give any inclination that he'd heard him.

"I've never met anyone more dramatic than me," the imp continued. "It's actually very cute when you get all worked up about things, like that woman who wore pleather."

"That was an abomination," Isaac said, ear still pressed to the side of the lamp.

"But I also think you're kind, funny, have very good taste—"

"That's true," Isaac agreed.

"And you get me. You get my cattiness, my level of snark, my wit."

180

"Wow, super humble as always," I said.

"You didn't judge me when I told you how I worked for the Devil all those years. You told me my bed and breakfast was beautifully decorated, and I appreciate that you have a good eye for things like that."

"I do," Isaac said. "I really do."

"Oh, for the love of god." Why this surprised me, I didn't know. They were actually perfect together. "You two deserve each other."

"Anyway," Martin said. "I just wanted to see if maybe I could take you out on a proper date sometime. It's a new thing I'm trying: dating, instead of just sleeping with you and never calling you again."

"That would be an improvement," I mumbled.

"Yes," Isaac called out, hitting the walls. "Yes, Martin, I will go on a date with you!"

"Really?" Martin called back. "Oh, good. Well, okay. I'm not exactly sure how to take you on a date, since you're stuck in a lamp. But, semantics. Clara will hopefully free you soon. Where is Clara, by the way?"

Isaac opened his mouth to answer, then stopped and turned to me, eyes wide. "I-I think I figured out how to right a past wrong."

"Hello?" Martin called out. "I do need to know if we're going on a date because this green skin doesn't get luminous on its own."

"Just a minute!" Isaac yelled back.

"What do you mean?" I asked. "How are you going to right anything? My mother is dead, the damage is done."

Isaac stood, pacing. "I haven't been honest."

"Shocking," I said drily.

"No, I mean, I did want The Wish List to begin with. I wanted to take it from your mother, I wanted to take it from you."

I threw my hands up in the air. "I knew it. That's why you were so interested in learning how to grant wishes, why you always wanted to be out in the shop when clients came in."

Isaac shook his head impatiently. "But I don't want that anymore."

"Just like that?" I had a hard time believing anything Isaac said at this point.

"No." Isaac arched his neck, looking up at the top of the lamp, like he could see Martin, see some future I couldn't. "It's been a transition, I mean. When you first freed me and brought me to the shop, all those feelings of want flooded back. But then I got to know you and Remy and this community you've created. I met others, like Martin and Helen and Myrtle, who's crochety and grumpy, but in a cute kind of way."

"What's your point?" I asked.

"I thought The Wish List was all I could have in life, that no one would want *me*, but that's not true. Martin wants me." Isaac gestured to the air. "Remy wants me. She said so."

I scuffed my shoe on the floor when he didn't mention anything about me. I hadn't exactly been welcoming to Isaac. Far from it, actually.

"And I think maybe once I get free, I might find Greta, see if she's still alive and if we could have a relationship after all. Though she'll really have to suck up to me to earn my forgiveness."

"That would be nice," I said. "For you. And Greta, probably."

Isaac nodded. "I don't want to push people away anymore, and I don't want to take your shop from you. You can have it." He paused. "Also, I'm sorry for saying your shoes were ugly."

"You didn't say that . . ." I trailed off.

"Oh." Isaac gave a little laugh. "Oops. Let's just forget about that. My point is that I don't want to be afraid anymore."

I pushed off from the side of the lamp. "Afraid of what?" I asked.

"Living. Afraid that if someone gets too close to me they'll leave." He pointed upward. "Remy's worth that risk. So is Martin."

"Martin, really?" I asked.

Isaac arched an eyebrow.

"Sorry, continue." I gestured.

"I don't want to steal your life away. I just want to live mine."

The lamp started vibrating around us, shaking so hard I fell to my knees. Swirls of magic surrounded Isaac, circling around and around and around, so fast it was dizzying. A wind picked up in the lamp, whipping my hair past my face and against my shoulders.

"What's happening?" Isaac yelled.

"Hello?" Martin called in the distance. "What is going on in there?"

Fear shone from Isaac's eyes, and I tried to get up, but the strong winds pushed me into the floor.

"Clara?" Isaac asked.

"Just, don't panic," I assured him.

"Too late!"

The magic encompassed Isaac until I could no longer see him, then it vanished, along with Isaac, leaving me completely alone. A smoky blue tether appeared, stretching toward me. I scrambled from it, pressed my back against the wall, but it followed me, slithering across the ground like a snake until it wrapped itself around my ankle. It looked like the lamp had a new master—me. And I had no idea how I was going to fix this.

Chapter Twenty-Nine

"You've got to be kidding me," I mumbled, then called out, "Hello?"

"We're here," Isaac said, then I heard smooching noises.

"Seriously? Are you two making out in front of the lamp right now?"

Martin scoffed. "You are ruining what is supposed to be a very romantic moment."

"This is not a romantic moment," I yelled back. "I'm stuck in this lamp, and I have no idea how to get out."

"You have to right a wrong!" Isaac said.

"But I haven't done anything wrong." I kicked the lamp and pain shot up my leg. "Dammit, why do I keep doing that?"

"Clara," Martin said. "You can't honestly believe you have no wrongs to right."

"I've already righted them. Remember? Facing my past? Practicing magic? Telling my daughter the truth about her heritage?"

"Yes, so now you're perfect," Martin said, the sarcasm thick.

Perfect. I hadn't been perfect for a long, long time. I slumped against the side of the lamp, sniffling. Now I was trapped—did that mean? I stared at the blue tether cuffed to my ankle. Was *I* a genie? Oh god. The thought of living out my existence in this tiny golden prison made my blood go cold. I couldn't be a mother to Remy while stuck in here. I couldn't run The Wish List. I couldn't live my life.

Tears slipped down my cheeks, and I wiped them away, but not fast enough as they kept coming, my cheeks wet, the tears salty on my lips.

"Pull yourself together, Clara," Isaac said. "Listen, you did try and help me get out of the lamp, even if you were going to bind me to the basement. But I forgive you for that."

"She was going to do what?" Martin asked, and I thought I heard Isaac whisper to him. Whatever he said worked, and the imp quieted down.

"Now, tell me about your regrets," Isaac said. "Maybe recent ones. Let's work our way backward."

"No." I lay on the bed, hands resting on my stomach. "Isaac, I appreciate your help, but this is something I have to do myself. And I need some peace and quiet to think. So if you and Martin could maybe just go find Remy and let her know that I will be at the parade as soon as possible, that would be great."

"That star she made is so good," Martin said.

"You made the star," I replied.

"Right. I did, didn't I? Well, it's absolutely beautiful."

"We'll be back later," Isaac promised. "We're going to get you out of here and return that lamp to Alisandra."

I nodded, even though they couldn't see me. Their feet pattered against the floor, and the bell rang, then the door clicked shut. I was alone.

Who was I kidding? I deserved this. I'd pushed Preston away, pushed Emerson away, didn't fulfill my promise to Dara, didn't even try. And I'd just attempted to trap Isaac forever in the basement. I was as bad as my mother at this point. Well, maybe not as bad. I didn't think I was evil, but I was a woman pushed to the edge. I shook my head slowly. That wasn't right. Nothing pushed me to the edge. I did that all on my own. But why?

My mind felt like this tangled mess that I couldn't figure out.

I stood from the bed and walked around the little space. It was sparse, not much here to do . . . but hadn't Isaac mentioned he'd discovered he could summon things he wanted with his thoughts?

Clearly I wasn't getting anywhere, so I might as well take a break. I squeezed my eyes shut and thought about what I wanted right now, in this moment. I opened my eyes, and laying there in the middle of the bed was a large book.

No. I walked toward it. Not a book. An album. A picture album.

I hadn't asked for that. I asked for something comforting. I figured I'd get a tub of chocolate chip ice cream or a TV to binge some new Netflix show, not a freaking album. I approached it cautiously, almost afraid it was a trick or something.

I stopped in front of the bed, staring at the album, the front cover with a picture of me . . . and my mom. I'd never seen this before, didn't even know it existed. Was this the lamp's doing? I reached out a shaky hand and opened it up. Pictures filled the pages, and I flipped through them, not taking my time, devouring it all, wanting more. I got to the end and then went back again, starting on the first page.

Pictures of me and my mom on my first day of high school. She'd stayed home from a trip because I was so nervous about going to high school, about making friends, about classes. So she'd snuck me in early in the morning, when it was still dark out, before anyone would arrive. She took me through the school, to each classroom, telling me stories upon stories about her time there. By the time the sun was rising my worries had melted away, and I'd been tired but exhilarated, ready to take on this new adventure.

Later that day, my mom had left for her trip, and I'd come home to an empty house.

I flipped to the next page, full of pictures of my mom and me on a trip to a nearby town. She'd woken me up early one morning and whispered, let's go. Witches rarely flew on their brooms, but my mom exclusively traveled on hers everywhere she went. We'd mounted her broom and flew for hours. I had no idea where we were going, but I'd held on tight, arms twined around mother's waist, excitement building over where we might be going.

There'd been a small town of supernaturals that didn't have a Witch Granter, and my mom was traveling to that town for the day to grant wishes to any resident who'd like one. She did this every once in a while, and this time, she was going to let me help grant the wishes. We'd spent the day doing what we loved, then hiked in the hills around the little town, taking pictures and spending time together before we flew back home. It had rained on us. That flight home had been miserable, and I'd caught a cold from it.

The next page was of me and my mother at my high school graduation. My gaze caught on one particular photo of me and Preston. Mother hadn't liked us together, thought he distracted me too much from becoming a better, more powerful witch, but on that day she'd taken a photo with me on one side, Preston on the other, all of us smiling big, so much hope and promise for our futures. Preston and I had been holding hands behind my mother's back, not featured in the photo. But I remembered the way his hand gripped mine, so steady and sure.

And I kept flipping, spending who knew how much time on each page, letting myself sink into the pictures, remember the sounds, the smells, the tastes that surrounded my mother and I until I was finally at the end, at what must've been the last picture we'd taken together. Right here, in The Wish List. My mother had given me the keys to the shop, said it was mine, for the weekend, at least. She was leaving on some business trip, and for the first time ever, I was going to be running The Wish List. It was a big responsibility, one she'd trusted me with. So before she left, we'd taken a picture together. It was only a few days later I'd learned the truth about my mother and her dark dealings. That she was granting wishes she shouldn't have been granting, collecting people's souls for her own twisted purposes. Purposes I still didn't understand.

But in that moment, life had been perfect.

I let that sink in. Perfect. No, that wasn't right. Just that morning, I'd gotten in a fight with Preston over coffee. Coffee of all things. He'd said he was going to bring me a latte for my first big day running the shop, but he'd stayed out late the night before, slept through his alarm, and forgotten about his promise of coffee, prompting a few angry phone calls until I'd finally woken up him. We hadn't yet made up by the time this picture was taken because I had to get to the shop to open it.

I flipped back through the pictures, the cracks beginning to show in each one. I'd been happy in these pictures, yes, but certainly not perfect. Because everyone was right. Of course they were. I was chasing perfection when it didn't exist. And I'd messed up so many things in the last few weeks because I'd been too stubborn to listen to everyone, too afraid.

But what was I afraid of?

I still didn't know.

The bell to the shop rang somewhere in the distance. Crap. I'd forgotten to tell Martin to lock up before he left.

"Um, we're closed," I called out, even though it was probably futile.

"Clara, *what did you do?*"

I stood up straighter. "Helen?"

"So Martin was telling the truth. You freed Isaac and got yourself trapped in there."

"Well, I didn't actually free Isaac," I yelled. "He did that himself."

"Tell me what happened," Helen said firmly.

So I did. She knew a lot of it thanks to our group chat, but I filled her in on everything that had happened since she dropped me off at that dock with Martin and his rowboat.

"But Clara." I didn't have to see Helen to hear the exasperation in her voice. "Why would you try to hide Isaac away again? You had to know that wouldn't work."

"I just wanted things to go back to the way they were," I said miserably, slumping down onto the bed, fingers grazing the album cover. "You know, Remy and me, together, at The Wish List, practicing magic and granting wishes, renovating our home and making it our own."

"You mean like the two weeks between when the mayor almost burned down The Wish List and when you found the lamp?"

"Yes!"

"When Martin was annoying the crap out of you because he kept texting you tips for helping your teenager transition to a new school?"

Oh. I'd forgotten about that. Martin had gone full mom mode and was worrying nonstop about how Remy would transition to a brand-new school her senior year.

"And the constant noise from the recent demon attacks?"

I had been sleeping poorly because of all the demons we'd seen lately around Whispering Willows.

"And you hiding every time you saw the mayor to avoid any awkward interactions?"

"What's your point, Helen?"

"Life wasn't perfect then and it's not perfect now. You're chasing something that doesn't exist."

"Yeah, so I've learned," I mumbled.

The bell rang again. "What the feck? The imp was telling the truth, then? You're a feckin' genie now?"

That would be Myrtle.

"Is Martin telling the whole town about this?"

"Pretty much," Myrtle said. "In between making out with the genie." She paused. "Well, guess he's not a genie anymore, is he?"

I groaned.

"Really, Clara, what were you thinking?" Myrtle asked.

"We're trying to work that out at present," Helen said.

"Oh god," Myrtle mumbled.

The bell rang again.

"Who's there?" I asked.

"I'm looking for my wife," the Serpent said.

"Nice to see you too, Gene!" I yelled, but I all I heard in response was a grunt.

"You're going to miss the parade," Gene said, presumably to Helen. "You love the parade."

"Well, I'm trying to help Clara figure out why she's trapped in the lamp as fast as I can."

I threw out my arms. "I don't need to know why I'm trapped in the lamp. I need to know how to get out of the lamp! Riddle me that!"

I opened the album again, wanting to look at all the pictures, relive these memories I made with my mom before everything went to hell.

"Clara, what are you doing in there?" Helen asked.

I swallowed, my gaze stuck on a picture of my mom standing over our cauldron, performing a spell. "Just looking at some pictures of my mom and me. Good memories. You know, before I found out she was evil and I was forced to go on the run to hide from her."

The bell rang again. "Is she still in there?" Martin asked.

I rolled my eyes.

"You know it did take me fifty years to escape, so . . .," Isaac said. "Just saying."

"Most of the time, I'm really happy I married you," Gene said, presumably to Helen. "But moments like these I question my life choices."

"Oh, you don't regret marrying me," Helen said. "Even through all the bad." I could picture the way she was probably playfully shoving him, the way he was rolling his eyes, and then the way he'd plant a kiss on her head.

Regret. My heartbeat slowed in my chest, my breathing filling my ears, the whole world shrinking in on that one word. Regret. I stared at the pictures of me and my mom. Thought about the moments that made up my life. I looked at picture after picture, frantically flipping now, like the answer might lie in one of these memories. I didn't regret any of them. Not a single moment. No matter the heartbreak, the hardships, the trials. I wouldn't take it back, none of it.

Life didn't have to perfect. But I was afraid of what would happen if it wasn't.

I was afraid.

I was afraid of going through all the heartbreak again.

But so what if I did? I'd survived it once. No. I didn't just survive. I thrived. Got married, had a daughter, made new friends, came back home, found a community.

The bell rang again, and my head snapped up at the interruption. "I swear to god, Martin. Who else did you tell—"

"Clara?"

My heart stopped. "Preston."

"I overhead Martin telling Remy you might be late, that you were caught up with something. You'd never miss that parade, not if Remy has a float in it."

He knew me well.

"I knew something was wrong and came here as fast as I could."

"I think that's our cue, everyone," Helen said, and it wasn't the first time I was grateful for her.

"Why? It's just getting good," Myrtle said.

"Yeah, I wanna stay," Isaac added.

"My wife has spoken. Out," Gene said to everyone, and I heard their footsteps as they padded toward the door, everyone mumbling and murmuring, until it was silent.

Just me and Preston, and it suddenly became so clear what I needed to do. I just hoped I had the courage to do it.

Chapter Thirty

"You still there?" I asked Preston.

"Yeah, I'm still here."

I thought about how I'd acted over the last few weeks. "I don't deserve for you to be."

"No, you don't. But I'm here anyway."

The words shook me to my core. He was still here. No matter what I'd thrown at him, how I'd hurt him. When I really needed him, Preston came. He was the steady, the calm in my stormy seas. I didn't deserve him, but I'd work every single day to prove that I did. I'd do a lot of things differently moving forward. Starting with this. Because this was going to be the key to setting myself free from this lamp. No one could save me at this point but myself. So here went nothing.

I blew out a big breath. "I'm afraid, Preston. Life wasn't perfect. It never was, but I wanted to pretend that I'd gotten everything I wanted because that would mean I wouldn't have to risk anything again."

Just like Alisandra. The siren and I had more in common than I'd wanted to admit, and if I expected her to put herself out there and reconnect with her clan, then I had to take my own risks.

"Like what?" Preston asked, and I could hear the confusion in his voice.

"My heart, for one. But stability. Safety. My dreams. My heritage."

"Okay," Preston said, and I knew it wasn't enough. I had to tell him more, tell him everything.

"After the whole debacle with the mayor, life wasn't perfect like I'd convinced myself—it was safe. And that's what I wanted. So I pushed you away, I tried to ignore the lamp, I yelled at Emerson. But you know what I realized?"

"What's that?" Preston asked, and I thought I could hear him stepping closer to the lamp.

"I realized that safe is worse than messy. Safe means I'm not putting myself out there, it means I'm not allowing myself to love, to be loved. It means I'm doing terrible things, all because I'm afraid."

"What terrible things?"

"I almost convinced myself it would be okay to let a man stay trapped in a lamp for all of eternity. I wouldn't listen to Emerson when she needed my help, and now she might be in trouble."

"That all sounds pretty bad," Preston said.

"I know! And that's not me. That's something my mother would've done—did do." She trapped Isaac because she was afraid to take a risk. Instead of trying to help her twin brother, she doomed him to a life in this lamp. "I know I'm not my mother." I started pacing. "But I almost did something terrible because I was so determined to keep my 'perfect' life."

After I'd discovered my mother was using her witch granting powers for evil, I don't think I truly ever felt safe. Not even in my suburbia life in Portland where I was far away from magic, from Whispering Willows, but especially not since I'd returned here. And that was hard to admit. Because I loved my life here, but I felt like I was always looking over my shoulder, waiting for something else to go wrong, so I figured if I ignored it that meant it would go away. How stupid. It sounded so dumb when I actually talked through it in my brain.

"I've been wearing these blinders to pretend that life is great because I think if I admit that it's messy that means admitting that I may never be completely safe. Remy may never be safe."

"Safe? From like demons and mayors who fake date you?"

I laughed. "Kind of, but no? I mean, safe from heartbreak and anger and fights and big emotions."

"Ah." Preston paused. "I get it, Clara. After everything you've been through, change can be scary. You've made some huge leaps in a short time, and it's okay to be scared. But I'm here for you. Helen is here for you. Myrtle is here for you. Martin is even here for you, in his own weird way."

I sniffled. "I know, I know. I didn't get it." My gaze flicked to the album still laying on the bed. "But I do now. I'm so sorry, Preston. I'm sorry for hurting you twenty years ago, and I'm sorry for hurting you again now."

"Clara." His voice rumbled, low, like a caress down my spine. "What are you saying, exactly?"

"I love you," I burst out. "I've always loved you. It never went away. And it's scary and not going to be easy and you're going to have to deal with all my drama, and possibly a genie that just got released from a lamp after being trapped for fifty years." I paused. "And his possible new relationship with Martin, which is so weird but oddly seems like it actually might work?" I shook my head. "But I love you, Preston. And I want to take you out on a date. A proper date that doesn't involve golden lamps or mermaids or bars with Emerson there insulting everyone. Oh! Emerson. I need to find her as soon as I get out of this lamp. Well, first I need to see Remy's float in the parade, and then I need to find Emerson. But I love you. I want to be with you, give us the second chance that we deserve."

Preston was silent. Oh god. I'd just completely rambled. That wasn't even romantic—it was just word vomit all over Preston. Of course he wouldn't want to be with me. What kind of romantic gesture was that? I should've written out something that sounded coherent, not like a woman on the verge of a breakdown, which, let's be honest, that's what I was—

The lamp started vibrating underneath my feet, the same swirls of magic that surrounded Isaac now rushing and circling around me, filling me and making me feel light, like a balloon that could just lift in the air. The magic spun faster, faster, dizzying to the eye, until I couldn't see anything but blue and green in a tornado of color. It shot up my nose, into my ears, in my mouth. It whipped at my hair, lifted the edges of my shirt, and I closed my eyes, letting the magic take me. It filled my veins, flowed through me, a tickling sensation creeping through my body. Finally, it lifted me, and my body became weightless.

Then I slammed toward the ground.

My feet felt steady, solid under me, the magic fading from me. The air felt different, less stale, more open. I sniffed, smelling the familiar scents of cinnamon, rosehip, lavender. The Wish List. I'd escaped. Relief swelled big and strong like a wave. I was back in my shop, back home.

Hands cupped my face, but I kept my eyes closed, reveling under the roughened skin and the way it felt against my cheeks. Then I felt his breath, warm and puffing against my lips. His lips grazed mine, barely touching them, hovering, hovering. I opened my eyes, and Preston rocked back on his heels, a devilish grin on his face.

"What just happened?" I asked, touching my lips, still dazed by our almost kiss.

"You're gonna have to work for the rest," he said, his grin so sure and cocky.

"Am I now?"

He nodded. "Oh yeah." He grabbed my hand and pulled me to him. Our bodies pressed together in a way that made my knees go weak. "Besides, I don't think you're quite ready yet."

"Not ready?" I asked in disbelief. "For you?"

He pointed at his mouth. "For these lips. I've learned a few things in the last twenty years." He tugged me out the door of the shop, the parade now in full swing as a float in the shape of a witch hat glided past us.

"Learned a few things . . ." I echoed, still dazed by everything that had happened. "Preston, I really think I can handle—"

He pulled me into an alleyway and pushed me against a brick wall, his mouth inches from mine, his voice low, his arm braced over my head. "When I kiss you again for the first time, it's not going to be rushed, it's not going to be in your damn shop, and it sure as hell isn't going to be something you'll forget any time soon. So we're waiting until the perfect moment."

"There is no perfect moment," I said, the slightest whine to my voice. "I've learned that better than anyone recently."

His mouth lingered by mine for half a second before he pushed off the wall, shot me a smile, pulled away, and walked back out onto Main Street.

Well, okay then. Get Preston Hammond to kiss me. Challenge happily accepted.

Chapter Thirty-One

Preston and I shoved through the crowds of people lining the street, trying to get a good spot so I could see Remy on her senior float. I didn't see Emerson anywhere, and my stomach dropped lower and lower. Cursed. Isaac said Emerson was freaking cursed. I just broke my own curse and now I needed to find Emerson so I could help her break hers. No more being afraid.

"Here," Person said, grabbing my hand and leading me back into another alleyway tucked between The Velvet Box and Potions & Things.

"Preston." I twisted around, arching my neck so I could look back at the street and the growing crowd. At this point, it was impossible to see the parade. It didn't even matter that I was here, I hadn't arrived early enough to get a good spot. "We're going the wrong way."

"No we're not," he said, and we ducked into a little slip of a street behind his mother's shop.

I glanced around warily, not ready to see Marjorie again.

"Relax," Preston said. "We're not here to visit my mom."

We came to a stand in front of a ladder that ran up the building and all the way to the roof.

"What are you up to?" I asked as Preston started to climb.

I guess I had no choice but to follow.

I gripped the ladder, and it creaked. "Are you sure this thing is solid?" I yelled up after him.

"Just get up here." Preston got to the top and hopped off onto the roof.

I gulped and followed, and when I reached the top Preston grabbed my hand and pulled me along the sloped tiles. We crouched low, both of us scaling the roof up the peak and then down toward the edge. Preston slowed, sitting and tugging me down next to him above a gutter. Main Street spread out before us, the parade in full swing as floats glided past: a float in the shape of the sun, a float covered in leaves, a float in the shape of a basket, everyone standing inside of it dressed up as a different type of vegetable or fruit. I smiled. And there at the end of the line was the senior float, a half moon, half sun, covered in stars, some glittery, some silver and smooth, some bright and golden. Remy stood on the float waving as the crowd cheered for the senior class. My heart warmed when my daughter caught my gaze and waved, the smile on her face bright and big.

This entire day had been a complete disaster, but this moment more than made up for it.

"She's really something," Preston said.

"She is."

"A testament to the woman who raised her."

I stared at Remy as she blew kisses to the crowd. "No. She's who she is despite the woman who raised her."

"You have to know that's not true." Preston inched closer, his thigh touching mine.

"I guess I did some things right," I said, not taking my eyes off Remy. The senior float moved down the street at a steady pace. When it neared I let out a loud whistle that made Remy wince.

She gave me a look that I think meant I needed to take it down a notch. So naturally I only whistled louder.

Preston laughed.

"You know, you've done a good job too," I said to him. "I'm proud of you, of this life you've built for yourself. You sure you're ready to let me come in and bulldoze it down?"

Preston grabbed my hands, gathering them in his lap. "You're not going to bulldoze anything. You're exactly where you belong."

Remy continued to smile at the crowd as her float moved further away, every once in a while glancing back and catching my eye. Preston gave my hands a squeeze. Down below Martin and Isaac stood side by side, watching the parade, Isaac's smile bright enough to rival Remy's. There was a lot to unpack there, but watching Isaac I realized Emerson wasn't the only one I owed an apology to.

I turned to Preston. "I think the genie and I need to have a chat."

"Right now?" Preston asked, and I nodded.

"It's important."

He leaned over and pressed a quick kiss to my cheek. "Go on, then. I'll be here. I'm not going anywhere."

His words filled me with warmth as I climbed over the roof, down the ladder, and walked through the alleyway, ready to make the second apology in a list that was quickly growing.

I tapped Isaac on the shoulder, and he turned.

He looked the same as he had in the lamp, just more grounded. Literally.

"Oh, Clara, you escaped." He looked at Martin. "Told you she'd figure it out."

Martin grumbled and pulled a wad of cash out of his wallet.

"You bet on whether or not I'd make it out of the lamp?" I asked.

Martin handed Isaac the money. "I really didn't think you'd do it. I told Isaac you're not very self-aware, unfortunately."

"Thanks, Martin," I mumbled, then looked at Isaac. "Can I talk to you for a minute?"

Isaac stuffed the money into his pocket. "I suppose we should probably have a chat."

We both looked at Martin, who stared at us. "Do I not get to listen in on this?" he asked.

"Martin, go away," I said.

He scowled at me. "You're very testy for someone who just escaped eternity in a lamp." He huffed. "Fine, I'll just go stand over there. Isaac will tell me everything when you're done anyway."

I just rolled my eyes as the imp walked away, and I faced Isaac, staring into a face that was so familiar but somehow belonged to almost a complete stranger.

"I want to apologize," I said.

Isaac rose his nose in the air and sniffed. "For wanting to keep me trapped in a lamp for all of eternity, you mean?"

"Um, yes. For that. And for not wanting to help you escape in the first place."

"What?" His voice rose almost three octaves.

"I'm sorry! To be fair, I hadn't met you yet at that point. I thought maybe my mother trapped something evil in the lamp, something she didn't want getting out."

That wasn't the entire truth, though. I took a deep breath.

"And I also thought if I ignored the lamp, ignored you, then I could pretend you didn't exist, that life could just continue on as it had."

Isaac's normally sharp features softened. "I suppose that's understandable. And I'm sorry too. I wasn't really going to take The Wish List from your mom, and I wasn't trying to kill her. In that moment, I just got so angry she had this amazing life that I didn't. That she got to grow up in this magical town with this magical little shop, and I got, well, kidnapped."

I thought about my grandfather, how horrible he'd been to my mom growing up, how much he hated her magic. I never understood why he'd married my grandmother in the first place if he detested magic so much.

I shook my head. "Isaac, your feelings are valid. Of course you felt robbed, and you were just a boy. But . . . life wasn't easy for my mother. And it might not have been easy for you either if you'd never been kidnapped. Did . . . did Greta treat you well?"

Isaac's eyes welled with tears, and he ran a hand through his thick red hair. "Yes, other than her awful taste in clothes. It was a crime the way she dressed me before I could dress myself." He shuddered. "I need to burn my baby pictures so no one can ever get a hold of them." He sighed. "But she was kind, and other than lying to me for my entire life up to that point, she loved me. I felt it everyday in everything she did."

I put a hand on his arm. "That makes me very happy for you. Listen, you can stay with me and Remy as long as you need to get on your feet.

And I'll teach you how to use magic, how to grant wishes, all of it. Anything you want to know."

"Really?" Isaac asked.

I nodded. "We're family, Isaac. You're a Westfold, and we'll always be here for you, no matter what."

He fanned his eyes. "Okay, well, my allergies are really bad right now, and um, I need a tissue—"

"It's okay." I reached into my purse to pull out a tissue and hand it to Isaac.

He blotted at his eyes. "I'd really like everything you said, but I think I need to find Greta first, get some closure from her and hopefully find out why she took me in the first place."

I raised a finger. "I have a theory about that."

One that literally just came to me.

Isaac stared, curiosity in his eyes.

"I think maybe my grandfather asked her to. He hated magic, hoped his kids would be born without powers, like him. I think the thought of two kids with magic would've killed him. So he pretended you died in the hospital, lied to my grandmother about it while she was out of it and on pain meds, and asked Greta to take you."

Isaac put a hand to his head. "That's quite a theory."

I scuffed my foot against the ground. "Well, it's a work in progress, but I truly don't think my grandmother would ever have let anything happen to you. She would've loved you."

He bit his lip.

"I mean that would be good news in the context that Greta wasn't just some madwoman who stole you away from your family."

"That does make me feel a little better."

I smiled. "Good. Now go have fun with Martin. Not too much fun," I warned, which made him laugh.

He slung an arm around my shoulder. "I have a feeling you're going to be my favorite niece."

"I'm your only niece."

"Eh, potato, po-tah-to."

I leaned in for a hug, wrapping my arms around his waist as he brought his arms over my back. We stood in an awkward silence, both clutching each other before Isaac stepped back.

"Nope that was awkward."

"We're not there yet," I agreed.

"Definitely not."

I stuck out my hand. "Handshake, then?"

He eyed it, then took it and shook gently. He let go and walked back to Martin, who had been standing suspiciously close the entire time. Those two really did make a good pair. They linked hands and walked down the sidewalk.

Another small weight lifted from my shoulders. But I had another relationship to mend, and I hoped it wasn't too late.

Chapter Thirty-Two

I walked down the busy parade street, the floats now gliding off the route and vendors filling the area. The scent of freshly baked pies filled the air, and I was tempted to stop and buy one for me and Remy, but no, I had a mission, and I wouldn't ignore it anymore.

Time to rock the boat. Time to be comfortable rocking the boat.

I hoped maybe Cruz had helped her with whatever she was running from, that maybe this curse she was under had lifted, but now I had my doubts. I'd shed my curse, but what about Emerson? I couldn't imagine how she'd even brought a curse upon herself. She must be so scared, feel so alone, and I'd just pushed her away. Like a terrible friend. And what had that gotten me? Trapped in a lamp.

Screw it. I'd scour this entire town until I figured out where Emerson—

"Clara?" I turned and saw Dara standing there, gray hair hanging in a braid down her back.

She smiled big at me. "You did it. You really did it. Emerson is staying, and she's—she's happy. I think we might actually have a chance."

Guilt twisted at my gut. "Um, Dara, about that..."

She rushed toward me. "It took a few days, but she really came around. I have my daughter back. It feels like—" She paused. "Well, it feels like how it was before her dad died. I have hope for the first time in a long time. It turns out I didn't need a wish. I had you."

"Dara, I'm so happy for you. For Emerson. But I didn't do anything. I wish I could tell you I had, but, well, I didn't want Emerson to be my problem. So I didn't really try. Not like I should have. And I'm so sorry. If you want a wish, another one, it's on the house. I mean, you still have to give a piece of your soul and everything, but I won't charge you any money for the wish."

Dara just shook her head. "Why do I need a wish? I have everything I could want." She laid a hand on my shoulder. "And, Clara, you need to start giving yourself more credit. You came to the funeral, you went out with Emerson to The Brewery. You did enough." She gave my arm a squeeze. "You carry around so much weight on those shoulders. You don't have to, though. Lean on everyone around you. They're here for you, including Emerson. Including me."

I smiled at her, tears welling in my eyes. "Thank you, Dara." I tilted my head. "Do you know where I can find Emerson, by chance?"

I didn't know if Dara knew her daughter was cursed, wasn't sure if anyone knew. It didn't seem like Emerson had been forthcoming about it. Maybe there was a reason for that.

Dara nodded. "She's at the beach, with Cruz. At their place."

That was all she needed to say. I knew their place well, had been there with Emerson many times.

"Thank you, Dara."

I gave her a hug and ran toward the beach.

Ran was a bit of an exaggeration. More like I speed-walked toward the beach, arms pumping by my sides. Soon I saw Cruz's truck parked in one of the small parking lots along the coast, and I increased my speed, working up to a jog toward his vehicle and waving both arms. Emerson caught my gaze from inside, her eyes widening. She turned to Cruz, who nodded at her, and she opened the door and stepped out of his truck.

"What are you doing here?" she asked, getting closer to me.

"I'm so sorry about earlier," I said. "I turned you away when you needed me the most. I didn't support you. I was a terrible friend."

She shook her head. "I'm the one who's been a terrible friend. I was rude, mean." She smiled. "I was a bitch."

I grabbed her arm and led her to a bench overlooking the ocean, and we both sat down. "I have to ask you something. Are you in any kind of trouble?"

Emerson bit the inside of her cheek, tugging on a strand of long, blonde hair. "What do you mean?"

I gasped and pointed at her. "That's your tell!"

"What are you talking about?" she asked.

"You always bite the inside of your cheek when you're lying!" Good to know some things hadn't changed.

"It's—well." She licked her lips. "Um . . ."

"Were you . . ." I looked around, then lowered my voice. "Have you been cursed this entire time you've been back in Whispering Willows?"

I almost didn't believe Isaac when he'd said it, but now, talking to Emerson, I realized maybe he was telling the truth.

A big wave crashed against the rocks in the distance, the slightest mist coating us.

Emerson's eyes widened. "How did you know that?" she whispered, like she was afraid someone would hear.

I gasped. "So it's true!"

She nodded, swallowing a few times, opening her mouth to speak, but no words came out. She tried again, but all that came out was a raspy croak. "I can't talk about it right now. Maybe it's a story I'll tell one day. When I'm ready."

"But you're okay? The curse has lifted?"

Emerson donned a thoughtful expression. "I will be."

Well, that didn't answer my question, but it wasn't my place to press. Not now.

"She stared out at the ocean in the distance. "I'm sorry I ran away so long ago without saying a word to you. It was shitty."

I looked down at my hands, not saying anything.

"It's okay, you can say it. It was a terrible thing to do."

"It was," I agreed, then grabbed her hand. "But I'm ready to move forward, to be friends again."

That brought a smile to her face.

"And what about LA?" I asked. "Your job? Your boyfriend?"

Emerson shuddered. "Please don't call Gary my boyfriend ever again. I want to forget he exists."

There was definitely more to that story, but now didn't seem like the time to ask for details.

She nudged me. "What about you and a certain ex-boyfriend of yours?"

I couldn't help the smile that came to my face now, and Emerson just shook her head with a rueful grin. "I knew you two were going to get back together."

"Oh, we're not officially together," I said, which sounded ridiculous even to my ears because I'd literally told him I loved him.

Emerson's nose wrinkled. "What do you mean?"

"He wants me to work for it, to earn a kiss."

She waggled her eyebrows. "Sounds like fun foreplay."

I gave her a light shove as she laughed. "It's going to be torture. But I'm ready to put the work in."

"'Atta girl."

We sat silent for a moment, the sound of the crashing waves surrounding us, the sky darkening as the sun sank lower over the horizon.

"So what now?" I asked.

Emerson turned to face me. "You know how I always loved fashion and decorating?"

I nodded.

"Well, I think I want to open my own interior design shop. I have so many ideas for spells I can create to help give people the perfect spaces for their homes, offices, storefronts."

Now that I thought about it, that would be a great fit for Emerson. She'd always had an eye for design. If only I had her skills. I could whip something up and transform our awful basement in time for Remy's—

"Oh!" I gasped, grabbing Emerson's arm. "Oh my god. I can be your first customer."

"What?" Her brows furrowed.

"Remy's birthday is in one week, and I want to completely renovate the basement at The Wish List and give Remy a girl cave. A place where she can practice magic, study, hang out. Her own space. Do you think you could help with that?"

Emerson tapped her chin. "You know, I think I just might be able to. I'll have to come check it out tomorrow, and we're going to have a lot to do in a short amount of time . . . but yes." She gave a firm nod. "We can definitely make it happen."

"So what are you and Cruz doing tonight?"

Emerson jumped in her seat, like she was just remembering Cruz was there. "Cruz! Oh my god. I have to go. We promised my mom I'd be back soon, and now she's probably worried—"

"Go, go." I shooed Emerson toward the car. "Have a fun night. Not too much fun," I called after her, and she just winked at me and sashayed toward the werewolf's truck, Cruz's gaze drinking in her every movement. I wondered if those two had worked things out yet.

I watched as they drove away into the distance, then turned my gaze back to the ocean in front of me, finally feeling at peace. Taking risks wasn't so bad after all. I'd gotten myself an almost-boyfriend, my best friend back, and I'd discovered a long-lost uncle. I could finally relax and focus on Remy's upcoming birthday.

Well, almost. I just had one last thing to do.

Chapter Thirty-Three

The wind swept past us as Remy and I flew through the sunny blue skies.

"This is so cool," Remy shouted in my ear, my hands clutched tight to the broom we rode on, hers clutched tight around my waist.

Far below the sparkling blue ocean spread out, sun glinting off the peaks of the swelling waves.

Then I spotted what I was looking for: a little alcove tucked between two tall cliffs. Remy and I veered downward toward the rocky beach.

My stomach lifted to my throat, like I was on a rollercoaster instead of my broom. Remy squealed in delight behind me.

"When do I get a broom?" she shouted.

"One thing at a time," I said over my shoulder, though the wind picked up my words and carried them away.

Remy getting her license at sixteen had already been enough to give me a heart attack. The thought of her flying a broom? That needed to wait until she was at least twenty. Scratch that. Thirty. Thirty seemed like a good age to get a broom. I definitely would not be telling her that my own mother taught me to fly on a broom years before I ever learned to drive. That would only add fuel to a fire I had no interest in stoking.

As we neared the little rocky beach, I saw a siren laying there, tail flipping in the sand as she lifted her face toward the sky.

"Wow, is that her?" Remy asked, and I realized this might be the first time Remy had ever seen a mermaid.

I glanced behind me, and Remy's eyes had widened to saucers. She stared at Alisandra as we got closer and closer.

Finally we reached the beach, and I slowed to a stop until our feet hit the pebbly sand.

Alisandra sat up straighter. "Witch Granter, you came back."

I nodded and gestured to Remy. "This is my daughter."

"It's nice to make your acquaintance, little Witch Granter," the siren said, her purple tongue darting out between her lips. The sun shone down on her scales, and they shimmered beautifully in the light.

"I have something for you." I reached into the satchel strung across my back. "I have to be honest. We thought about destroying this thing."

Alisandra's eyes widened. "Oh?"

I nodded. "It has the potential to trap a Witch Granter, turn them into a genie. That's dangerous, evil magic in the wrong hands."

"So what changed, then?" Alisandra asked.

"I realized that after what happened to your Vi, you would never let another Witch Granter get trapped in here. You'd guard this thing with your life."

Also, there was absolutely no information anywhere about how to destroy an ancient, magic lamp, so I didn't even know if it would be possible to do such a thing.

I reached out the lamp and handed it to Alisandra, who accepted, clutching it to her chest. "Thank you," she said. "Thank you, thank you, thank you."

A harsh wind snapped at us, and the waves rushed up on the beach, cold and a shock to my skin. I shivered and drew Remy into me.

"So what now?" I asked the siren.

She looked out to sea. "I'll retire my siren song. But as for me"—she shrugged, hugging the lamp—"I don't think there's anything for me beyond this little beach where I've been banished to live."

"Actually." Remy stepped forward. "My mom told me all about your banishment. You can't stay here all alone for the rest of your life. You deserve more. I never met your Vi, but from what my mom said, she sounded like an amazing person. She wouldn't want this life for you."

Alisandra's eyebrows raised. "You think I should appeal my banishment?"

I nodded, and Alisandra shrank into herself. My stomach sank. She couldn't continue to stay here, alone.

"You don't have to lure people here to talk to you anymore," I said. "You can go and live your life. I, um, I talked to some of your clan members. They're willing to make amends if you are. They'll accept you back. I think they miss you." I thought of Karissa and the rest of the mermaids, the sorrow in their eyes as Karissa told me Alisandra's story. "I know they do."

She wriggled in the sand, her tail swishing and splashing up water at us. "I like it here. It's—"

"Safe," I finished for her. "It's safe, Alisandra. But you're not truly living your life. You're holding back because you're afraid that what you might find will be scary, hard, heartbreaking?"

Her eyes widened, and her hand fluttered to her throat. Remy smiled at me and grabbed my hand, squeezing it tight.

"How did you know?" Alisandra asked. "How did you know I felt that way?"

I thought of my own fears these last few weeks, how many people I'd pushed away to try and keep my own life safe and easy. "I know a thing or two about being afraid. But let me ask you this: would you change anything about your relationship with Vi? Would you take it back knowing how it ended?"

Alisandra shook her head, a fierceness taking over her features. "No. No, never."

"Exactly. So yes, heartbreak may be in your future, sadness, loss, but you'd do it all anyway because that's how you know you're truly living."

Alisandra's throat bobbed. "Okay," she said. "Okay. I'll at least talk to my clan."

Heads bobbed in the water in the distance. I had a feeling Alisandra might change her mind. So I maybe, kind of, took a big leap and asked her clan to come to this beach, to speak with her.

I gestured to the mermaids heads peeking in and out of the swelling waves. "I'd hoped you'd say that."

Her blue eyes widened, fear shining in them.

"It's going to be okay," I assured her. "You don't have to live this life alone. Not anymore."

Alisandra nodded and shimmied toward the sea, diving in without looking back. Her tail flapped in the water before sinking down and disappearing with the rest of her.

Remy snuggled in closer to me. "Do you think she'll be okay?"

I stared at the ocean, tumultuous and writhing, waves hammering relentlessly against the pointy rocks jutting out from the water. "Yeah, I do. Life isn't going to be easy for her," I said, thinking about my own life. "But I have a feeling that's what going to make it so good."

Chapter Thirty-Four

I kept my hands wrapped around Remy's eyes.

"Seriously, Mom, what's going on?".

"No peeking!" I said.

"Not possible," Remy replied as I guided her down the creaky stairs toward the basement of The Wish List. "You've got an airtight grip around my head."

Martin stood in front of Remy, holding her hands as she went step-by-step down the stairs.

Emerson had spent the last week completely renovating our basement using custom spells she created, and she'd done a fantastic job.

We finally made it to the bottom, half the town of Whispering Willows gathered in the little space. Martin released Remy's hands and took a few steps back, bumping right into Bones, whose head touched the ceiling.

All the boxes were gone, the floor epoxied with a shiny gray finish, the walls painted a bright sky blue—Remy's favorite color. Emerson had spelled the ceiling with bright silver and white stripes. A big desk sat against one wall with a silver cushioned chair. Bookshelves now lined the walls, filled with spell books and enough space for Remy to curate her own collection. Fluffy pillows lay in one corner with twinkle lights overhead, a little book nook for Remy. My gaze traveled to my favorite part of the room: the opposite wall from where her desk was. A hearth was cut into the wall, a glowing purple cauldron sitting inside. The same cauldron my mother had used long ago. Emerson restored it, and now I saw the star sitting in the center, the Westfold family crest.

"Surprise!" everyone yelled as I removed my hands from Remy's eyes.

I looked next to me at Remy, who stared in shock, her mouth dropped open. Her gaze slowly moved around the room as she took in all the details of her new space.

"This is all for me?" she asked, hand fluttering up to her chest.

"I wanted you to have your own place," I said. "Somewhere you can flourish as a witch, practice your magic, study, relax." I gestured toward Emerson. "Emerson decorated it."

Remy and Emerson had become fast friends over the last week, bonding over their love of fashion, design, and gossip. Emerson even wrangled details out of Remy about her vampire crush, details that Emerson wouldn't divulge to me. She said some things were sacred and that Remy would tell me when she was ready. We'd been just a little busy over these last few weeks, but Remy told me everything, so I had a feeling she'd spill eventually.

Remy hugged Emerson, thanking her as Cruz came to a stand next to his girlfriend, both of them glowing. They'd been glowing since finally admitting their feelings for each other after the parade. Now they looked like the perfect couple: the tall, dark, and handsome werewolf and the beautiful blonde witch. I was happy for them, even if Emerson had still kept the details of her curse vague, telling me that she'd share her story one day, when she was ready.

Helen and Gene approached, and Remy hugged them both next.

"Happy birthday, kiddo," Helen said. "Well, I guess you're not a kiddo anymore."

"I can still be your kiddo if it makes you feel better," Remy said, and Helen laughed.

Gene flashed one of his rare smiles, sharp fangs and all. It only looked slightly terrifying when the Serpent attempted to smile. "We're proud of you and the witch you've grown into," he said.

"Thanks Uncle Gene," Remy responded, wrapping her arms around him. He stiffened, still not entirely comfortable with showing any kind of affection. He'd get there. He'd have to with Remy—she was definitely a hugger.

"Oh for feck's sake," Myrtle said, appearing by Gene's side. "Who let the vamp in?" She jabbed a thumb at Gene.

"You know, I could say the same about you," he replied in his surly voice.

"Are they always like this?" Emerson asked, looking between the werewolf and the vampire.

"Yes," everyone said in unison, which made us all laugh.

"You get used to it," Remy said cheerfully, drawing Myrtle into her hug with Gene.

"No, no, I draw the line at hugs with werewolves," he said, stepping back, his gaze flicking to Cruz. "No offense."

Cruz flashed a dazzling smile, dimples pecking his cheeks. "None taken, Serpent. I think your prejudice is against one particular werewolf, not all of us."

Well, that was true. I just shook my head and pointed at Myrtle and Gene. "Behave. It's Remy's birthday, and we're not going to tolerate any fighting. Today we are celebrating."

Isaac stood near the hearth, having an animated conversation with a leprechaun. He'd moved into our house, much to Remy's delight, who loved that our family was growing. She'd had so many questions lately about our family tree, distant relatives we could reach out to, connect with. I wasn't sure I was ready to go down that path—finding out my mother had a twin brother she'd hidden from the world had been enough of a shock. I needed time to recover before trying to track any others down. Besides, I wasn't even sure there were others to track down. According to my mother, everyone was dead.

"Happy birthday, girl," Myrtle said, giving Remy's shoulder a squeeze before moving toward another werewolf to talk with.

Two hands squeezed my shoulder, and I smiled immediately, coming face-to-face with Preston. "Well, hello, there," I said, trailing a finger down his chest.

"Nuh-uh." Remy stepped in between us. "Wand's length apart. At all times when you're in my presence."

"Or mine!" Myrtle shouted from behind us.

"Or mine," Martin added.

I rolled my eyes. "Oh please. You have no room to talk." I raised my eyebrows at him.

I'd walked in on him and Isaac making out on our brand-new living room furniture the other day and had to set some very strict boundaries. And also clean my entire couch.

"I think you two are sweet," Helen said, a twinkle in her eye.

She'd been so happy when I told her Preston and I were together. Well, kind of. We still hadn't actually established anything, or kissed, or done more than just have a lot of long conversations and meaningful glances that Remy said made her want to gag. I didn't know exactly how I was going to get Preston to kiss me, but it would happen. The man didn't have *that* much self-control. At least I hoped he didn't. I'd been busy preparing for Remy's birthday, but now that all the drama with the lamp was over, I had time to focus on Preston and building our relationship. I also had Emerson back by my side, and that girl had a lot of game and was ready to be my "wing woman," as she put it, which both excited and terrified me.

Preston gave me a quick kiss on my cheek and excused himself to catch up with a friend. Everyone around us melted away until it was just Remy and me, standing in this new space of hers, looking around at those who'd come to celebrate her birthday.

"I'm sorry I've been acting a little crazy lately," I said, nudging her.

"A little?" she asked. "I still cannot believe you got yourself trapped in a lamp. It's a good thing I didn't know about it, because I would have freaked, Mom." Her voice wobbled. "I already lost Dad. I can't lose you too."

"Oh. Oh, Remy." I pulled her in for a hug. "I promise I'll be more careful. I was trying so hard to keep up this perfect facade I didn't stop to consider how my actions were actually making things so much worse."

"It's okay. I get it. We've been through a lot over the last couple years. But we've survived."

"Yeah, we have. I just don't want to survive anymore. I want to live."

Remy gestured to the basement around us. "I'd saying we're doing plenty of living these days. We've only been in Whispering Willows for three and a half months, and look at everything we've built so far, despite the setbacks."

"Yeah." I looked around the room at our friends, our family, everyone here for Remy and her special day.

Life might not be perfect, but it was ours, and it was all I needed.

Epilogue

Remy and I sat inside the diner, both of us sharing a heaping plate of chili cheese fries.

"Oh my gosh, I forgot to tell you," Remy said through a mouthful of fries. "The Samhain ball is next month, and I need to find a dress!" She paused. "Maybe Emerson can help with that. Or Isaac. If he's not gone visiting Greta."

"Um." I pointed a fry at her as a fairy flew through the air, face red as she held a tray full of food over her head. The tray dipped, and another fairy flew to rescue her. Together they safely delivered the food to a nearby booth. "What about me?" I asked. "I can help you pick out a dress, too, you know."

"Or maybe Martin is available," Remy murmured. I threw a fry at her and she laughed. "I'm sorry, but you do not have the best fashion sense, Mom. It's just a fact."

"Oh really?" I pointed to my jeans and tucked in blouse. "This is called a French tuck, and it's very in right now. Also flattering."

Remy rolled her eyes. "You learned that from Queer Eye. You don't have the innate fashion sense I'm looking for."

"Fine," I said. "Take Emerson or Isaac or Martin. I'm sure any of them would be happy to help you pick out a dress." I dug a fork into a mound of chili. "So . . . do you have a date for this ball?"

Remy's cheeks turned pink. "No, I'm just going with friends. As a group. Not doing dates."

I remembered the vampire crush she'd told me about after her first day of school and realized life had gotten so busy I'd never asked her about it. "So not going with a certain vampire, then?"

Now Remy's cheeks darkened even more, and she ducked her head. I was so used to confident, brazen, know-what-she-wants Remy that I didn't know how to handle this shy, bumbling girl.

"Remy!" I said. "What's going on? You know you can tell me anything."

"He asked, and I said no," she blurted out.

Oh, wow. Clearly I had missed a lot the last few weeks. "I didn't even realize you two were talking."

Remy took a sip of her Coke. "We've been lab partners in science, and we've had a lot of time to get to know each other. It's not a big deal."

I shifted in my seat as a fairy zoomed by with a pot of coffee, refilling cups at various tables, splashes of the dark liquid spilling out.

"Whoa, whoa, whoa. Why do I feel like I'm missing something, here?" I asked. "You've been lab partners, you've had time to talk and get to know each other. He asked you to the Samhain ball. You said no. What led to all this?"

Remy's shoulders slumped, and she met my gaze. "I think maybe I was scared to say yes."

"Why?" I asked.

She popped a fry in her mouth. "Because what if he realizes I'm just this dorky girl and not remotely cool enough to date him?"

"Oh, Remy." I reached a hand across the table.

"He's like one of the most popular guys in school."

Her words brought me back to my own high school crush on Preston. It had been very similar: he was the jock, popular, smart, ambitious, and I, well, wasn't any of those things.

"Listen to me," I said. "If this vampire, whose name I still don't know, by the way, doesn't appreciate how amazing you are, then he's not someone worth your time. You are beautiful, brilliant, hardworking, caring. Frankly, if he can't recognize that, he's an idiot. But"—I paused —"if he's asked you to the ball, then it sounds like he already has a pretty good idea of how awesome you are." I shook my head. "I let my fear of taking risks get me trapped in a magical lamp. Don't let the same thing happen to you."

Remy cocked her head. "Don't get trapped in a lamp?"

I swatted at her with my napkin. "You know what I mean. Don't let fear hold you back. I've been doing way too much of that lately, and look where it's gotten me."

Remy nodded. "Good point."

"That's my girl. So you'll talk to your vampire, tell him you've changed your mind?"

Remy pursed her lips. "I think so. Thanks, Mom."

A group of goblins broke out in laughter on the opposite side of the diner, one of them slamming a hand on the table, making the entire diner tremble.

"You know," Remy said, and I already didn't like the tone. It was her calculating tone, the one she used when she was about to rope me into something I wanted nothing to do with. "You're probably going to have to go dress shopping too."

I crossed my arms. "And why is that?"

"Because Mr. H is chaperoning the ball. He's going to need a date."

Oh. Well, I hadn't expected that. Then again, maybe it wasn't a bad idea. If Preston still hadn't kissed me by Samhain, and lord I hoped that wouldn't be the case, I could seal the deal with the right dress.

"You just worry about your own date." I settled back into the booth.

She tapped her chin. "I don't get what's going on with you two."

Well, that made two of us. I still didn't understand what Preston was waiting for, but he assured me he was all in. He just wanted to take it slow. For whatever reason.

"You guys are so weird," Remy continued.

Again, couldn't argue with that. But I liked our weirdness. It's what made us work.

The door to the diner opened, and a crisp white letter came zooming through the air.

"Incoming," someone yelled, and everyone sprang into action.

The goblins in the corner ducked. The fairies fluttered behind the counters.

A few patrons dove under their tables. Remy and I both lay down on our booth seats. The mayor had started a new program, where mail could now be delivered directly to the person it was addressed to. He'd gathered some local witches to spell our mail delivery system. But it had caused all sorts of problems. Nasty paper cuts. Mail getting lost or destroyed because it was delivered at an inopportune time. So the mayor rolled it back, said they still had some kinks to work out, but every once in a while, a stray letter still made its way out into the wild, much to everyone's displeasure.

I heard the soft thud of paper against table and slowly sat up, blinking a few times at the little rectangular envelope bouncing on the table in front of me. The letter was addressed to me. No return sender.

My stomach twisted.

"Who's it from?" Remy asked as the diner slowly returned to its normal activity once everyone realized they wouldn't be maimed by the stray envelope.

"I don't know." I grabbed the letter, running my fingers over it, not recognizing the handwriting on the front. Loops and curls, messy but readable.

I slowly opened the envelope and pulled out the letter. I stared, my heart beating in my chest, picking up pace the more I read.

"Mom? You okay? You look like you've seen a ghost."

My eyes stuck to the paper, reading the letter again to be sure I hadn't somehow misunderstood something.

"Mom, who's it from?"

I swallowed a few times. "My dad," I finally choked out.

"Your dad who your mom said was just a one-night fling?"

"Correct."

"Who Grandma claimed she tried to search for?"

"Correct again."

"The dad who she told you had died by the time she finally did find him?"

"That would be the same dad," I said.

"So what does the letter say?" Remy leaned forward, her fingers twitching like she wanted to rip the paper from my hands and read it herself.

"My dad is alive . . . and he's coming here, to Whispering Willows."

. . .

THE END

Want more of Clara and Preston? **Scan the code below** and you'll get access to this YOUR WITCH IS MY COMMAND bonus story!

Haven't had a chance to read the first book in the series? **Read Be Careful What You Witch For now.**

Keep reading if you'd like a sneak peek of book three, coming soon!

Witch Fulfillment: A Sneak Peek

My daughter stood in front of the full-length mirror, twirling in a circle as the bottom of her shimmering blue dress fanned out at her ankles. The dressmaker bustled around her, dipping her wand in a vial that sat on a small table nearby, then touching the wand to specific places on Remy's dress. She tapped the waist and it cinched tighter, then she tapped the thick shoulders, which fitted to the muscle and bone. Each tap of her wand made the dress form to Remy like a glove. I couldn't believe my eighteen-year-old daughter was going to her first-ever Samhain Ball. After I left my life of magic behind at the young age of nineteen, I never dreamed I'd witness something like this. Sure, I knew I'd see my daughter go to prom, homecoming, and every other high school event under the sun, but I never thought I'd see her attend a witch ball. It brought up memories of my own Samhain Ball, a night I'd never forget.

I held back my tears, not wanting to make this moment about me and my feelings. Remy turned, examining her figure in the full-length mirror. I knew this was a momentous occasion for her as well. She'd just discovered magic was real four months ago, and now here she was, learning magic, attending a magic academy, dating a . . . vampire. Well, I thought she was dating a vampire. She hadn't exactly updated me on that situation.

I settled back onto the pink couch sitting near the back of the room. Silk brushed my ear and I looked behind me at a rack lining the wall, stuffed with dresses of all colors.

"So is this the one?" I asked, my attention straying back to Remy.

The dressmaker stepped back, pressing her wand to her chest.

Remy stared at herself in the mirror, a smile on her lips. "I think so."

I squealed. "Oh Remy, you look absolutely stunning."

She tugged at the spaghetti straps and pulled the A-line up. "Do you think he'll like it?"

She didn't say his name—she still hadn't told me that little tidbit. But I knew who she was talking about. Her mysterious vampire crush.

"He'd be crazy not to, Remy," I said, standing and walking toward her. She turned to me and gave me a tight hug.

"Okay good. I kind of still have to tell him I want to go with him, but you know . . ."

"Remy!" I pushed her to arm's length. "You still haven't said yes! He asked you a month ago!"

She bit her lip. "Well, Mom, it's complicated."

I clearly didn't understand teenagers and their weird dating habits. "How? He asks you to the Samhain Ball. You say yes."

"Except I said no!" Remy said, twisting her hands together.

She'd told him no when he first asked, afraid that one of the most popular boys in school asked her to a dance.

"Yeah, but I thought we talked through that whole situation? You said you were going to tell him how you changed your mind."

Remy looked down at her feet. "I know, I know. I just . . . he's been so moody toward me, so distant. And that kind of made me mad. I mean, I know I turned him down, but he's acting so immature about it. Makes me question everything."

I laughed. She might've been eighteen, but sometimes I felt like my daughter was at least a decade older. Other teenage girls might pine after their crushes, do anything and everything to get their attention, forgive easily, overlook red flags, but not Remy. She was wise beyond her years.

"Listen, kiddo, you just have to talk to him," I said. "You hurt his feelings, his pride."

She opened her mouth to argue, but I continued, my words gaining speed.

"That doesn't excuse his behavior." I tucked one of her wild brown curls behind her ear. "All I'm saying is that people aren't perfect. Don't start making excuses to shut him out before you've even given him a chance."

Remy blew a big breath out. "I guess maybe you're right."

"I'm sorry." I put a hand to my chest. "Can you say that again?"

The door to the little dress shop burst open, Martin standing in the doorway, phone out, no doubt recording this moment. "I knew it," he declared, his green skin shimmering as he huffed and stomped into the room. "I knew you were here."

"Are you recording right now, Martin?" Remy asked. "I thought we talked about this."

"You told me you'd already found your Samhain Ball dress, but I was walking down the street, and who did I see through the window? A certain Remy." He sent me a pointed stare. "And a certain Clara Westfold."

I rolled my eyes at the imp. He could be incredibly dramatic. "Martin, I'm sorry we lied to you."

He crossed his arms.

"We just wanted a nice mother-daughter outing is all. I know you wanted to be there for Remy's special moment."

He circled Remy with his phone, tears pooling in his eyes. "Oh, you're so beautiful."

Remy's expression softened.

Ever since we'd arrived in Whispering Willows four months earlier, the town had seemed to adopt Remy, looking out for her, loving her, wanting to be a part of her life. I appreciated that everyone loved Remy so much, but sometimes, they took it too far, invading parts of our life that we just wanted to keep for ourselves. We'd agreed that it would just be Remy and me going dress shopping. She might have teased me about how she wanted someone with more fashion sense to go with her, but at the end of the day, she said she didn't want anyone else by her side. We knew it might hurt some people's feelings, so we told a little white lie. Clearly, that had been a mistake.

Martin stopped his video and started snapping photos of Remy with the flash. She threw her hands up in front of her face to protect her eyes from the blinding light.

I shook a finger at the imp. "No, no, Martin, boundaries. You can't just sweep in here with your compliments and make Remy feel bad about not inviting you to this."

"Fine." Martin stuffed his phone in his pocket. "Why didn't you just tell me the truth and save us all of this heartache?" He put a fist to his mouth, stifling a cry.

I resisted the urge to roll my eyes again. I rolled them so much around the imp that at some point they were just going to get stuck up there.

"Well . . ." I threw out my hands helplessly. "We didn't know how to tell everyone we didn't want them to come. We didn't want to hurt your feelings, okay? So we just figured it might be easier to make something up, spare everyone. Happy?"

Martin frowned. "No, I'm not."

The door burst open again. "What's this about Remy going dress shopping?" Myrtle stood in the doorway now, still in her wolf form, blood dripping from her mouth. "I'm on a hunt and I get a text from the imp about Remy getting fitted at Best Dressed.

I whirled on Martin. "Who else did you text?"

The imp twined his hands behind his back, avoiding eye contact, his pointy ears wiggling. "I might've texted the group chat."

"Are you kidding me?"

That meant he'd told Helen, Gene, Myrtle, Bones, Isaac, and Emerson. They couldn't all show up. Remy didn't want all that attention, and I didn't want this special day of dress shopping ruined for my daughter.

Remy groaned from behind me. "I'm like half-naked right now. I don't want Uncle Gene to see me like this." She grappled at her dress, trying to pull it up and cover her bra.

"Don't worry, girlie," Myrtle said as she slinked into the room, her muddy paws leaving prints on the soft white carpet that made the dressmaker look like she might faint. "Busy fighting demons. Helen and Gene won't be able to make it. Is my snout bleeding? Oh, bollocks." Blood dripped from her nose onto the floor, and she let out a string of curses in what I guessed was her ancient Gaelic language.

The dressmaker's face was now a deep shade of purple.

"I'm so sorry," I said. "Just let me deal with this." I gestured to

Martin and Myrtle. "And I promise I'll get my best cleaning spell in here to take care of the mud and blood."

The dressmaker didn't say anything, just continued to stare.

"You two, over here, now," I whisper-yelled.

Myrtle approached with her tail between her legs, and Martin strode over, nose high in the air. "I'm sorry we lied to you about dress shopping, okay? But Remy just wanted it to be me and her today, so can you two please go? Remy already said you all could come take pictures of her in her dress before the Samhain Ball, at our house. Let's just stick to that plan."

I looked behind them to see if I should be expecting anyone else. Luckily Isaac was out of town, so we didn't have to worry about him intruding, and I assumed Emerson knew me well enough to know we might not want that kind of intrusion. Myrtle said Helen and Gene were busy fighting demons. So that left . . .

The door opened again, Bones looming tall over us. The half-giant frowned down at everyone, shaking his black bowl cut.

Remy shrieked. "Bones, you can't see me like this!" She dove behind Myrtle, and her dress tickled the werewolf's side. Myrtle jumped about a foot in the air, getting her claws tangled up in a rack of nearby dresses.

Bones's head skimmed the ceiling, and he had to duck to enter further.

"Bones, you idiot!" Martin shouted. "I told you you wouldn't fit inside the shop!"

Bones flicked the imp, easily half his size, and Martin flew back into the mirror, cracking it.

The dressmaker put a hand to her head, her eyes flitting from Myrtle, still tangled in all the dresses, now smearing them with blood and mud, to Martin, laying on the floor as shards of mirror fell all around him.

"Oh god," I said.

"Out," the dressmaker burst. "Out, out, out now!"

"I'm so, so sorry." I stood frozen, helpless. "We really didn't mean to make any messes."

"Out," she shrieked again, her voice rising three octaves.

"Okay." I scurried to Remy and covered her while she shimmied out of her dress, pulled on her jeans, and threw on her T-shirt. Myrtle finally disentangled herself from the dresses, and Bones picked Martin up by his collar.

"Bones," Martin gasped. "You're choking me."

The half-giant paid no mind to the imp as he carried him from the shop.

"Get. Out!" the dressmaker yelled, chasing us all from the shop and out onto Main Street.

"Well, that was a little dramatic," Martin said.

We all jumped when the door to the shop slammed behind us, glass rattling in its pane.

Remy sank down onto the curb. "Well, there goes my favorite dress so far."

I sat down next to her. "We'll find you another one. I promise."

I shot a glare at Myrtle, Bones, and Martin, all looking properly chagrined.

"Just go. You three have done enough for one day."

"We just wanted to see the girl," Myrtle said with her thick Irish accent.

"We wanted to participate in Remy's special day." Martin kicked at Bones, who finally dropped the imp to the ground.

Bones grunted in agreement. I didn't think I'd ever heard the half-giant talk. I never even asked why he didn't speak, just accepted his grunts and moans.

Remy turned. "I love you all, and I always want you to be part of my special moments, but I just wanted to get a dress with my mom today. And now, I don't even know where I can get another dress."

"We'll find another dress shop in a nearby town." I nudged her. "It'll be fine."

"Sorry, girlie." Myrtle nudged Remy with her snout before crossing the street.

"We're sorry, Remy." Martin leaned down to press a kiss to her head, and Bones patted her shoulder with his giant hand.

They walked down the street, disappearing around the corner and out of view.

Remy leaned into me. "I went from having no one but you for two years to having a whole community to love me. And I love Whispering

Willows, and I love that everyone cares so much about me, but sometimes it's a lot."

I roped an arm around her shoulder. "I know, I know. I didn't have my mother growing up, and everyone kind of became like a surrogate parent for me. I forgot how smothering they can be, even if it comes from a good place."

Remy smiled. "I know. It's fine. I don't know if I was really feeling that dress anyway."

A salty sea breeze flowed past us, rustling my shoulder-length brown hair, the exact same shade as Remy's, but while hers was wild and curly, mine was stick-straight.

I raised an eyebrow. "Are you just saying that?"

"No, I think there's something else out there for me. Something that will wow him."

"Uh-huh. You know, you're gonna have to tell me his name before he comes to pick you up for the Samhain Ball."

"What, so you can cyber stalk him to death?" Remy shook her head. "Pass."

I just laughed, my expression sobering as I studied my daughter. I truly loved that everyone in this town had adopted Remy so easily as their own, but sometimes I just wanted her to myself. More and more, I felt like I was losing her. After this year, she'd be out of high school, out in the world. She might decide to move out, to travel, to go to college.

Remy looked up at me. "Whatcha thinking?"

"That we need to get home for lunch." I stood and pulled her to her feet.

I wouldn't think about that. She was mine. For just a little while longer. And I'd make the most of it.

About the Author

Tee Harlowe writes paranormal and fantasy romance focused on women and their strength, grit, and determination. After years spent traveling, Tee settled down to start writing her own adventures. When not writing, Tee can be found wrangling her children, attempting to bake, and losing to her husband at pretty much every game they play.